Slightly Murderous Intent

A Southern California Mystery

SLIGHTLY MURDEROUS INTENT

A Southern California Mystery

by Lida Sideris

To MomV, my enthusiastic critic, from her fan-daughter

Contents

Praise for SLIGHTLY MURDEROUS INTENT

"A smart caper with a heroine to match."—*Kirkus* Recommended Review

"I highly recommend this cozy mystery to anyone who enjoys a feisty heroine with laugh out loud sidekicks."—*Kings River Life* magazine

"…An excellent read. It has everything needed for a cozy afternoon curled up on the sofa – murder, mystery, humor, and plenty of action. The plot is extremely detailed and so well written that I found myself hooked on page one."—*Readers' Favorite*

Chapter One: Target Practice

The last of my patience dripped onto the concrete floor beneath my feet. My fists clenched, my jaw tightened and my stomach rumbled like the start of an avalanche. I'd officially reached the cracking point.

"Today was V-day for us. Victory with a big fat V." Los Angeles Senior Deputy District Attorney Bruce Beckman stood at the head of our table, arms raised high. The first two fingers of each hand formed a "V". Meanwhile, everyone's dinner sat in front of them. Everyone's, that is, but mine. All I had was an empty plate and an empty stomach.

"Where's our server?" I whispered. The beachside diner was packed. "Did they run out of food?"

Beckman dropped his pose and glared at me so fiercely, my cheeks glowed from the heat.

"Sorry," I mumbled. What did he expect? His mac n' cheese was half eaten. I licked my lips.

"The case came close to swinging in the opposite direction," Beckman continued. "But it didn't. Know why?"

A hand shot up from the small, wiry guy sitting across from me. D.A. Investigator Ramsey had squinty eyes, little ears and a short neck that belonged on a ground squirrel. Beckman scowled at Ramsey until his arm slunk down.

"We couldn't have won today's trial without this guy." Beckman gestured toward the deputy D.A. sitting next to him.

I half stood and peered past the other diners. No sign of our server.

"Slacker," I mumbled. I slammed my napkin down beside my plate.

"Have some of mine," Michael whispered. "Please, Corrie."

If anyone else had offered, I would've cleaned his plate in thirty seconds. At least half of it, anyway. But Michael was my oldest friend slash newest boyfriend, and I loved him dearly from his dark floppy hair to the Chuck Taylors on his feet. We sat in a crowded hipster restaurant in Santa Monica, a hop, skip and a jump from the sparkling Pacific Ocean. Michael had barely touched his burger, waiting on my dinner with me. His stomach growled right alongside mine.

"Obviously, I picked the right man for the job," Beckman said. "And gave him a few tips. Quite a few, actually." He chuckled.

Weak laughter trickled around the table, followed by a groan. Did that come from me? Beckman shot me his signature scowl. I managed a shadow of an apology, and his attention returned to the man on his left. My hunger pangs took a brief hike while I assessed the object of Beckman's praise. Assistant Deputy D.A. James Zachary flashed a grin. He was a sight for sore eyes. Or any eyes, for that matter. His deep-dish dimples caused female passers-by to slow down in appreciation. Tall, athletic and brawny, James was devilishly handsome.

"Thanks to James," Beckman continued, "defense counsel didn't stand a chance."

Cheers erupted. I clapped and wriggled around in my seat. My stomach rumblings grew even louder. That's what happened when my last meal was breakfast.

"I'll be back," I whispered to Michael and shoved away my chair.

We sat around a table of five. Three of us were members of the world's oldest profession. The oldest after toolmakers, farmers, the military and doctors. We were lawyers. I was the only lawyer unaffiliated with the D.A.'s office.

"Wait." Michael took my hand.

Michael Parris wasn't a lawyer, but he was the associate dean of the computer science department of a private tech college near downtown L.A. The other non-lawyer was Investigator Ramsey. We'd gathered together tonight to celebrate with James, Michael's other bestie…and my one-time high school crush.

Michael's lips were moving but shouting voices, clanging dinner plates and background music swallowed up his next words.

"What?" I leaned in closer, sniffing a sweet combo of sandalwood and fresh laundry that made my empty insides tingle.

He wiped his mouth on a napkin and said, "Stay here. I'll go to the kitchen. Help yourself to my burger while you wait. I promise I won't return empty-handed."

"No, you stay. I want to make sure they get my order right." I touched his shoulder. "Be back soon."

We locked stares and his hazel eyes softened. "Two minutes. If you're not back, I'm coming after you."

I'd insisted my tablemates eat without me, figuring my meal was on its way…fifteen minutes ago. I aimed for the kitchen, wading sideways between packed tables when I bumped into our server. She tried to push past, but I blocked the way.

"I'm still waiting," I told her.

"No, you're not," she said. "You got served."

"Crispy chicken sandwich with spicy slaw and chili cheese fries, hold the onions. It's not on our table." I pointed my thumb over my shoulder.

"I brought all the orders out personally."

"Not mine."

"You wanna talk to the manager?"

"I *demand* to talk to the manager."

She tipped her head and pitched it to one side. "Big Sam's up front by the cashier."

I moved out of her path, and she hustled past. I continued my sideways trek, filing between chairs and dodging scurrying servers. I paused by a table. A couple was engaged in a cozy tete-a-tete, ignoring the grilled turkey clubs sitting in front of them. I debated reaching across to grab some cheesy fries, but decided against it.

It was stop-and-go all the way to the front. Nearly closing time and the place was still hopping. I slowed and looked back at the kitchen. Maybe I'd get somewhere if I talked to the cook. I was about to swivel around when I spotted a manager-type; a stocky guy with a shaved head and goatee, chatting up a group of wannabe diners near the bar. He wore a short-sleeved, floral print shirt over jeans. Muscle-bound with a wide stance, he looked like he could hold his own in a wrestling match.

I headed for him and waited behind the blonde hostess. The cash register drawer popped open with a ping. She plucked wads of bills from beneath the drawer and shoved them into a vinyl bank bag.

"Excuse me," I said.

She jumped and turned to me, zipping up the bag and pushing it behind her. "Yeah?" Long bangs stabbed at her eyes.

I pitched my chin toward the stocky guy. "That the manager?"

"He owns the place. Big Sam Neely." Her attention went back to the bag. She unzipped it and continued stuffing bills inside.

I navigated closer to Big Sam and leaned against a pillar, waiting for a chance to butt into the conversation. Meanwhile, a lanky dude in a dark gray hoodie and faded jeans edged his way inside. His clothes were baggy; his hood was up and over his head. Only his nose, mouth and tinted shades were visible. Sunglasses at night weren't unusual in L.A. I stared out at the room. A couple of diners wore shades.

The guy in the hoodie flitted past me. On close inspection, he looked like he'd seen better days. His dry skin belonged on a lizard and veins popped out of the back of his hands. He threw out his anchor near the hostess. My heartbeat quickened. The cash drawer still gaped open.

I elbowed my way back toward him, half-expecting the guy's hand to dart out and grab the bank bag, but he ignored the money. Instead, he eased forward and stared out toward the back of the diner. My gaze dropped to the lower left side of his jacket. The bottom edge had latched onto the large violin shaped leaf of an ornamental ficus, exposing the top of his jeans. My heart hammered against my chest. The grip of a revolver stuck out of his pocket.

His fingers reached for the gun seconds after I hurled myself forward, arms extended, aiming for his waist. I'd knock him off his feet and grab the revolver. I missed on both counts and landed with a thud behind him. He raised his gun. I'd barely stumbled to my feet before he fired a shot. The rest of the scene unfolded in slow motion. The guy whirled around, dashing for the exit. I dove for him again when he streaked past. This time my fingers locked around his ankle. He kicked out and stumbled forward, dragging me along until I lost my grip. He catapulted out the front door and into the night.

Chapter Two: The Chase

Chaos ripped across the room and sparked a small stampede. I jumped to my feet and bulldozed my way out and after the shooter. If I didn't catch him right away, he'd disappear.

I scrambled onto the sidewalk and scanned Ocean Avenue. An older couple strolled along, and a group of women jogged by. No sign of the shooter. The entry to the building next door was on a side street. He'd still be running if he'd gone that way. No cars parked nearby. Only one other place he could be.

I hurried into a large parking lot adjacent to the diner. Zig-zagging between vehicles, my eyes were primed for any sudden movement. The only other exit was through the alley behind the restaurant, but he couldn't have made it there so quickly. I'd have seen him. Which meant, he was close by.

The opposite end of the lot wasn't an option. Too well lit by street lamps. I gulped and aimed for the area closest to the diner. Lighting was dim and shadows plentiful. Recessed doorways and outdoor stairwells served as bunkers where homeless souls hunkered down for the night. Large planters also provided bedding. I slowed beside an oversized, raised planter box running alongside the diner. A man lay inside the box, back lit by the streetlamp behind us. Long, matted dreadlocks spread against the dirt. His head rested on a slim backpack. A tattered blanket covered most of him. Another guy snoozed in a heap on the asphalt nearby, his light hair a tangled mess. A small brown dog lay sprawled by his side. The dog raised his chin and stared at me before lowering it with a shudder. He looked too forlorn to care about much. As I debated what to do, a metallic clanging broke the stillness behind me. I turned and scrambled toward the clatter.

Panting, I climbed on top of a cement block holding up one end of a chain that blocked cars from exiting into the alley. The shooter was here somewhere. Had to be. The blare of a car horn and the hum of traffic drifted by. There was only one way out by car and that was back onto Ocean. No vehicles had left in the past few minutes. I snapped my head in all directions. Still no sign of the guy.

I hopped down. That's when I spotted him. Thirty paces away, he raced toward the alley, hood over his head. I sprinted after him.

Just as he turned the corner, a backdoor opened right in front of him. The runner stumbled and nearly lost his footing, giving me a chance to gain some ground.

"Dammit." I had no weapon. I'd left everything in my purse beneath my chair.

I picked up speed as the guy powered off. Another set of rapidly tapping feet stomped behind me. I didn't bother looking back.

I'd nearly closed in on the shooter when he leapt onto an electric scooter and took off across Broadway, motoring back onto Ocean Avenue. I hotfooted it across the street after him, dodging an SUV that blasted its horn. I tottered around the corner and onto the sidewalk, sliding to a stop after stepping onto a pile of something soft and squishy.

"Crap!" I stared at my pump. False alarm. My foot was stuck in a cluster of oozing cheese from a half-eaten pizza. Thankful it wasn't what I thought it was, I kicked the box aside just as another runner swept past. We caught stares. "Michael!" He'd been hot on our trail.

"I'll get him." He panted away.

I scraped hunks of gooey cheese off my shoe with a piece of cardboard and took off again. Michael ran ahead, but I'd lost sight of the electric scooter. Could Michael still see him?

I caught up on the next corner. Michael was doubled over, breathless.

"Where'd he go?" I asked. The scooter lay on its side across the street.

Michael pointed down the road. "A black sedan...parked over there." He spoke between breaths. "Jumped off and into the passenger side. Door was open. No license plates. Sorry."

I put my arm around him. "If it wasn't for you, we wouldn't have gotten this far. You slowed him down."

"I did?" He straightened and stared down at me through dark and silky lashes.

"You slammed the door into him when you came outside the diner. You stalled his getaway plan." I linked my hand in his.

"But he still got away," he said.

"But I got a better look at him. He's not as old as I thought. Anything unique about the car?"

"I think so," he said. "No. Well, maybe. Looked like a first-generation Ford Focus."

"Good. That could be helpful." I needed to slow down my thoughts. The gunshot rang through my head. "What happened inside the diner? Anyone get hurt?"

"Not exactly."

"What does that mean?"

"I'll tell you on the walk back."

Chapter Three: Blister in the Sun

We did an about face and slow-jogged back to the restaurant. The gunman had aimed toward the rear tables where we'd been sitting. That much I knew.

"When you took off," Michael said, "I raced after you but you'd disappeared. Then I remembered the popular escape route used by all video game villains. Alleys. So, I ran through the diner and out the rear door."

"Who wasn't exactly hurt?" I asked.

"Beckman," Michael said.

"He was shot? Is he okay?"

"Didn't see any blood," Michael said. "Whatever happened, I'm sure it wasn't life threatening. Pretty sure, anyway."

We hustled back inside through the entrance and into the high-volume atmosphere. Everyone seemed to be in a panic except for a tanned, bearded guy in a T-shirt and jeans hovering near the bar. He munched on a pretzel and tossed me a glance before settling on a barstool. Big Sam stood on a chair just past the register, shouting over the din.

"I'll meet you at our table," I told Michael.

"Okay."

He wound his way to the back. I stopped near Big Sam.

"Everybody stay calm and we'll get through this. We will remain calm and collected, you hear?" He stared down at me. "Did you hear me?"

I nodded.

"Good, 'cause I think you're the only one who did." He jumped down.

"Is anybody hurt?" My heart pounded between my ears.

"Nothing serious," he said. "Paramedics are on the way. All in all, we're fine, considering."

"Thank goodness. Don't let anyone leave the building," I said. "They might be witnesses."

"Witnesses? You a cop?"

"No, but I'm the closest thing you've got to one right now."

"What does that mean?" Big Sam asked.

"I've worked with law enforcement." That's all I was saying, for now.

His eyes ran over me. "You a meter maid?"

"No." Just what kind of vibe was I giving out? "I've helped in a few police investigations."

He nodded. "You're undercover. Don't worry. I'll keep your secret. " He raised his chin and squinted at me. "Do something 'til the cops arrive, you hear? I'll seal the place up tight." He turned and marched toward the entry.

I fought the crowd and jabbed my way to the back. My tablemates were on their feet and huddled around Beckman who was on his hands and knees on the floor. He whimpered like he'd been stung by a bee. Okay, maybe a swarm of bees. D.A. Investigator Ramsey held his arms wide open, using a tablecloth to shield the bottom half of Beckman, while a guy in a suit bent over Beckman's rear end. The guy wore latex gloves.

"What's going on?" I whispered to James. "Is he a doctor?"

"You could say that," James replied. "He seems to have a…grip on the situation."

I stood on my toes and peered over the tablecloth. The doc's hand was on Beckman's bare behind. He was applying a small towel to a slightly bloody area. Looked like a flesh wound to me.

"Well, if you're going to get shot, you couldn't ask for a better spot," the doctor was saying.

"That's right." Big Sam showed up behind me. "This is a popular, well known dining establishment. It's no surprise we got a surgeon eating here."

"My ass!" Beckman grumbled. His belly hung over his belt; his graying hair sprang in all directions, thick and coarse, like steel wool.

"I'm actually a veterinarian," the doc told Big Sam. "But your chili cheese fries are exceptional."

"I wouldn't know," I mumbled. My stomach growled right on cue.

"Thank you, sir." Big Sam puffed out his chest. "Your next order will be on the house. And a *Yelp* review would be appreciated, at your convenience, of course."

Beckman cranked his neck around and moaned. "It feels like you're pressing a hot poker to my butt. That means an infection is coming on. I'll probably be dead by dawn. Where are the paramedics?"

"It's not life threatening in the least," the doc said. "And infections take hours, sometimes days to develop. This wound is superficial."

"Maybe to you it is," Beckman said. "But for me, it runs deep."

A paramedic burst through the back door, and Big Sam waved his arms. He pointed down at Beckman. "Man down over here. Nothing serious, folks." He looked around the room.

I glanced around and stepped away. "Where's Michael?" I climbed on top of a chair.

James stood by my side. "Didn't he come back with you?"

"Yes, but I don't see him." I climbed down. "Bet I know where he is."

While the paramedics took care of Beckman, I made my way over to the back exit, James at my heels. Michael was probably revisiting the alley. Maybe the shooter had left something behind.

A uniformed cop entered just as I reached the door.

The officer held up his hand. "No one leaves yet."

"We're missing a member of our party." James flashed his D.A. badge. "He was here before the shooting, but we can't confirm his whereabouts."

"Description?" the cop asked.

"Six feet tall, dark and handsome," I said. "He has an aversion to violence, a low threshold for pain, and only lies when forced to." I whipped out my smartphone and showed him a photo. "That's him. Michael Parris."

The door flew open again, and Michael stepped inside.

"Where have you been?" I asked.

His wide-eyed gaze flashed from me to James to the cop, who darted away. "I went out to check for evidence the shooter might've dropped after I hit him with the door." He ran a hand through his wavy hair.

"You hit him?" James asked.

"By accident," Michael said. "I didn't know he'd be running past. Then I raced after him."

"You what?" James asked.

I knew where James was coming from. It was hard to believe Michael had chased the guy. Michael was a thinker, not a man of action, especially when it came to guns and bad guys. I gave James the run-down.

"Don't you realize how dangerous that was?" James asked. "From here on, you two stay out of this investigation. Leave it to the professionals."

That's what James always said. I'd never listened before and I wasn't going to start now. And he knew it, too.

"I had to go after him," Michael said. "Especially when Corrie got stuck. I thought if I could just slow him down, someone else could nab him. I could've run a little faster, but I wasn't sure if I'd need to duck or hide or yell. I'm not good at dodging bullets—"

"The gunman jumped into a car," I said. "And they drove off."

"He had an accomplice?" James asked.

"A wheelman," I said. "Or woman."

"Any idea where he went?" James asked.

"He shot up Broadway and made a right," Michael said. "That's the last I saw of the car."

James threw up his hands and shook his head. "We don't have much to go on."

"Actually…" Michael held out his hand. "We've got this." He showed us a piece of crumpled paper. "I found it in the alley. It fell out of his pocket when he took off. The getaway car was a Ford Focus circa 1998." He turned to me and moved a loose strand of hair out of my face. "You okay?"

"Exceptional." We were alive, and he got the make and model of the car. My gaze flicked to the paper in Michael's hand. I took it and unfurled it. "Santa Monica Travelers' Inn. A motel receipt, dated yesterday. Paid in cash, room seventeen…"

James grabbed the paper out of my hand. "Stay here. Don't leave the diner."

He headed for the front of the place and planted himself next to a woman at the entry talking to Big Sam. Her long brown hair was pulled back into a ponytail, and a yellow blouse livened up her black pantsuit. She focused on Big Sam, which led me to tag her as a junior detective. Seasoned detectives were like periscopes, slowly eyeballing the room while they talked. Since there was no murder, they'd sent in a junior team member.

"It was a robbery attempt," Michael said to me. "Don't you think? He fired randomly to scare people while he grabbed the money and made a run for it."

I pictured the lanky dude next to the hostess. "The cash register drawer was open when he walked in." He must've noticed. "Wasn't money he was interested in." I slid over to the wood-paneled wall behind our table and eyed the bullet hole. Michael joined me.

"Once the police get the bullet out, that'll help ID the shooter, right?" he asked.

"Maybe. If the bullet has a unique imperfection. But…" I said, stepping back. "Could be a .40 caliber from a Glock."

"Is that good or bad?" Michael asked.

"Too common."

"If Beckman was the target…what if he wasn't? Maybe the shooter was after…" Michael looked over his shoulder. "…someone at that table."

I flipped around and eyed the table of four across from ours. Three men and a woman stood around it, talking with big gestures. "Why would you say that?"

"They're off-duty officers. That's what Beckman said." Michael turned to me. "Think he was aiming for them?"

"Could be," I replied. "If he was a terrible shot. The gunman took aim …and fired. Quickly, confidently. Then again…"

"Yes?" Michael's Adam's apple bobbed up and down.

"He might've been aiming at our table."

"I was afraid you'd say that," Michael said.

Chapter Four: Details

Nothing was obvious when it came to the attempted murder. Who was the target? What was the motive? Why not go after the target in a more isolated setting? And where the heck was my dinner?

"I have a question." I regarded my dining mates. Beckman had been taken by ambulance to Santa Monica General, but Ramsey and James had reclaimed their seats. The junior detective had asked everyone in the restaurant to return to their tables and wait for their statements to be taken. I knew little or nothing about James' D.A. associates. "Anyone here ever been threatened by a criminal?" Besides me, that is. But that's what I got for being the daughter of a well-known private investigator.

The group swapped glances.

"Beckman wins the bragging rights," Ramsey said. "A lot of criminals would love to turn him into a buffet for bugs and bacteria."

Michael wriggled uncomfortably in his chair. James' gaze caught mine. He rolled his eyes.

"Some would say I come in a close second." Ramsey made a loose fist and stared at his fingernails.

"Maybe it's a friend or family member of someone he recently put away," I said. "Like someone in today's trial. Beckman got the verdict he wanted. Maybe the defendant got a little angry."

"I'd say he was more than a little angry," James said. "But that's not unusual."

James' win had involved a local drug dealer who'd beaten a customer for haggling with him. The case should've been assigned to a bigger fish like Beckman or even the chief D.A. herself. But James had finessed it fine, considering he was new to the Westside office, having recently transferred from Orange County. His win meant the bad guy would be locked-up for a respectable amount of time, which could make Beckman….and the rest of the D.A. squad…prime targets.

"What was Beckman's role in putting the guy behind bars?" I asked.

"He did a great job of slouching in the back of the courtroom," Ramsey replied.

"I know what you're thinking," James said to me. "You're wrong."

He flashed a quick grin and dropped his chin down a moment before recapturing my gaze with a look that could soften a hunk of metal. I discreetly checked my pulse, keeping my hands in my lap. It beat at a normal tempo. There was a time when that look made me melt like a sliver of ice in the hot sun. But those days were history.

"If a barracuda wants to show how tough he is, he's not going to swallow a goldfish like me," James said. "He'll go after a fifty-pound tuna. Something that weighs the same as the barracuda."

"You don't want a barracuda after you," Michael said. "They sit and wait in ambush before snapping their victim in two."

"How do you know?" Ramsey asked.

"I'm a trivia nerd," Michael replied.

"He's my go-to source." James beamed at Michael. "The trivia king."

"Whoa," Michael said. "King's a big word. More like a duke or an earl."

"What letter does Dame Judi Dench's character use in the Bond movies as her name?" Ramsey asked.

"M." Michael threw a hand at him. "Dude, you need to pick a harder question."

I held Ramsey's squirrely stare until he dropped his gaze to the frothy mug of lager in front of him. His copper-toned skin looked rough around the edges. He leaned close to me.

"You haven't been around the legal field very long, have you?" He snickered.

How did he know I was a newbie lawyer? "Elementary, my dear Ramsey. You looked me up." All he had to do was check the State Bar website to find how long I'd been in practice.

"What are you…like twenty-one?" Ramsey asked.

"That was so five years ago," I said. What kind of D.A. investigator was he?

"Fact is," Ramsey leaned back. "Any one of us could've been the target."

"You don't seem too rattled," I said.

"I'm not going to worry about what didn't happen." He focused his small round eyes on me.

James grunted. "The target was Beckman."

"It could be me," Ramsey said. His squinty eyes never left mine.

"Because you're the investigator?" I said.

"That's right." He uncorked a wide-mouthed smile. "I work in the shadows with the questionable types, straight outta the underworld. Mobsters, lockpickers and no-gooders. A lot of people want to tango with me."

"Wow," Michael said. "You sound like a comic book character."

I rose and walked around the table. "It's no coincidence the shooting took place the day of James' win in court. I need a list of everyone who could be angered by the verdict. Another member of the D.A. legal team could be next." It was James I was worried about.

Ramsey stood. "Do you really think today's defendant would be dumb enough to send someone to tangle with a group of D.A.s in a crowded restaurant the day of? Chances of getting caught were high."

"He didn't get caught," I replied.

"These kinds of criminals lie in wait," Ramsey said. "They hit you when you least expect it." His shiny black orbs glided around the table to make sure he had everyone's full attention. "They climb in your bathroom window and wait until the middle of the night, when everyone's sleeping."

"You probably never get any sleep," Michael said.

"I haven't slept since 2017…" Ramsey said, "…without one eye open. These types of felons…" He planted his palms on the table, taking turns to make eye contact with each one of us. "…make sure they're not caught. And they know how to use a gun. This shooter didn't know what the hell he was doing. I say it was random."

"That's a bunch of—" I started.

James stood and took my arm. "Let's take a quick walk to the front. You, too," he told Michael.

James strode between us while he whispered to me, "Let's keep our opinions to ourselves."

"Since when?" I asked.

"Since Ramsey's not a team player," James said. "The less information we share with him, the better off we are."

I had to skip to keep up with his long strides. Ramsey enjoyed being the center of attention, that's for sure. "He knows more than he's sharing."

"James is saying we're not going to squeeze any answers out of him," Michael said. "And he could make trouble for you at the studio if you persist because he knows the right people. Am I right?"

James gave a quick nod.

As if I'd not had enough trouble already. For the past few months, I'd been working in the business and legal affairs department at Ameripictures Film Studios in Culver City, a few short miles away. I'd had more than my share of trouble on the lot, so I couldn't imagine Ramsey making life any rockier.

"He may be withholding important information," I said. "Could be—"

"Listen. I'll handle Ramsey." James stopped near Big Sam and the junior detective I'd spotted earlier.

"That's her," Big Sam told the detective and pointed to me. "She's the one that chased the guy."

The detective held out her hand and smiled. "Detective Abigail Rosewater. Call me Abby. Nice to meet you."

"Corrie Locke." I shook her hand.

Abby had high cheekbones and high heels. Her grip was firm. She traded in the smile for a frown.

"Glad you weren't hurt," she said. "Chasing criminals is risky business."

"She's no stranger to danger," Big Sam added. "That's what she led me to believe, anyway. She's some kind of detective."

"No, I'm not," I said and turned to Abby. "You're going to want the ballistics on the shooter's gun, and details on the vantage point. I can help. I was close by when it happened."

"Are you trained in law enforcement?" she asked.

"My father was Monty Locke."

"Am I supposed to know him?" She looked at the others. "Doesn't sound familiar."

"He was a private investigator who worked with L.A.P.D., as well as neighboring jurisdictions and a federal agency or two," James said. "Might want to look him up. Corrie's no dummy, and she's trained as well as any member of law enforcement."

I looked around. That sure sounded legit, but was it really me? I was plenty good at being a dummy. Who let the shooter escape?

"Assistant Deputy D.A. James Zachary." He traded cards with Abby.

Meanwhile, the detective's slacks had tiny bows along the hem and her silk blouse looked pricey. Her skin was smooth and dewy, like she'd just come off a facial at a Beverly Hills spa. Abby didn't dress like any police detective I'd ever seen. Her gaze flicked to me.

"Sounds like we could use your help in finding tonight's guy." She handed me her card.

I clenched my teeth to keep my jaw from dropping. This was a first. Usually, law enforcement did their level best to shoo me away from the crime scene and out of the picture. It was like living in an alternate reality.

"I never disappoint," I said. Not too often, anyway.

"You're the one who found the motel receipt?" she asked me.

Michael stepped forward and passed on his business card. "That would be me, Detective. Only because I was helping Corrie. Not that she needs any help. You don't know this yet, but she's L.A.'s best kept secret weapon when it comes to solving a crime. And I'm perfectly capable of handling myself in a case, as long as I'm with her."

"Good to know. Let me tell you a little something about me." She ran her eyes over all of us. "Out of the ten or so assignments I've had in the last year, a lot were solved. Even though I mostly helped. Meaning I wasn't the lead. But I could've been."

Michael flicked me a look. "Awesome record. But with Corrie, there isn't any case she hasn't solved. That's just the way it is."

He was right, almost. I'd never found the person who poisoned my father.

Abby grinned again. "Working together, we'll wrap this up in no time."

"I saw the suspect aim and fire," I said. "I tried to stop him, but I…" Failed was such a harsh word. "Didn't." It's not a failure if you learned something. I learned that I should keep my purse…and my weapons…with me at all times. I shifted onto my other foot. "We need to confirm who the target was."

"Agreed." Abby scanned our faces. "You can all go back to your table." Her gaze rested on mine. "After you give your statement to the officer, come see me."

A cop stormed up to us and spoke to the detective in low tones. They turned their backs to us. I slid closer.

"Let me know once he's inside," she told him.

I stepped forward. "Inside the motel?"

Abby cranked her head around. "We'll chat in a bit."

"Don't you think the receipt was too obvious a clue to leave behind?" I asked. "Maybe it's a trap." My hunches were flowing freely tonight.

"What makes you say that?" She stepped closer to me. "Do you know something we don't? Because I don't think these criminals have enough brains to set a trap. They're dropping clues all the time. One dropped his credit card after robbing a convenience store last week."

"This one knows what he's doing." I knew what her next question would be.

"Now how do you know that?" She crossed her arms against her chest.

"He knew his target would be here tonight. And there had to be some planning involved if he was able to escape the way he did."

"Not necessarily. He could've been lucky."

I gave her a briefing on the scooter and the driver waiting.

"Okay, maybe he's got some savvy." She planted her hands on her hips. "He stuck to a plan, but it was nothing special." She turned to the uniform. "Let me know when you hear something."

She marched to the cashier. We wound our way back to the table.

"Why was she so cooperative?" I asked.

"She's a junior detective with a decent reputation," James said. "Hardworking, solid work ethic and favors the color yellow."

"How do you know that, bro?" Michael asked.

"I asked one of the officers."

"Something's off." Actually, several things were off. I needed to figure out where the shooter was aiming. And exactly at who.

We returned to the table and took our seats. One by one, we were called up to a small office by the rear door. Finally, the only ones remaining were Michael and me. I went first.

Officer Nolan Fisher looked friendly in a Dudley Do-Right kind of way and was in his late thirties or so. He wore a ready smile, a thick mop of brown hair, and a cleft in his square chin. He sat on a barstool next to my chair, making him a lot taller. He left the door to the space open giving us a clear view of the back of the restaurant. The questions rolled out, starting with the basics. Then he turned to the harder stuff.

"D.A. James Zachary mentioned you stood close to the shooter when he made his move. Why'd you go upfront?" Fisher asked.

"Everyone at my table was eating, but me. I did what any famished onlooker would do. I hunted down the manager. To complain."

"Don't tell me you ordered the crispy chicken sandwich with—"

"Spicy slaw? Yes. How'd you know?"

"Happens every time." Fisher shook his head. "I stick to a burger and fries for that reason."

I leaned in a little closer to him and pointed to the side of his nose. "You have a little something…"

His hand flew to his nostrils and he wiped each with a finger. He grinned. "You got me. I couldn't resist eating a few fries. Some of my buddies were sitting at the table across from yours." He pointed. All heads belonging to the off-duty cops leaned toward the middle. Much of their food was uneaten, which reminded me, I was still hungry.

Fisher turned serious and refocused his clear blue gaze on me. "You see the shooter up close?"

"All the parts that weren't covered up." I replayed the scene in my mind. The guy never looked right at me. All I saw was his profile. "Wasn't much to see."

"Anything unusual about him?" Fisher asked.

"Tall, slim and his nose was hooked like a hawk's. He pulled the gun out of his left pocket with his left hand. No gloves." Who doesn't wear gloves to commit a crime? Either a very confident criminal, one that didn't care or a dummy, like Abby said. There'd been nothing unusual about him, except… "I'm not sure, but…"

"Yes?"

"The index finger on the left hand seemed different." I replayed the scene in my head again. "Like he was missing the top part."

Fisher stared at me, mouth open for a few moments. "Okay. That's more detail than I'd expected." He shifted around on his stool. "Do you have a photographic memory?"

"No." I stood.

"So you could be mistaken."

"That's right. Are we done?"

"How is it you're able to provide details and none of the other…fifty or so people eating or drinking here could? And you chased the guy? Who does that? You're either extremely cool under pressure or…"

I blew out a sigh. "I worked with Monty Locke."

"The private investigator?" His brows shot up.

"AKA Dad."

His head tilted back as he understood. "You helped him solve—"

"Yes."

"Sorry about your father. He was a world class P.I. He worked a lot of high-profile cases with L.A.P.D."

"Are we done? Because I'd like to eat a little something." My voice rose. Hunger brought out the Attila the Hun in me.

"Sorry. Go ahead." He stood. "If you have anything else, contact me, okay?" He handed me a card.

Michael joined us. "Everything alright?" He looked from me to the cop.

"Peachy." I rose to my feet.

Michael whispered, "There's a burger and fries waiting for you. Fresh from the kitchen. With a banana chocolate sundae."

"Oh, goodie." I grabbed him by his shirt and looked up into his twinkling eyes. This was one of many reasons why my heart belonged to Michael. I planted a kiss on his lips and headed to our table.

I wolfed down dinner and was polishing off dessert when Michael showed up.

"Was that a traditional police interrogation?" he asked. "Because your interrogations are a lot more interesting. He could use a few tips from you." He dipped into my sundae with his spoon.

"That's because I'm not a police officer, so my interrogation skills are looser." More like all over the place. I licked my spoon. A shadow fell across my ice cream bowl. I looked up.

"We need to talk." Abby stood over me.

Chapter Five: Criminal Profiling

Junior detective Abby Rosewater escorted me to a corner table and took the chair next to mine. "You've got a history of handing over cases to the police. Three in the past six months." She slapped her palm on the tabletop and grinned. "That's amazing."

My gaze scoured the restaurant while she spoke. Most of the diners had been sent home. "Just trying to do my civic duty." More like satisfy my endless thirst for dangerous encounters. Getting bad guys and girls off the street? There's no thrill quite like it.

She followed my gaze for a few moments before zeroing in on me again. "Can you walk me through the shooter's moves?"

"I can."

"That would be awesome." She looked around. "I could use a cupcake. Think they have any here?"

Was she for real? "They've got milkshakes and sundaes. What do you want to know about the gunman?"

She snapped her head back to me. "Plenty. But when we're done here tonight, you're done. I'm sorry, but I can't keep you involved with my investigation." She looked more disappointed than I was.

"What happened to us working together?" I asked.

"Wouldn't that be cool? Two strong, go get 'em types not afraid to break a fingernail in the name of justice, setting a positive example of how law enforcement and civilians with sharp skill sets can work side-by-side to haul in criminals and toss them in the slammer." She inhaled. "That would be us." She put up a hand to stop a passing server. "I would love a chocolate milkshake, please." She turned back to me. "Except when I ran the idea of our teaming up by my boss, the head detective, he said, 'Nothing doing.' As far as he's concerned, you're a liability. That means—"

"I could get you into trouble if I don't follow the rules to the letter. I'm familiar with lawyer speak." Had I crossed paths with her boss and possibly annoyed him a little? Or a lot?

"He's a by-the-book, old school detective who handed me this case. And..." She leaned in closer. "...he thinks he's got me under his thumb, but he really doesn't." She leaned back. "Can we keep this between us? This is my first case on my own and it's important I do it right. My boss doesn't want me to get into any trouble, by bringing you in to help."

"I get it. He's a control freak and doesn't like that he's got no control over me."

"No, I mean, yes, he...that's actually true. But we...I have a case to solve. I may or may not come to you for suggestions or theories," Abby said. "But that'll be on the down-low."

"Deal." I didn't care about theories. I cared about solving the case under the radar, which was my favorite way to fly.

She relaxed her arms. "Good, we're on the same page." She held out her fist and I obliged with a bump.

"Unless, I discover, that's an uppercase 'I'..." Wait, that didn't make sense, did it? Too late. "That the target wasn't Beckman."

"You think it wasn't?"

A milkshake landed in front of her and she took a long slurp.

"Don't know yet. But I go full throttle if I discover it was James, Michael or me."

"I didn't hear that. But, I understand. You're looking out for your tribe and yourself. Even so, the identity of the target is for my department's eyes and ears only. Which means..." She crinkled her nose. "No sharing with you. Once I find out." She leaned in closer and whispered, "But there's a good chance he was aiming for the table of off-duty officers across from yours."

"Detective." Officer Fisher stood behind her.

Abby pulled back and stood.

Fisher cracked a grin my way. "Hi, again."

I flashed a smile.

His gaze snapped back to Abby. "Did you know she's the one who found—"

"Can you please focus, Officer?" Abby told him. "We have important business here. A gunman is on the loose. And I'm here to interrogate Ms. Locke about it."

"Sorry, sir…I mean ma'am." He turned somber. "I just came to tell you, we've finished questioning everyone."

"Fine." Abby whirled around to face me. "Officer Fisher, escort Ms. Locke to the front. Have her wait for me there." She strutted away.

Fisher widened his eyes and called his grin back. "You'll probably figure this whole thing out in no time."

"I think…" I said, "Detective Rosewater's the one who'll figure it out."

"She's new around here. She could use some help."

I glanced at his uniform. "You're a level…"

"…two officer." He cupped his hand to the side of his mouth. "I'm going for detective trainee."

"You'd be a good detective." I wasn't too sure about that, but one thing I knew was he could be useful to me. "That's too bad about the Travelers' Inn." There was a chance his tongue would wag with a bit of prodding.

"I know," he said, then lowered his voice, "who knew it'd be a set-up?"

Correction: there was a huge chance he'd wag. "Was anyone hurt?"

"The officer noticed the trip wire just before he was about to—"

An older officer showed up next to me and addressed Fisher. "Detective Rosewater wants to know why you didn't escort this young lady to the front?"

"On our way."

Officer Fisher waved me ahead, leaned down and whispered, "You have a knack for finding things out, don't you?"

I grinned and looked up to see Abby watching us with a worried expression. Fisher led me to the front and scurried away.

"You're the only person here who got close to the man with the gun. Which makes you…" Abby leaned into me, "…valuable. Can you retrace his steps?"

In moments, I stood by the front door and recalled the guy wearing the hoodie. I hunched my shoulders slightly, lowered my chin and looked straight ahead, just like he did. Then I moseyed over to the cash register. Abby appeared next to me, nervously looking around. I towered over her in my three-inch heels.

"He waited here for about five seconds." I turned my head slightly. "The register drawer was open. He could've grabbed the money and run, but he didn't. He stared ahead and lifted his chin like he was looking for something, or someone, in the back." Just like I was doing. I took a few more steps…like he did and caught my breath. "Wait." He didn't have a clear shot to the table where the off-duty cops had been sitting. A tall, wide wooden post blocked the right part of his view.

"What's happening?" Abby asked. "Don't zone out on me." She leaned sideways, so she could get a better look. "Is this where he stood when he fired the shot?"

I pressed my lips together. I liked to mull things over before sharing. I waited a few beats and made my decision. I'd play it straight this time. Stepping back, I said, "Here. Take my place and tell me what you see."

Abby slid into my spot, held out her hands like she was holding a gun, and stared ahead. "Are you sure he stood here?"

"Positive. Don't move, okay?" I didn't wait for her answer. Instead, I dashed over to our table. Michael and James sat in their chairs. Officer Fisher stood where Ramsey had been sitting. I took my place.

"What are you doing?" James asked.

I waved my arm over my head and looked at James. "Call Detective Rosewater and ask her what she sees."

A minute later, Abby joined us.

Officer Fisher straightened up and stood at alert.

"I'm going to have to try the food here. Smells delicious. I heard the chicken pot pie is dreamy." Abby's gaze circled the table. "Is this how you were all sitting before the shooting?"

"Almost exactly," Michael said. "Except Beckman was sitting where the officer was."

"See if you can get D.A. Beckman on the line," she told Fisher and turned to James just as Ramsey skidded over to the table.

"What did I miss?" He grabbed a seat.

"Are you with the D.A.'s office?" Abby asked Ramsey. "I need to know who sat at this table tonight."

"Because you want to re-enact the scene?" Michael asked.

"Uh…yes. That's what I'm doing," she replied.

I mentally rolled my eyes. What was she doing?

"What kind of proof do you have that he's after one of us?" Ramsey asked.

"That's classified," Abby said.

"Was the crook one of the diners?" Ramsey's fingers gripped the edge of the table.

"Also, classified," she said.

"Lady, if I'm a possible target, you need to declassify," Ramsey said. "How else are we going to protect ourselves and bring the guy in?" He crossed his legs and turned away. "You're wrong, anyway."

"Look, I might be wrong in believing it'll rain tomorrow or that my apartment will be miraculously clean when I get home," Abby said. "But I'm not wrong about this. It's possible Beckman wasn't the target."

Ramsey's lips curled upward. "Ah ha! That's what I thought."

"He could've been a bad shot." James leaned back in his chair and spoke slowly. "Missed me by nearly three feet."

Michael's gaze widened and his stare locked onto James. "Bro—"

"We don't know that James was the target," I said. "Or anyone else." We needed to act as if we were all targets, but I didn't want to worry Michael. "Besides, no one's getting hurt. We'll wrap this up in no time."

"I like your attitude," Abby told me. "We will wrap this up, but like I said…" She smiled kindly at me. "…there's no 'you' in the 'we' part. Can't risk a civilian getting hurt during our watch. Especially during my watch."

"Where do you think most of your relevant information came from?" Michael asked.

"You can't be the hunted and the hunter at the same time," she replied.

"She's done that plenty of times," Michael said. "She's flexible that way."

"Which one of you doesn't understand the role of the L.A.P.D.?" Abby slapped her palm down on the table. "We're here to protect and to serve, and that's what we're going to do, dammit."

Michael and I swapped glances.

"You're right. We'll sit this one out. Too dangerous." Michael practically winked at me.

"I am a licensed investigator," Ramsey said. "I'll be investigating this shooting vis-a-vis the D.A.'s office. Share information now or I'll get a subpoena issued."

Abby's face lit up. "I like the sound of that. Makes me feel powerful. I've never been on a power trip before."

"Did you know…" Michael said to Abby, "James put away a big drug dealer today? He's the one that needs protecting."

"You're a college professor, right?" she asked. "Computer science? When I need questions answered regarding my hard drive or my mouse, I'll come to you. Otherwise, stay out of it."

"Associate dean, actually," Michael said.

"Gotten any death threats lately?" she asked him.

"No," Michael said.

Abby's gaze swung between us. "The target might be anyone at this table, except the computer professor." Her gaze lingered on James. "In the meantime, you all need to sit tight while we resolve this issue."

"Don't worry, Detective." It was James' turn to stand. "We'll leave this to the professionals to handle. The D.A.'s office will do everything to cooperate."

I caught James' stare. I knew what he was thinking. We'd come up with a plan that didn't involve Abby.

"I suggest you go home, have a nice cup of hot cocoa, preferably with marshmallows and a shot of brandy, and be extra aware of your surroundings until we catch our man." She turned on her heel with Fisher close behind.

"That's it?" Michael was on his feet. "She should at least post a guy at your place."

"Let them handle it their way," James said quietly. "And we'll handle it our way."

Chapter Six: Second Chance

Michael and I followed James home to his pad on the Redondo Beach Esplanade, a popular seaside stretch hosting condos and apartments overlooking the Pacific. A short wall ran along the top of the beach, serving as a spot to perch and enjoy the white sands, teal-blue waves and dazzling sunsets.

We motored onto a cement driveway, past a plain boxy apartment building straight out of the sixties. James pulled his SUV into a narrow spot. Michael parked in a nearby lot off to the side of the building. Our mission was to keep James safe and watch for tails.

Michael tagged behind James as he powered up a flight of concrete stairs flanked by steel railings. I slipped out of the car and into the shadows of a eucalyptus tree at the foot of the staircase. Voices floated down from a nearby unit. A breeze rustled the branches above my head and clawed at my blue silk blouse and slacks. I gripped my gun in my hand.

Minutes later, I crouched and stepped away from the tree, tiptoeing toward the front of the building. I'd nearly made it when a soft tap-tap drifted my way. I froze. Pressing my back against the wall, I waited. It was hard to hear past cars whizzing by and the whirr of the wind, but the tapping seemed closer. I hid behind a hydrangea bush and held my breath. Could be a cat. I straightened up and my heart stopped. There he was. The man in the hood and the shades. He scampered up the driveway like a dog returning home after being let out to do his business.

A door slammed and hurried footsteps pounded above me. James and Michael reappeared at the top of the stairs.

I lunged toward the shooter for the second time that night; this time I had a weapon. Fingers clasping the barrel, I raised it high and slammed the grip down toward the back of his skull. He ducked and rolled before I made contact. Hopping to his feet, he rocketed off, with me in hot pursuit. I shoved the gun in my pocket and pulled a five-pointed shuriken out of my belt. Holding it between the thumb and knuckle of my index finger, I threw it vertically like a knife, adding a last-minute flick in my wrist.

The throwing star stuck to the back of his left shoulder, but he didn't flinch.

"What?" He should at least slow down. Instead, he reached his opposite arm behind him and yanked out my star. It clinked to the ground.

He tore around a corner and into an alley. So did I. Footsteps beat the pavement behind me. I glanced over my shoulder. James ran about ten feet back.

"Call Abby," I told him.

"Can you get a clear shot?" James yelled.

That was the burning question. No one else was around. Firing my gun seemed to be the only way to stop him. I yanked it out, raised and aimed…but before I could fire, the runner cut a sharp right toward the courtyard of an apartment. I couldn't take a chance on hitting a bystander. He raced into a well-lit enclosure, leading back to the Esplanade. He flew down the curb, into the street and toward a black sedan double-parked near James' building. The passenger door swung open and the shooter dove inside. The car dashed up the Esplanade and out of sight.

Chapter Seven: My Bodyguard

"You kept yourself busy while we were upstairs." James spoke between breaths, doubled over next to me on the sidewalk.

"The blood." I paused to catch my breath. "Did you get—"

"Michael has your throwing star," he said. "Police are on the way. We'll have to get creative."

Since shuriken weren't legal in California, I couldn't turn it over to the law. Or let them know it belonged to me. "I need to switch it with…"

A smattering of footsteps tapped the ground behind us. Michael put on the brakes. "You guys okay?"

I straightened. "Where's my—"

He pulled it out of his pocket. "Your weapon of choice?" He held the shuriken up in a small plastic bag. "Or should I say your Excalibur." He grinned.

I grabbed the bag and held out my hand. "I'll need your knife. We can tell the cops I threw it…"

Michael pulled his knife out of a small leather pouch and handed it to me. I wiped my right hand all over the grip, then pulled out a tissue from my pocket. I took the shuriken out of the bloody bag and dropped the knife inside, using the plastic to smear the blood over the blade. Sirens blasted nearby.

"Let's head back," James said, leading the way to his apartment.

We put on the brakes at the bottom of the staircase.

"Get anything?" James asked me.

"Same outfit he wore at Big Sam's," I said. "Must've come to finish the job."

"You think he was aiming for James in the diner?" Michael asked.

"Hard to say," James said.

"Seems obvious to me," I said.

"Now he's messed up twice," Michael said. "He must be mad."

"He either knew where you lived or followed us," I told James. I was positive we hadn't been shadowed.

"He's a damn good tail if he did follow." James grunted.

"Man, oh man," Michael said. "This guy means business. But it's three against one, right?"

"He had a driver again." I told them about the car.

"It's the same Ford Focus. Has to be," Michael said.

"Absolutely." All signs indicated that he'd been plotting this for a while, which meant he had a head-start and a plan in place. We had neither. But who drives an old subcompact as a getaway car? Someone practical…and cheap.

Nearly thirty minutes later, an unmarked white Crown Vic rolled up the driveway and parked in the middle. Detective Rosewater stomped out and marched up to us. I stood at the bottom of the stairs. James was one stair up, and Michael two stairs behind him.

"A little too soon to be holding a reunion," she said. "Wouldn't you say?"

"Not if you want to surprise someone," I said.

Two uniforms joined us. Abby's gaze wandered around then focused on me. "Is that for me?" She pointed to the plastic bag. "Aw, you shouldn't have. Want to tell me what happened here?"

I recounted my story, replacing the part where I used my shuriken with my using Michael's knife. I handed her the bag.

"Amazing." Abby passed the bag to a cop. "That you were the one to chase him again. And to lose him again." She squinted my way. "How do you know he wasn't after you?"

"I wasn't at the table when he fired at Big Sam's, remember?" I mentally rolled my eyes. "And I don't live here. Why would he expect to find me at James' place?"

She turned to James. "Guess it's safe to say he was after you."

"Don't need a detective to figure that out," James mumbled.

"Let's go to the station for a little chat," Abby said to him.

"I expected as much," James said.

"That's great news," Michael said. "Because he needs protection."

"Maybe," Abby said. "But the only way to protect him would be to throw him in jail, which we can't do without arresting him. We're not exactly running a bodyguard service."

"But once he's released the shooter'll try again," Michael said.

"Steps will be taken…" Abby started.

"Michael, go with James," I said. "Take his car and afterward, drive him to your place. I'll drive your car home, and we'll meet up later."

"Don't you want to join us?" Abby asked. "I've got questions for you, too."

I took a step and limped. "I hurt my ankle. I'll need to ice it. And if that doesn't work, I'll see a doctor."

"But, you—" Michael said.

"I'll be fine," I said.

"Detective," James said. "Mind if she's escorted home?"

"So not necessary—" I said.

"Easy peasy." Abby turned to one of the officers. "Follow Ms. Locke home and take a peek inside." She returned her gaze to me.

"I decline that kind, but unnecessary offer." I didn't need law enforcement breathing down my neck.

"If D.A. Zachary says you need protection…"

"I'll go with her," Michael said. His voice turned low and slow, almost James Bondish, except without the British accent and the tux. "I'll see her safely inside. Then I'll drive to the station to give you my version of tonight's events and I'll escort James home." He took the steps down smoothly, edging James aside, cautious and confident as a jungle cat. He linked gazes with Abby. "That's how I roll."

James gave a grin of approval and Abby raised a brow.

"Seriously?" Abby asked. She folded her arms over her chest and gave Michael the head-to-toe. "Aren't you just—"

"The protector, that's right. See…" He took a step closer. "You got me all wrong. It's true, I run the computer science department at L.A. Tech by day, but when hunting down criminals, I'm someone else entirely."

He was someone else, alright. Full of surprises.

"Oh, and don't forget that Indiana Jones was a college professor," he said. "Which I'm not, by the way. I'm dean—"

Abby put up her hand. "I don't have time for this." She turned to me. "You're declining a police escort and that's fine. It's your hide." She regarded James. "Let's go." She turned and trekked down the driveway.

James flicked us a look and followed her. "Catch up with you two later."

When they were out of earshot, Michael turned to me. "We've got a gunman to catch."

"And I know just the team that can do it."

Chapter Eight: We're Not Going to Take It

Michael eased his ride down Catalina Avenue and hung a right on Pearl toward Coast Highway. Meanwhile, I kept my eyes peeled for a tail. Michael had played the part of superhero to a T tonight, but he still drove like his dear old granny. At the speed limit and behind limit lines all the way. And going through a yellow light? Not an option. I was pretty sure I'd need to join Eye-rollers Anonymous after this trip.

"You think he'll make his next move soon?" he asked.

"Within twenty-four hours." Likely less. I expected Ramsey to be next, but maybe that was what the shooter wanted us to think. "Turn left down Sixth and make your way to my place from there."

"Is that code for take the longest route ever?" he asked. "I get it. These little side streets make it easy to spot a tail. The shooter may think he knows what he's doing, but you know a whole lot more."

"I don't know nearly enough." I needed to think like a gunslinger. The angry, vengeful type, hellbent on taking out members of the D.A.'s office…if he could shoot straight. "Who is this guy?"

"You get to know him better, and I'll continue to dominate technology in case we need social media or a deep computer search to get closer to him," Michael said. "The computer is my comrade in arms, as you know."

"Is there something you're not telling me?" I asked. Michael seemed more confident than usual.

"What? No." Michael flashed me a worried look. "I'm just stepping up my game. You know, I've gotta be on my toes. To show this criminal we're not going to let him point guns and shoot innocent people. And, I want to be the best man I can for you."

"You're already the best," I said. I'd watched him grow from boy to man and from man to an unconventional criminal catching side-kick with all kinds of practical skills. While I was trying to improve myself for him, he'd been doing the same for me.

"I'm a work-in-progress." He turned onto Longfellow Street.

"Drive past my place and park a few duplexes away. Across the street."

"Noted."

"We've got to make sure all three possible targets are at the D.A. offices tomorrow," I said. "If Beckman's in proper working order, that is."

"Are we going to dangle some bait to bring the shooter in? I can work with James to make that happen," Michael said.

"No baiting for now. But don't use your cell phones. All communication should be in person."

"Check."

"Make sure you're both armed."

"Check. I've got my tranq gun, but my knife is on its way to police headquarters."

Tranquilizer gun and water pistols aside, Michael wasn't keen on shooting guns at anyone…or accidentally shooting himself in the process. I wasn't worried about James. He was always packing a little something and knew how to use it.

Michael cruised past my crib while we eyed the neighborhood. I lived in a cozy little bootleg unit in the front of a duplex on Longfellow Avenue, a few blocks from the golden sands of Hermosa Beach. I could almost hear the waves splashing from my pad. *Almost* being the keyword.

I shot a glance at Michael. "Thank you."

"I need to thank you." He shot glances at me between maneuvering into a spot up the street. "I wouldn't be who I am if it weren't for you. I used to be this geeky dude who never took risks outside of video games…"

"And now look at you." I grinned.

"I never dreamed I'd get so much character building from the woman I love."

"Why do I feel like a boy scout leader?"

"A beautiful, smart scout leader of a one-man troop."

"All I need is one." We kissed and I cleared my throat. "We've got a criminal to catch."

He turned off the car and sat up straight. "Right."

"Wait two minutes then follow me, but don't take the same path," I said.

"I'll make my own." He reached over and kissed me again.

I tore myself away and jay-walked across the street, drifting in and out of the shadows. I bolted up the walkway toward my place. I was certain villainous eyes weren't on the lookout, but I wasn't taking a chance. I tiptoed past to my back door, and dove into a row of evergreen bushes lining one side of the slim walkway. I waded through, tiptoed across and padded up the stairs. I unlocked the door and slipped into my kitchenette. I posted myself next to the living room window, a pair of night vision goggles pressed against my eyes. The goggles belonged to the arsenal I'd inherited from Dad. Parts of the collection were in a locked metal box in the garage, but the rest spilled over into my hall closet, also locked. Weapons, gas masks, tear bombs…I had it all.

I knelt by my window and peered between the slats of my blinds. Michael's car door opened. He edged out. Michael 2.0 was back. He crouched and padded quickly down the street. But it was the old Michael who crossed at the crosswalk after looking both ways a few times. But once he did, his confident march returned.

"I made it without incident," he whispered when he stepped inside.

He hustled around to take a quick look. Quick because the whole place could fit into a sardine can, with the sardines intact. The furnishings were sparse; just a futon, coffee table and lamp, along with the dartboard hanging on the wall, for shuriken practice. The kitchenette hosted a small table and two chairs, plus an appliance or two. He rounded the corner into my bedroom.

My gaze remained fixed on the sparse nightlife outside, but I moved aside after a minute. I had nothing to show for my surveillance, except for a cat scurrying under a car.

I slid into my kitchenette and grabbed a large bag of tortilla chips. I ripped open the top and started munching. Once I started, stopping was not an option. I pulled out a jar of tomato salsa and entered snack heaven. My bedroom closet was overstuffed with clothes and blankets, and shoeboxes filled the space beneath my bed. That left the dresser. There really was no place to hide in my bedroom, which explained why Michael showed up moments later.

"Chips and salsa time," I said.

"Most important meal of the day." He munched a chip. "I'd sure feel better if I stayed here tonight." He peered out the blinds, into the street. "I know you're capable of handling yourself, but when you're alone—"

"I'm never alone," I said between crunches. "You should know that by now." I grabbed my purse and turned it upside down. Out spilled the contents: my pistol, pepper spray, lip gloss, a hair brush, a bag of trail mix, crackers and a stun gun.

"No wallet?"

"No room." I reached into a kitchen cabinet over the fridge and pulled out a small knife. I handed it to Michael.

"Your substitute."

"Thanks." He took out his knife holder and shoved the new one inside.

I passed him my bag of chips and stared down at my fingernails. Boy, could I use a manicure.

"If I hadn't asked you to come to James' celebration tonight, you'd be sleeping peacefully right now." He dipped and crunched more chips.

My gaze stepped up to his. "Number one, I never sleep peacefully. A beetle walking across the floor wakes me. Number two, I would've been so disappointed if I'd missed all the action." A tingle of excitement flitted up my spine. I had a case to solve and a man I loved standing in front of me. "And I wouldn't be enjoying this tasty snack with you, would I?" I took my bag back. "You'd better go." I wanted him to stay, but he was needed elsewhere.

"I almost forgot about James." He stepped away to the door and flipped a U just before he turned the knob. He rejoined me and we shared a parting kiss. He left minutes later.

I kept up my post at the window a little longer, mulling over the events of the night. When only a few broken chip pieces remained in the bottom of the bag, I plopped onto the futon. I'd downed enough to feed six people. "Nice going." I hiccupped.

The next time I opened my eyes, strips of light peeped through the blinds. I stretched out my arms and shook my head. The seeds of a plan were finally forming.

Chapter Nine: Meet Me Halfway

The triggerman still had a job to do, which meant the four of us needed to act fast to get him off the streets. Four of us being Michael, James, me and Veera. Veera wasn't just my legal assistant at the movie studio. She doubled and tripled as my friend, confidante and life-hurdles consultant, when she wasn't working in business and legal affairs, or attending online law school at night. We were between jobs at the studio while our new boss was off filming a documentary in India, so we had truckloads of time on our hands. What better way to fill that time than nipping on the heels of a shooter on the lam? That's what I told Veera when I called her.

She answered with a yawn, then perked up. "Did I hear you right? You got us a case? 'Cause I'm so ready. Give me ten minutes to get my game face on."

I could almost see her rolling up her sleeves and packing up her pepper spray and duct tape, which always came in handy. She'd bought a legitimate set of cuffs, too, since mine were never around when we needed them. There was quite a racket on Veera's end while I gave her a run-down of last night's events. Drawers clanged open, mattress springs squeaked and something whirred.

"That's what I like about you," she said. "Most people go out to eat in a restaurant and all they get is a meal. You go out to eat, don't get your meal, and get served crime á la mode instead. And what I like most of all? You don't waste time. You take action. Thanks for offering me a piece of that action."

"Let's meet at ten in the diner," I said. "We'll eat there."

"Okay by me, Boss. We'll get some grub and dig around the scene of the crime."

***

A pair of joggers, sweatshirts and sneakers permanently resided in the trunk of my age-old BMW, along with a couple of hats and sunglasses. Veera kept a spare change of clothes in my trunk, too. Disguises and comfort wear always came in handy for P.I. work. I planned to stop by the day job later, so I dressed like the movie studio lawyer that I was…or wasn't, at the moment. I slipped into a fitted, sleeveless V-neck dress that landed just above my knees. The side slit came in handy in case I needed to make a run for it. Kitten heeled pumps were not so handy, but easier for sprinting in than three-inch heels.

I motored to Big Sam's Diner with an hour to spare, and parked in the adjoining lot. Daylight gave a whole different perspective to things. I hadn't noticed a short, neatly trimmed hedge that separated the lot from the sidewalk. The gunman could've been hiding in there. A police car parked across the street. Nothing looked out of the ordinary.

A hostess stand was set up beneath a large blue umbrella, just outside the front entry of the diner. Tables with blue and white checked cloths were scattered around. A server offered me a menu and I ordered two breakfast burritos to go, then followed him inside. Not a customer in sight. The wait staff huddled near the kitchen. I ducked when I spotted Big Sam by the back door. There was business to handle before we made contact. I quick-stepped outside, and waited until the server passed me the bags of food.

I strolled through the mostly empty parking lot and landed in front of the planter box where the homeless guy'd been sleeping last night. Empty. No sign of the man snoozing on the ground either, or his dog. Pieces of bark were sprinkled along the surface of the box, mixed with cigarette butts, litter and parts of old newspapers. I scanned the bark for signs of personal effects from the previous occupant, but all I spotted were an old sock and a crushed soda can. Both looked like permanent fixtures.

A wide strip of green lawn and waving palm trees beckoned me to Pacific Park across the street. The park spanned a few blocks that overlooked swoon-worthy views of the ocean. The lush seaside terrace that perched atop sandstone bluffs was home to uber-fit joggers, energetic kids and tourists. It also doubled as a hangout for the growing homeless population. I hopped onto the Ocean Avenue crosswalk and eyed the transient occupants on the green steel benches in the park, directly across from Big Sam's. A good place for me to conduct business.

A mild breeze ruffled my thick, somewhat manageable hair. The sky was a brilliant blue and the air smelled salty and fresh. I hung back and eyed the loaded shopping carts parked near the benches. My gaze stopped when I spotted the brown dog from last night. He lay beneath a bench where his master sat, staring at me from a weather-beaten face topped with scruffy hair.

"Spare any change?" the man asked when I approached.

He was younger than I expected. Maybe just a shade or two older than me. His clothes were scraggly; his eyes were pale blue slits. Dried blood stuck to a nostril and his cheek was red and swollen.

"I brought you lunch." I held up a bag. "Mister..."

"Harley." He peered up at me a few beats before snatching the bag away. A big toe stuck out of a hole riddled sneaker. The musty chokey smell of unwashed clothes and sweat mingled with the salty scent carried by the breeze. I took a step back.

He flashed a gap-toothed smile and devoured most of the burrito in a few bites. He threw pieces of chicken and tortilla bread at the dog and licked his fingers. The dog gobbled it up.

"I need your help," I said.

He chewed loudly, mouth open. "No, Lady. I need *your* help. You're not living on the street."

"I'm looking for the man who tried to shoot a friend of mine last night, in that restaurant." I pointed to Big Sam's. "That's where your burrito came from."

He dropped what was left of his meal on the grass. The dog dove for it and swallowed it whole. Harley grabbed his backpack and shot off, pulling the grunting dog behind him.

"Wait." I trotted after them and he picked up speed. What just happened? "Hold on."

He scrambled toward the north end of the park, aiming for a cliffside path, away from the joggers. I raced past the straggling brown dog and gripped Harley's arm. He tripped and fell on the grass with a thud.

"We need to talk," I said.

He slowly rolled onto his back and held up his hands. "You don't look like the fuzz."

I paused to catch my breath and noticed a fresh cut along one side of his neck. I moved in closer. "Who cut you?"

His hand slapped against his neck, trying to cover the spot, as if I'd forget I'd seen it.

A light burned brightly above my head. "I know all about it. Last night…the guy who slept in the planter wasn't really homeless, was he?"

Harley's eyes narrowed even more. I could almost see the wheels in his head, slowly turning. The truth didn't come easily to him. I could relate. At least I could a month or so ago.

"You're not a criminal, Harley," I said. "Not like the man last night. He raced into the parking lot from the diner. You were sleeping, weren't you? The planter box is warmer, softer than the ground. He shook you awake and when you tried to make him go away, he slashed your neck and threatened you."

Harley wiped his nose and struggled to sit up. His eyes welled up and the brown dog lay down beside him. "Might as well put a bullet in my head. I'm as good as dead." He pointed to the dog. "So is he."

"What did the man say to you?"

"That he'd kill us, if I told anyone."

"But you didn't tell. I already knew." I knelt next to him and placed the second bag of food near his hand. "Help me catch him and I'll find a way to help you...I'll get the guy and you'll be safe."

His head snapped up at me. "You're a big fat liar."

"Seriously?" I said. "Take a chance on me. Because I'm going to take one on you."

What curveballs had life thrown at him to bring him to this downtrodden state? I needed to do something to help at least this one fellow human.

"To show my good faith, after we talk, I'll take you and your dog somewhere safe." I let that sink in, but I could tell he didn't believe me. I barely believed me.

He lifted his butt and tried to scoot away in reverse. "He sent you. To test me and kill me if I talked."

"Why would I feed you first? All I want is a few questions answered. You were never in any danger from me." And that was the truth, so help me God. "But if you threaten or lie to me, all bets are off. Understand?"

He sat up and gave me a slow nod. The dog stared up at me. I reached into my purse and pulled out a small pack of saltine crackers. I ripped it open with my teeth. The dog eyed me with a long face. "What's his name?"

"Hollister."

"That's different," I said.

"Holly, for short."

"Holly want a cracker?" I asked the dog. He licked his chops and I fed him a couple. I turned back to Harley. "What did last night's man look like?"

"Mean. His fist was made from cement."

"What color eyes? Hair? Any scars?" Come on, give me something I can work with.

"His eyes were covered..."

"By sunglasses?"

"Yeah."

This was going nowhere. "Anything else?"

"No."

I stood and blew out a sigh. "Fine."

"We have the same chain."

"We do?" I touched my neck. It was chain-free. So was his. "You mean the man from last night?"

He stroked Holly's head. "Who else would I mean?"

"What kind of chain?" I asked. "A necklace?"

"This kind." Harley reached into an inside pocket of his tattered sweatshirt and pulled out a long, silver ball chain with dog tags hanging from the end. "I saw it when he slugged me, before he knocked me out." He stuffed the chain back inside.

He's former military? "What was printed on the tags?"

"It was old," Harley said. "That's all I know."

"How do you know it was old?"

"I joined up five years ago." Harley took his time getting to his feet. "Got my tags during basic training, but I was kicked out before I saw any action. For smoking weed and a few other stuff. We didn't have no social security numbers on our tags."

Could be a solid lead. "Thanks." I turned around to leave.

"You said you're going to help me," he said.

"I'll have to make some calls," I said. "Where will I find you?"

"You're standing in my summer house. During the winter, I sleep inside a blue cabin across the street."

"Cabin?" I gazed across the street at the block of restaurants and hotels.

"The garbage bin in the alley."

Wow. "I'll be back. I won't forget about you." I swiveled and wound my way toward Big Sam's. I stopped by the bench where Harley had been sitting and eyed the other bench occupants nearby. No one paid me any attention, except for a dusty little woman with a round face and a nearly toothless grin. She pushed a battered baby stroller filled with plastic bottles and blankets. Her hair was gray except for the ends where a bit of rusty color hung on. Deeply etched lines ran across her forehead and danced a half circle around the corners of her eyes.

She waved me over and slid behind a tree. I came closer and she retreated into thick shrubbery with only her head and shoulders sticking out.

"Are you hiding from someone?" I asked. Maybe she'd run into the shooter as well.

"Your mama."

"Okay." I could understand that if she'd met my mother. Mom could be intimidating. "You know Harley?"

She slapped a gnarly hand over her mouth, then slowly lowered it. We stared at each other for a long minute, until I stepped back.

"Glad we had this talk." I turned when she said,

"I know a secret."

What were the odds the two transients had a run-in with the shooter?

Chapter Ten: Could've Been

"I saw you." The woman's sparse brows shot up.

"When?" I faced her again.

"In the dark. Running faster than a Jamaican buffalo man."

Was she crazy or not? Why hadn't I spotted her? "Where were you?"

"Warming my hands on a car engine."

The clanging noise in the parking lot last night. It was her. I sucked in my breath. "I wasn't the only one running, was I?"

She gave a shrug. "He woke up Harley and socked him good. One, two, three." She put up a dirty fingernail for each count. "Mean scuzzball."

"What did the mean man look like?" I asked. It was like talking to a child. What would a child see?

She wrinkled her face which made the bags under her eyes puff out. She held out a palm.

Great. I looked around for an ATM while I dug my hand into my purse. Not a bank in sight. I unzipped a pocket and pulled out the small bag of trail mix. I handed it to her, and she snatched it away.

"I'm no squirrel!"

I dug around some more and came up with two bills. I handed them to her.

"Two dollars? Is that all you get for your allowance, girly?" She stuffed the money into her bulky sweater.

"These are tough times," I replied. "After he hit Harley, where'd he go?"

She squeezed her lips together.

I straightened up. "Never mind." I turned on my heel.

"Earrings," she said.

My hand shot to an earlobe. I wore silver toned, crystal studs shaped like leaves. I took them off, handed one to her and cradled the other in my palm. "Tell me about the man."

"He took Harley's bed." She ran a calloused fingertip across the crystal.

"The planter box?"

She nodded.

He'd been in front of me the whole time, just like I'd thought…too late. I replayed the scene in my head. I couldn't have spent more than a few minutes in the parking lot. He'd waited 'til I'd moved far enough away and rocketed off. That's when Michael entered the scene. The dreadlock wig was probably stuffed inside his baggy hoodie. But what about the blanket?

"You took his blanket." I was taking a chance she wouldn't say more, but I had to be sure.

She shook her head fast. "Not me, not me." She popped back over to her stroller and hobbled off.

Chances were the blanket was stuffed in her stroller. My inclination was to run to the cop parked on Ocean, but I didn't know how much more he'd get out of her. Plus, he'd probably take her and the stroller in. She'd never see it again. I hurried after her. "I'm Corrie. What's your name?"

She held out her palm. I dropped my other earring in.

"Daisy," she said. "Don't be crazy. Blanket's mine." She shook her head rapidly again and limped off.

"Oh, brother." I whirled around toward the diner. The shooter threw me off by sleeping in the planter, covered by an old blanket. I should've known the dreadlocks were a wig. "So dumb." I *was* off my game." If I hadn't been, I would've noticed that his head rested on a skinny backpack. The homeless population carried overstuffed backpacks overflowing with all of their belongings.

I hurried across the street and into the parking lot. I made a beeline for the planter box and stared down at it. Just an assortment of trash…nothing to link to the gunner. I strolled around the planter, stopping to scrutinize the ground. More of nothing.

I retraced his steps to the one-way alley. Litter dotted the asphalt and pressed against all vertical surfaces; nothing seemed incriminating. No nearby windows, but a camera stuck over the gate of a parking garage of an apartment building a good six car lengths away. Probably picked up the back of a man running. Another longshot in a case brimming with longshots.

I dragged my feet to Big Sam's and cruised through the entrance. The place was a graveyard, except for a couple at the bar. Veera joined me minutes later. She'd poured her curves into a short-sleeved, confetti printed jersey dress with a ruffled hem and scooped neckline. She looked movie studio, legal department ready. I told her so and told her about Daisy and Harley.

"It's a good thing you didn't know it was the shooter sleeping in that plant box," she said. "He could've taken you out right then and there if you'd tried anything. Were you carrying a weapon?"

"No. It was one of those rare occurrences, like no traffic on the 405."

"Yo!" A shout flew across the room and slammed into my ears. Big Sam stood near the kitchen. He waved his bulky arms over his head and waddled over to us.

"I've been wanting to get a hold of you," he told me. "You're the only one who got any answers last night. Seems like these cops don't make a move without checking this or that, and they still get no answers. Good thing for me you're not a meter maid."

"What?" Veera asked. "You must mean parking control officer. They do important work. Before I worked in the security and legal fields, I managed parking control at Long Beach Memorial. Would've been chaos without us officers directing parking lot traffic. And it's not just females that take on that kind of challenging work."

Big Sam's gaze travelled over Veera, all six feet of her. Plus sized and proud of it, her honey colored hair was pulled back into a high ponytail and her caramel hued complexion glowed. Big Sam ended the trip over planet Veera with a big grin. He didn't make any attempt to hide his admiration. "They're lucky to have you. All of your former jobs."

Veera raised her chin and glowered at him. "Push your eyes back in your head before I do it for you."

Big Sam wiped the grin off his face.

"That's better," Veera said. "We work with law enforcement…" She shot me a glance. "Both of us."

"On a case-by-case basis," I said. "This is Veera Bankhead."

"Pleased to meet you, Miss Bankhead. It's Miss, isn't it?"

She leaned forward with a grimace. "My personal life isn't any of your business."

"Any man would be lucky to have you, I mean to know you, but I was kind of hoping there were no men in your life," he said. "That's why I asked."

"I'm here on a professional level, got that?" she said.

"Well, let's get this professional business done then." He turned to me. "You've gotta take my case." Big Sam waved his hands around. "Look at this place. People usually gotta wait forty minutes to get a seat. How am I supposed to conduct any business?" He lowered his voice and said, "I asked that fine looking lady detective for your number and she wouldn't give it to me."

"Wait a minute," Veera said. She turned up the glare. "What's her looks gotta do with her being a detective? That's irrelevant."

"A fine-looking female is never irrelevant." He ran a palm over his short buzz cut. "Isn't a fine-looking gent relevant to you?"

Veera backed off. "Can't argue with that."

"Don't you think there are more important things to discuss?" I asked.

"You mean like where all my customers disappeared to?" His gaze roamed the room and landed back on me. His cropped goatee was low maintenance like his hair. But the rest of him seemed high maintenance. "That's why I require your services."

"Go on," I said.

He leaned into me, shooting glances at Veera. "Way I saw it, you handed the police most of what they needed to know last night."

"Happens every time." Veera beamed proudly at me.

"What does that mean?" he asked her.

"It means, we'll take your case," she said.

"You will?"

"There's a lot of work that still needs to be done," I told him. "We have no real leads on the shooter yet."

"But we'll need expenses upfront, and complete cooperation from all of your employees," Veera said. "And regular meals to keep up our energy."

"As long as you bring this whack job in," Big Sam said. "He's gotta understand that I don't take kindly to gunfire in my fine eating establishment."

Veera narrowed her dark eyes and surveyed the room before returning her gaze back to him. "You look kind of familiar." She stared at Big Sam. "Haven't I seen you somewhere before?"

"This is no time to throw pick-up lines at me," he said.

I put out an arm to hold Veera back. "We're here to gather more evidence about the man with the gun."

"Let me get something straight first," he said. "You're not police officers, not meter maids, I mean…" He flashed a glance at Veera. "…parking control officers. That would make you…undercover operatives, right?"

"Look," I said. "We do P.I. work. The problem is we're not licensed." There, the truth was out.

"But we're not afraid of criminals or danger," Veera said.

"That's right," I said. "We welcome both." As long as we're armed.

"Okay," he said quietly at first, then his round eyes lit up. "Okay! Good enough." He pointed to me. "Far as I'm concerned, you've got what it takes to find the guy who's ruining my business. And I'm gonna make it easy for you to bring him to the law." He looked on either side of him, turned to me and dropped his voice. "I'm going to hand you your first lead so you can gather evidence or whatever it is you need to lock him up."

"How did you get a lead before she did?" Veera asked.

"Are we talking about the same guy?" I said.

"Maybe it wasn't the man holding the gun, but I know the chump behind the scenes," Big Sam said. "I also know he wasn't aiming to kill anyone."

"You recognized the shooter?" I asked.

"Didn't need to. I recognized his boss and the motive. The he-devil wants to scare my customers away."

"Why would he want to do that?" I asked.

"Because…I'm his biggest competitor."

Here was an angle no one had considered. Probably with good reason. Big Sam didn't know that the shooter had come after James last night once we'd left the diner. "What makes you think he'd do something so extreme?" I asked.

"I hear he's got some major investor who's not happy with his numbers." Big Sam dropped his voice. "He opened up his place on the pier two years ago, and still can't beat my business. Doesn't even come close."

"You think the gunman was hired by another restaurant owner?" I asked.

"That's right. On the pier."

There were three eateries on the Santa Monica pier. A fish shack, a Mexican restaurant and a newer, upscale Asian Mediterranean Middle Eastern fusion place.

"Now I know where I've seen you before," Veera said. "You were that TV chef that went around to mom and pop food places…"

"That was seven years ago, woman, before I settled down here. I didn't let any of that fame or fortune get to my head, if that's what you're thinking. And I used the funds to finance my own diner, which has been a big hit. Until last night." He lowered his voice some more. "I've got loyal customers. If it wasn't for my place, he'd be making bank. The sooner he's caught, the sooner my customers return."

"Who are you talking about?" I asked.

"Gordon Joshua, of course. With a name like that, he should be running a beauty parlor."

"He's that British celebrity chef," Veera said. "He critiques amateur chefs on his show. How do you know he's got anything to do with last night's shooting?"

"Oh, it's him, alright. You'll see. Let's go. I'll get my hat." Big Sam turned around and headed toward the back.

I hurried after him with Veera close behind. "It's not him."

"You don't know that," he said.

"There was another incident last night after we left the diner, and it involved another one of the district attorneys," I said. "It can't be who you think it is."

Big Sam turned to face me. "That would be just like him. To throw you off his scent." He zipped around and cut a path toward the kitchen.

"What do you expect us to do?" I asked.

"Make him fess up, and I want to be there when you do."

"Hold on," I said. "We're not going to his restaurant."

"You don't have to eat there. I'll feed you when we get back."

"It's not that," I said.

"You got a better idea?" Big Sam tossed his frown between Veera and me and broke into a smile. His gaze had pushed past us to the entry. "Looks like we won't have to go to his place, after all. Here comes little Gordy now."

Chapter Eleven: Make it Real

"You got some nerve," Big Sam said, greeting his visitor.

"Thought I'd drop by to see how you were faring. Heard about the trouble you had." Gordon Joshua's British accent had softened by living stateside too long. His brown hair was streaked with blond highlights and a diamond stud sparkled from his left lobe. He wore a forest green button down, tan slacks and a sunburn. Everything about him was round from his ocean blue eyes to his physique. He took his time gazing around the empty restaurant. "What a shame. Did you spook the customers away?"

"No, you did, chump," Big Sam shouted so loudly, people walking across the street turned their heads. "After that stunt you pulled last night."

"Hold on," I said to Big Sam, and turned to Gordon. "Mr. Joshua, do you own a gun?"

"Who are you?" he asked, stuffing his hands in his front pockets. His gaze swung from me to Veera.

"That's none of your concern," Big Sam said. "But if you don't cooperate, they're gonna haul your sorry ass into the police station as soon as—"

Veera shot him a look that buttoned up his mouth.

"Do you own a gun?" I asked again.

"I do. So what? This isn't England. Do I need my lawyer?"

"What kind of gun?" Veera crossed her arms against her ample chest and arched a brow. She looked like she could take him down before he pulled his hands out of his pockets.

"A custom Smith and Wesson revolver in a locked drawer in my business office," he replied. "Why are you asking?"

"We're investigating the shooting last night," I said.

"You don't think that I—"

"Oh yes, they do," Big Sam said.

"We don't." I cut him the evil eye. "We're asking everyone the same routine questions."

"I see." Gordon flashed a tight smile at me.

"You keep your gun at your restaurant?" I was ready to move on to the employees. Someone might have seen something noteworthy.

"That's right," he replied.

I stepped away and refocused on the back of the room. "Do you own any other guns?"

"There are firearms sitting in a safe at my residence. I live in a condo down the street."

I reclaimed my spot. "And those are…"

"A Ruger and a Glock. All permitted, of course. Along with a rifle."

Big Sam's dark eyes bounced between us and settled onto me. "Shouldn't you be turnin' him in? He's got weapons and he's got a motive, which makes him a prime suspect. What are you waiting for?"

Veera turned up her glare.

"Where can you be reached in case we've more questions?" I asked Gordon.

He took his hands out of his pockets and passed me his card. "That's my cell, Miss…"

"Corrie Locke."

"You're with the police?"

"I'm not."

"Are you a private eye?" he asked.

"I'm a lawyer."

His blue gaze widened, his ears turned red and he stepped back. "You tricked me," he told Big Sam. "You all did. If I'd known who she was, I never would have—"

"That's right. You should be shiverin' in your Gucci loafers after what you did to my place. Don't think I'm not coming after you." Big Sam shook his fist.

"I only dropped by to be a good neighbor." Gordon puffed out his chest and stormed out.

"Good neighbor, my ass." Big Sam spun around to me. "You didn't say you were a lawyer."

"Never said she wasn't," Veera said.

"Besides the law, we do investigation work on the side…when we find a case worth taking on," I said.

"A modern-day Perry Mason. You got my full attention," Big Sam said. "What are you going to do about Gordy?"

"Nothing yet," I said. "Let's focus on what happened right here. Start with everyone who was on duty during the shooting."

"Think it was one of them? I've a mind to fire them all, if I was up for doing the work myself. Which I'm not. I still think it's Gordy."

"We'll take a closer look at him," I said. "Meanwhile, one of your employees might've noticed something that could lead us to the shooter."

"Something to prove it was Gordy?" Big Sam said. "Let's find out."

***

Big Sam called the staff together and instructed them to answer all questions. Then he left Veera and me to talk to anyone who'd worked the shift the night before. I asked each one about a tall, lanky male customer missing the tip of a finger. Forty minutes later, we had nothing. No one saw or heard anything, although the bartender showed us his missing baby toe. By then the rich warm smells of toasted rolls, burgers and coffee sent us to the nearest table where we polished off our lunches.

"Holy comfort food, this revs up the soul," Veera said about her meatball sandwich with smoked mozzarella.

I had no complaints about my chicken pot pie.

"Now what'll we do?" Veera pushed away her empty plate minutes later. "Might as well stick around. It's not like anyone will miss us at the studio. Never thought I'd say this, but I almost miss working for that sorry excuse

57

of a back stabbin' senior VP ex-boss of ours."

She referred to Marshall Cooperman, Vice President, Legal and Business Affairs at Ameripictures. He excelled in barking orders, then changing his mind minutes later without telling us the new plan.

"Seriously?"

Veera burst out laughing. "Heck no. I'd rather pet a tarantula with my bare hands." Her eyes widened. "Should we go to the pier and spy on that British chef?"

"Wait a minute," I said. My eyes wandered around the ceiling and rested on a corner of the bar. Positioned near the ceiling, above a long mirror, a security camera faced out toward the cash register. "How'd I miss that?" I needed to get my mojo back.

Veera clicked her tongue. "The former security guard in me should've noticed that camera right off the bat."

She'd worked in parking lot security before becoming my assistant. She'd traded in the parking lot for the studio lot and hardly looked back since, though her security connections came in handy.

I swallowed my last bite and pushed back my chair. Moments later, we stood by a coltish blonde texting on her phone. The hostess from last night. She leaned back against a wall near the register.

"Excuse me," I said.

"Yeah?" She cocked her head in annoyance, her bangs poking her eyelids.

"Did the police take the security tape?" I asked.

She did a fast eyeroll. "Uh-huh. Last night. Big Sam put in a new one this morning." She resumed texting.

"Dang," Veera whispered.

I strolled around to one side and peered beneath the wide hostess stand. A monitor on a shelf beneath displayed a split screen, each showing live footage from two security cameras.

"Where's the second camera?" I asked.

"Near the back door." She didn't bother looking up.

"Veera," I said. "Stand right there."

I positioned her in the spot where the shooter had waited before moving forward to fire his gun. I raced over to the monitor.

"Genius." I looked at the camera above the bar. It pointed to the register, but the hooded man had paused just before the register. That's where I'd planted Veera, near a post, which neither camera picked-up. The post blocked the shooter from view. "He definitely knew what he was doing." Which meant he'd been to the diner before.

"Veera, I've got an assignment for you," I said when I returned.

"Ready and willing." She rubbed her hands together.

"A little over six feet, male Caucasian, slim build…" His face looked gaunt so I was willing to bet he was slender under the baggy clothes. "…hooked nose. He knew exactly where to stand to avoid the camera."

"Which means he'd scoped this place out."

"Check out footage from the past week and see what you can find. Ask around some more about the missing top joint of the index finger on his left hand."

"This is exciting. Kind of like being on a virtual stakeout surrounded by delicious food."

"Where do you keep the tapes?" I asked the hostess.

She pointed toward the kitchen. "Big Sam's office."

Veera bunched her lips. "He'd better not hang around in there while I'm working."

"You'll have to boot him out so you can concentrate."

"Guaranteed." Veera marched toward the back.

Minutes later, Big Sam appeared by the register. "Besides being a mighty fine-looking woman, your colleague knows what she's doing." He flicked his thumb behind him. "Smart and sassy is what she is, which makes her the sweet onion I'd like to smother over my grilled cheese sandwich."

"I suggest you keep that thought to yourself. Besides, we're on a mission, remember?"

"'Course I remember. You think I like seeing a bullet graze one of my customers' rear ends? It's like he shot me in the back during business hours."

"No, it's not," I said.

"Let's go."

"Where?"

"To burn that mother-loving restaurant of Gordon Joshua's down. I mean figuratively, of course."

"Why would we go there?"

"While Veera's looking for evidence here, we'll turn Gordy's place upside down 'til we find the evidence to prove that conniving he-devil shot the gun to improve his business and take down mine. Or hired someone to do the dirty deed."

"First of all, we need to know what kind of bullet the police dug out. Secondly, how do we know that his business has improved?"

"That's what we're going to find out."

"It's not him."

"Look, you're working for me and I want you to follow this lead, is that clear?"

"Okay. But first, you'll need to apologize to him."

"I'll never—"

"It's easier to take down an enemy when he thinks you're a friend."

Big Sam slowly nodded. "He'll never see me coming."

I pulled out my cell phone.

Big Sam took a few steps, turned toward me and stopped. "What are you doing?"

"I'm calling the D.A.'s office to get an update."

"You can call on our way. Then you can poke around while I distract Gordy."

I had two missed calls from Michael and one from James. I followed Big Sam out and called Michael first.

"Are all three potential victims in the office?" I asked when he answered.

"All three accounted for and on the third floor."

"Even Beckman?"

"It was just a surface wound that's been patched up. He had a few stitches so he's not sitting down much."

"Don't let anyone leave," I said.

"Roger that."

I called James next.

"It's the day after two possible murder attempts," he said by way of answering the call. "You think you might want to pick up the phone?"

"Not when I'm at the crime scene trying to uncover missing puzzle pieces."

"Find anything?"

"Yes, but all it shows is our shooter carefully planned the whole thing. He'd been to the diner before. Also, could be a former military man. What've you got?"

"Looks like the D.A.'s office has a job opening."

"You're leaving?" He wasn't the type to spook so easily.

"I'm not going anywhere. The job opening's for you."

"I'm a movie studio attorney, remember?" At least I will be once my boss shows up. *If* she shows up.

"This is a temp job," James said. "And one you'd rather be doing."

He had a knack for knowing what I'd wanted in the past.

"You'll be reviewing files of cases that could involve last night's guy."

I guess his knack was still going strong. "Don't you have interns to do that?"

"You need to come here," he spoke quietly.

He clearly had the wrong idea of how I felt about him. I needed to set him straight, once and for all. There was a time when I would've wanted him to say something like that to me. But not anymore. I'd let him down gently. I cleared my throat. "I don't think that's a good idea because—"

"We need to keep an eye on each other and compare notes. Michael's already here."

My ego was crushed like an eggshell in his hands. Served me right. "I'll be there."

"Besides, we have a lead based on your observations last night."

Now we're talking. "We do?"

"A possible match for your nearly fingerless man."

Chapter Twelve: Pier Pressure

I asked James to give me an hour while I trailed Big Sam to the Gordon Joshua restaurant, GJ's on the Pier. Big Sam was right. The place was flooded with customers.

"See?" Big Sam punched the fist of his right hand into his left palm, grinding the two together. "He's stealing my customers. I knew it."

"Pull yourself together and go inside," I said. "I'll follow separately, so I can get the lay of the land."

"Good thinking. We'll cover more bases that way. There's no telling which one of these people will be the first to crack and confess Gordy's behind the shooting. I'll keep him busy."

Big Sam wandered over to the back of the place, while I waited near the entry. I turned and smiled at a man in jeans and a T-shirt behind me.

"I can't believe how busy this place is." I put on my best innocent bystander face. "Is it always like this?"

"Dunno, it's my first time." He leaned in way too close. "You here alone?"

Time waster. "Beat it, Bud," I said, using my best Bogart impression. I elbowed past him and squeezed onto a crowded wooden bench with other eager diners. I sat next to a woman wearing a floral dress and bright lipstick. "Is this a good place to grab a salad?"

"The best," she said. "But, I would skip the salad. They've got the tastiest fish and chips, and the best strawberry lemonade."

I scoped out the dining area. My vantage point was spot-on to watch the staff. The hostess seemed more engaged with the customers than the blonde at Big Sam's. She chatted them up while keeping an eye on servers and busboys. All seemed in line…except for one guy that didn't fit in. Bulky, tanned and bearded, he'd stuffed his muscles into a brown suit and sat at the bar, facing the restaurant. When one diner seemed rambunctious, the guy leapt to his feet and escorted the customer outside. He was the resident bouncer. Why would a restaurant need a bouncer?

"And the clam chowder and lobster rolls are unbeatable," the woman next to me talked nonstop, pausing once to suck in air before describing the lobster rolls with the precision of a sushi knife.

"Is it always this crowded?" I asked during a breather.

"It's never like this." She leaned in closer to me. "I usually go to Big Sam's Diner on Ocean, but I was spooked by the shooting last night."

"There's free ice cream here today," the lady next to her told us.

"I'm a sucker for dessert. Thanks." I stood and squeezed my way through wannabe diners and over to the hostess area. I stopped next to the bearded guy in the suit. He raised his chin and stared down at me. Up close, his face was moist and all the scars were visible. The suit was too much for the warm summer day.

"You were at Big Sam's last night." I'd noticed him in the bar when I came back from the chase. There's nothing like hitting up a potential witness with a factual statement right off the bat.

He licked his lips and settled into an overbite that made him look like an angry rabbit.

"Who are you?" he asked.

"A customer waiting to be seated."

He stretched his neck closer. I could smell the spearmint gum on his breath. "You say you saw me last night? I saw you, too."

"How exciting was that?" I said. He sure got riled easily.

He leaned back. "Was what?"

"The shooting," I said.

"As long as it wasn't me being shot at." He snorted.

"Two questions. First, why does Gordon need a bouncer?"

"The man's a celebrity chef. People get excited around him."

"Okay. Second, why would you be at Big Sam's bar when you could drink for free, right here?"

"A guy needs a bacon martini, once in a while. We don't serve that here. Gordon's not interested in revving things up."

That was fair. "Something felt odd about the shooter last night. Can't put my finger on it." I leaned back as if in thought, but my eyes were stuck on his.

"Maybe because he came in for more than just the fries." He smirked and shifted his feet in a half circle to eye a group of guys by the entry, then returned his stare to me. "I saw you heading down the pier with Big Sam. And I saw you two walk in. You're up to something, don't think I don't know. Next time wear a disguise if you want to stand a chance of gettin' past me. And it better be a good one 'cause I see through all the tricks."

So he'd been working for Gordon for a while now. And he was sharp-eyed.

"Did Big Sam mention the stunt he pulled last month?" the guy asked. He wagged his finger near my face. "Tell him we don't play dirty even when he does." He gave me a nod and walked off.

Was Big Sam holding out on me? I scanned the place until I spotted him. Using sweeping arm gestures, he was arguing with Gordon near the kitchen. I waved my hand up in the air and caught his attention. I pushed my way outside, pulled out my sunglasses and leaned against the building. Foot traffic whizzed past every which way. Cars roared by on Ocean Avenue and a plane thundered overhead.

"You all done? Who confessed?" Big Sam joined me.

I straightened. "Why didn't you tell me what you did to Gordon last month?"

"What *I* did? I ain't taking the blame for that."

"Find yourself another investigator." I stormed off.

"Wait." Big Sam stumbled between sightseers to keep up with me. "That employee went rogue, and I fired her as soon as I found out what she did. I had nothing to do with it."

I slid over to another spot of shade. "Convince me." I figured I'd be more likely to get to the truth if he thought I knew the story already.

"I hired Becca from a foo-foo restaurant in West Hollywood. She'd worked there for sixteen years so I figured she oughta know something. I never thought she'd make a whole lotta phony reservations at Gordy's place. How was I supposed to know they'd turn away walk-in customers? That was playing dirty and I don't do that. Ever."

"You think he was behind last night's shooting to get back at you for that stunt?"

"Makes sense to me. He'd called me a filthy liar. He insisted it was fishy how an employee would do what Becca did without the order coming from the top of the food chain. He's just mad that my operation's more profitable than his. Before last night, anyway."

"If you want me to help, I need to know everything." I turned and hurried back to Ocean Avenue. He hustled to keep up with me.

"Nothing else to tell." Big Sam huffed and puffed beside me. "I apologized to Gordy, and we were good. Or so I thought. You get anything out of his crew?"

"They're serving free ice cream scoops today."

"Going for a customer grab. I'll show him…"

Veera stood in front of Big Sam's Diner, waving her arms.

"I've got some intel," she said when we got there.

"We're listening," Big Sam said.

"One of the busboys remembers a tall skinny guy coming in a few nights ago," she said. "He noticed the finger."

"Did you get a copy of the tape from that night?" I asked.

Veera dug a hand into her purse and pulled out a videotape. "You know how I feel about leaving empty-handed."

"Uh, no, I don't," I said.

"Really? Well, you're about to find out."

Chapter Thirteen: Any Way You Want It

We stood around Big Sam's computer monitor and watched a tape from four days ago. Last Friday night's activities, twenty minutes before closing. The place was packed.

"Ah, the good old days," Big Sam said, shaking his head. "Seems like yesterday."

"That's because it was," Veera reminded him. "Nearly." She forwarded the tape and stopped. "Watch that booth right there." She pointed to a corner of the screen.

A man slid into a seat, picked up the menu and kept his face away from the camera. He wore a baseball cap and tinted glasses.

"Keep watching." Veera fast forwarded and stopped seconds later.

The same guy stood, his back to the camera, and threw some bills on the table. He edged sideways toward the front of the diner. No matter how hard I squinted, I couldn't see his face.

"Suspicious, if you ask me," Veera said.

"The only way he could know exactly where to stand was if he spent time here, either eating, or..." I turned to Big Sam. "As an employee."

"None of our employees have that kind of physique," Big Sam said. "This guy's a beanpole. We're more robust around here. Solid and firmly established."

"We can't be sure he's our man. But if it's him, he could've been planning this for weeks or longer." I turned to Big Sam. "Isn't this a popular hangout for government workers and law enforcement?"

"That's right. I support law enforcement and the military. They get ten percent off. Used to be in the Navy myself."

"Should I check credit card payments around that time?" Veera asked.

I shook my head. "If you rewind the tape, you'll notice he paid in cash. I'm guessing he's been here a few times, paid in cash and planned this for a while. He was waiting for the right time."

"Gordy must've had something to do with this," Big Sam said. "That could be his man."

"I've gotta go," I said.

"Where?" Big Sam and Veera asked.

"To the D.A.'s office. Veera, can you stick around long enough to view a few more tapes?"

"Sure can. But there's some more footage you might want to see." Veera popped the tape out and inserted another one. She fast forwarded and pressed play. "This one's from a week before."

The scene opened with a gangly guy at the entrance. He wore a cowboy hat and dark shades. He turned his head and stared over his shoulder for a while, using his left hand to scratch his temple, shielding his face from the camera. And then I saw it.

"He's showing us the finger," I said.

"I won't tolerate that around here." Big Sam peered at the screen and blinked his eyes. "Wait. Something funky about that finger. I need my reading glasses." He turned to me. "That the guy you ran after last night?"

"Could be," I said. He dropped a motel receipt that led the cops to a dead end and now he was making sure his pygmy finger was clearly visible. Why?

***

The D.A.'s main office was in downtown Los Angeles, but James worked in a regional bureau, the Westside division, set up a block from the police department. The building housed several government offices and served as the gateway to a residential street lined with compact, older homes shaded by trees with leafy canopies. Wrought iron fences and window coverings were the norm. Not a welcome mat in sight. A grand gothic style church reigned across the street from the D.A.'s office, next to a two-story building that looked drab in comparison.

I entered the compact lobby of James' building. It was barren except for a couple of chairs. A black security dome stuck to the ceiling near the locked entry to the rest of the building. Access was granted or denied by a receptionist sitting behind a bullet-proof glass window.

I flashed my ID and she handed me a temporary badge. She buzzed me through the door and into an elevator. James had added my name to the guest list.

Minutes later, I sat on wall-to-wall, low pile brown carpet. My elbow touched Michael's shoulder as he reclined next to me. We were in James' private office. The hallway was musty, but it smelled nice in here. Like apples and licorice. There were bowls filled with each. But the furnishings? They looked like hand-me-downs from Gramps, if he'd been an old school government employee. Piles of binders and file folders were stacked on the floor with pathways leading to the desk. Both Michael and James wore suits. James went to court nearly every day, so I got that, but Michael?

"I wanted to fit in, like you two," he said when I asked.

James was suited up in a two-piece navy number that only heightened his good looks. Brown waves danced around his handsome face. I caught my breath at his stare. He gave me a nod and a close mouthed, lingering smile. I slowed my breathing and shifted my focus to Michael. In his dark gray suit, he looked sharp. Cary Grant had nothing on him. The top of a folded white hankie stuck out of the breast pocket of his jacket. His six-foot frame ended in black Converse sneakers that didn't diminish his being dapper. In my book, Michael had something James would never have, besides me, that is. Pure sweetness.

"I'll be right back." Michael dashed out. He returned thirty seconds later, a chair in his hands. "For you."

"Why, thank you." I sat in the chair.

"What'd you find out at the diner?" James asked.

I told him about the video footage and then I paused. "There's another really slim possibility." I told them about Gordon Joshua and the rivalry between the two restaurant owners.

"Don't waste your time on that angle," James said.

"Are you sure?" Michael asked. "Corrie always says to investigate every angle."

"I'm sure," James said without looking up.

Michael shrugged. "Okay, but facts can be sneaky things that tap you on the shoulder when you're looking the other way."

"Yeah, well this is not one of those facts," he replied. "This is a personal matter between two TV chefs blaming each other for poor business. Has nothing to do with the shooter."

I opened my mouth to lash back when Michael tossed me a glance that told me James was in one of his moods. The mood where he practically spewed lava. Probably hadn't slept much last night. The new, more compassionate me bit her tongue.

"You said you had a match for the guy missing the top of his finger," I reminded James.

He knelt next to a pile of folders and picked one up near the top. He slid it in front of me. "Take a look at the snapshots in the Nappy file."

I opened the folder and inspected the photo page belonging to Edgar Nappy, the man convicted yesterday. He was not only missing the top of an index finger on both hands, but the thumb, too. Did the shooter have all of his thumb?

"Well?" James asked.

"Maybe it was him." His thumb had been on the other side of the gun, out of sight. I scanned the guy's vital statistics. Nappy was twenty-nine, five-foot-six and a hundred eighty pounds. "Revise that to a no." I closed the folder. The gunman had papery skin on his cheeks and lines etched from the corners of his mouth to his nostrils. Veins stuck out on the back of his gun hand. "The shooter looked to be in his forties, but he moved faster than anyone else last night." Which reminded me…I told them about Harley, Daisy and the planter box.

"Are you holding anything back?" James asked. "You have a bad habit of keeping necessary facts to yourself."

"That's not fair," I said. Not too fair, anyway.

James grunted.

Maybe I used to keep a fact or two from him in the past, but I preferred to come clean these days. "Not holding anything back today."

"If Corrie's food had been served," Michael said. "She would've caught the guy right away. She doesn't do well on an empty stomach."

"Good thing she wasn't served," James said. "That's what made her go up to the front of the diner."

"Either way, I should've had my dinner." I picked up a folder and paged through it.

"There's always a chance, guys," Michael said. "That we'll never hear from the guy again. He took two huge risks last night. And came close to getting busted."

"It would be smart, Pollyanna, to act as if he'll try again." James rose and slammed a folder on his desk. "I plan to stick around for a little while longer."

"Of course you're going to be around," Michael said. "We guarantee you will."

"He shot Beckman," I said. "And came after you, right after. What's he thinking?"

"He was..." Michael said, "angry about missing Beckman and went for James instead, determined to hit a target. If it wasn't for you..." He turned to me. "...he could've shot..." His gaze landed on James.

"He's not afraid of getting caught," I said.

"Or thinks he's too smart to get caught," James said.

"Which means sooner or later, he's going to kill someone," Michael said.

"Don't be such a pessimist," I said. "We'll nab him before he does that." Meanwhile, we had to keep James safe. I grabbed another file. "Why would he display a defect that would be so unique?"

"Because he's throwing us off track," Michael said.

"Exactly," I said.

"But he can't because we've got magnetic wheels that stick. Besides, can you fake a finger like that?" Michael asked.

"Maybe not, but you can hide it when you need to, so no one would notice,"

I said. "Using a prosthetic. He's bringing it to our attention so we focus on the missing finger while he keeps it hidden during his everyday life." The wheels in my head were turning so fast I half expected them to shoot out my ears. "Did you look over all of your files?" I asked James. "For someone with a prosthetic finger?"

"No, I've been popping corn kernels all morning," he said. He dropped his chin to his chest and cast me a glance. "Sorry. This is one of those days where I should've listened to my mother and become a dentist. Looking into someone's mouth has to be better than waiting to be shot." His gaze stuck to mine. "No other files featured a criminal missing the top part of his index finger."

"A prosthetic wouldn't get through prison metal detectors," I said.

Michael snapped his thumb and middle fingers together. "But a partial passive prosthetic wouldn't have any metal in it. They're made of silicon material. I know from sitting in on robotics classes at L.A. Tech. But just to be sure, I'm going to look up a prosthetics specialist."

"And say what?" James gave Michael a killer look. "Done any index fingers lately?"

"Bro, we're trying to help," Michael said.

"Good idea, except his missing fingertip could be from decades ago," I said. "I'll ask Veera if she found anything else."

James slid to a window that looked out the front of the building. "I need to put myself out there. It's the only way to bring him into the open."

I grabbed a folder. "Let's find the motive first before we use you…or Ramsey, as bait." Ramsey would be better. There was something wormy about him. I pointed to the folders. "I want files on anyone you've put away and anyone paroled in the last three months. Especially if they're ex-military."

James' lips turned inward for a moment and he narrowed his gaze. He huffed and slid next to me. "Okay." He blasted through a stack of files leaving two on one side.

"I've got an idea." It was Michael's turn to get up. "I need to use your computer, bro."

James nodded toward a group of desks outside his office. "There's a laptop out there. I might need mine." Michael slipped out and James shifted closer to me. He plowed through a few more files.

"You sure you're not the target?" he whispered to me.

"What? No way. He shot at Beckman, remember?"

"He might have thought you were still at the table. There was a woman at the table next to us with hair like yours…"

He rolled his gaze over my hair. I slipped my hands under my thighs to keep from patting down the wild waves around my head.

"…and nearly the same length. You both wore blue tops."

"Why James, I never thought you noticed."

"I notice you alright." He turned to a file. "From a distance, he might have thought she was you. Then he spotted you next to him and misfired."

"Nope, I'm not the target. Besides, her hair color was different." I'd noticed James noticing her.

"You sure?" He stared up at me.

"My hair isn't so brassy." The shooter followed us to James' place. Was he after me? My little voice said no. "The timing tells me it's your team."

"You've been involved in more cases involving dangerous felons than I have."

"Are you jealous?"

"You need to take the possibility seriously."

"He could've finished me off in the parking lot and he didn't."

"Good point." He turned back to his files.

Minutes ticked by in silence until he spoke up. "I've narrowed it down to two possibilities," he said. "Cases involving tough dealers with decent networks." He handed me a folder. "You already met the first guy. The man we put away yesterday. Edgar Nappy. He's got a big network behind him."

"That would make it easy for him to put a shooter in place," I said.

"And take a look at Tony Tulep. AKA Antonio Tuleppo." He handed another file to me. "AKA El Cartero."

"The mailman?" That's about all I remembered from my high school Spanish class. "What kind of drug dealer name is that?"

"The kind reserved for a US born, former postal worker immersed in a life of crime. Fired for peddling coke on his route. And I don't mean the soft drink. Didn't do time for lack of evidence. He planted roots near Mexico City, came back to Southern California a few years ago and established himself as the drug dealer of choice to teenage customers living in affluent areas."

"That's dirty low down," I said. I took Tulep's file and thumbed through.

"He was convicted a month or so ago," James said.

"Did you work on his case?" I asked.

"Near the end, I made an appearance."

"That's when the appearances count. How long has Beckman been assistant chief deputy D.A.?"

"Since before we were born," James said.

At twenty-eight, James had a couple of years on me. That was a long freaking time in the D.A.'s office. "What about Ramsey?"

"Acts like a loon, at times." He sat behind his computer. "But he gets the job done."

"I don't get it. You haven't been around here long enough to make that kind of enemy impression. If I was the shooter, I'd go after those two." The motive had to be personal. Really personal. I skimmed a news clip in the Tulep file. "How involved does Team Beckman get in putting dealers away?"

"Those two cases are the only ones Beckman, Ramsey and I handled together."

I took the files and flipped through, mulling over the dealers and the victims. Michael raced in.

"I think I might have something," he said.

Chapter Fourteen: Brass Tacks

We huddled around Michael while his fingers danced across the keyboard in front of James' computer screen.

"Incoming printout." Michael looked up at James. "The shooter rode a Fly, so I called Fly, the e-scooter rental company, and mentioned I'm with the D.A.'s office. The manager answered all my questions. Just like that. I could've made the whole thing up. So cool."

Michael never lied. I was working on the never part.

"You said you're a D.A.?" I asked.

"I said I'm sitting at the Westside division of the district attorney's office and I've got a few questions." Michael gave James a fist bump.

"What did you find out, Sherlock?" James asked.

Michael leaned toward him. "You already know we saw the guy take off on an electric scooter parked at the end of the alley."

"For a fast getaway," I said.

"Right. Fly's a new e-scooter company with a small fleet all over Santa Monica." Michael reached behind him and pulled out a piece of paper from the printer. "I gave the exact coordinates and time of where he parked the e-scooter and where he'd abandoned it. Here's a list of everyone that rented a scooter yesterday and didn't bother returning it. All have coordinates near the shooter's scooter." He held up the sheet. "Two are students at Santa Monica College. But one name…could be our guy."

"He's not *our* anything," James said. "He's an attempted murderer that better be caught soon." He sank onto a side chair leaning against the wall.

I cruised over the list of three names. All males. All had driver's license information listed.

Michael turned to James and held up the list. "See the last name on the list? That's our man."

James eyed the name a second before turning away. "Not much we can do with a fake ID. Thanks, anyway."

Michael shot to his feet. "But what if he slipped up and didn't use a phony? We've got to try." He looked at me. "Right? Even a phony license could provide a clue."

"Good point." Even though our guy didn't seem like he made mistakes. "Once we confirm it's a fake, we can find the specialist behind it. Ramsey might know expert fake ID makers. And the not so expert ones, too." I picked up the list. "This is the best lead we've had so far." I turned to James. His teeth were clenched. "What's the matter?"

"We've had two chances to nab him and missed."

"You mean I missed," I said. It's not like I didn't try.

"He was in our faces each time," James said. "Should've expected him at my place."

That was a little far-fetched in my humble opinion. I would've at least waited 'til the next day. "How many open and shut cases have you seen?" I asked.

He heaved out a sigh and slumped lower into his seat.

"Can you get Ramsey to check the ID out? Please?" I asked.

He snatched the list and sauntered out.

"I've never seen him like this before," Michael said. "He doesn't get rattled so easily."

I'd seen him rattled plenty of times, courtesy of yours truly, so I didn't exactly agree. "He'll be his usual charming, yet irritating self, once this blows over. No one likes wearing a target on their back. It's itchy." I picked up the two folders. "We need to do background checks on everyone whose name appears in these files, including the dealers' flunkies, and the victims' families."

"Wait, you're saying a family member of a victim would go into a crowded restaurant and pull a gun?" Michael said. "Ordinary people don't do that."

"What makes you think these teens came from ordinary families?" I got to my feet. "Besides, people are capable of anything when they're mad."

"Mad crazy or mad angry?" Michael asked.

"The type of mad that makes you carry a gun and fire it in a crowded diner. It's a deadly, emotional play." I handed an open folder to Michael. "Edgar Dingo Nappy was sentenced yesterday."

"So he could've ordered the hit on the D.A. team."

"Maybe," I said.

"He could've been planning it for weeks in case of a guilty verdict."

"Doesn't work for me." I flipped open the other folder. "...Tony Tulep was..." I peered closer at the file. "Sentenced to twelve years in prison."

"Did you say Tony Tulep?" Michael asked. "Where do I know that name?"

"From a bulb catalog?" I grinned. "A tulip especially designed for drug-dealers."

"Funny. I mean I read something about him recently." He slid behind the computer screen and pounded away for a few beats. "Here it is. He was released on a technicality a few weeks ago. Something about a wrong signature on wiretap warrants. Hasn't been seen since."

I dashed over to the screen and skimmed the article. "Wow. Scot-free after serving less than three weeks of his prison sentence."

"He's the gunman, isn't he?" Michael asked.

I shoved both files under my arm. "I need to review these more carefully."

"If you're a free man, why shoot to kill in a crowded restaurant?" Michael asked. "Odds of getting caught are high. He wouldn't want to go back to prison."

Michael had a point. "Release would be an unexpected happy glitch in his crime-ridden life. He'd probably lie low once he got out, which is why no one's seen him," I said. "Unless he needed money. He could be lying low and dealing. But, you're right. He wouldn't go into a crowded diner." No way. I flipped open the file and studied Tulep's photo. Scruffy looking, glasses and a full-on beard.

"We've got two possibilities so far. Someone was either very unhappy about yesterday's verdict," Michael said. "Or very unhappy about Tulep's release."

James rejoined us.

"Tulep got out recently," I told him. "Did you know?"

"Why do you think I gave you the file?" he replied.

"He couldn't be the shooter," I said. Unless he shaved his head, his beard and lost a lot of weight since the photo, all of which could've happened. Or he could've hired a triggerman.

"Maybe since everyone knows Big Sam's Diner is a law enforcement hangout," Michael said. "And someone could've shot back, it would be the best place to do it. So unexpected. Kind of like Tulep's release."

"Good one," I said.

"The shooter didn't care if he lived or died," James said, perching on the edge of his desk. "Just wanted to hit his mark."

"He missed," Michael said. "So nothing was accomplished."

"Unless he missed on purpose. Or…" I said, "maybe he was aiming for Beckman's butt. He wasn't shooting to kill."

"Let's cut the speculation and get back to the facts," James said.

"What did Ramsey have to say?" I asked.

"The name's a fake and he'd ask around about the ID," James replied.

"Why is Nappy's middle name Dingo?" Michael asked.

"Short sandy hair, a pointy nose and an Aussie accent. He's a dead ringer for a wild dog." James stood and paced the room. "When yesterday's verdict came in, he wasn't shy about sharing his feelings."

"Oh, man. Did he threaten you?" Michael said.

"Said we'd made a big mistake and we'd be sorry." James scowled and knelt next to the folder pile. He opened another one. "Hired guns are part of his syndicate."

"Do you have a list of the hired guns?" Michael asked him. "We can narrow down the possibilities."

"Doesn't work that way," James replied, staring at the paperwork.

"What'll we do? You need protection. Big time," Michael said.

"That's where we come in," I said.

"Don't be ridiculous." Beckman stood at the threshold, taking up most of the space with his bulky form. He was slightly bent over, his mouth twisted to one side in a wince. He reached into a pocket, and pulled out a medicine bottle. He flipped open the cap, popped a capsule in his mouth and jerked his head back. "What kind of protection could you provide? Ever shoot to kill before? And I'm not talking about video games."

Michael and James stared at me.

"I don't play video games," I said.

"I've pulled the trigger before," Michael said. "A few months ago." He referred to a little incident at the college where he worked.

"Water pistols don't count," Beckman said. "Neither do flare guns."

"I'm offended," Michael said. "I don't own a water pistol and you'll find my flare gun in my trunk. Untouched."

Beckman rolled his eyes. "You have no idea who you're dealing with. Dingo Nappy is dangerous."

"How do you know it's Nappy?" I asked.

Beckman grabbed an apple out of the small glass bowl sitting on a side table. He tossed it in the air and caught it. "He grew up in the backwoods of Kentucky in a family of turkey hunters and horse traders."

"I think horse traders disappeared at the turn of the century," Michael said. "The last century, I mean."

"His family publishes a horse-trading magazine. He's also a former Eagle Scout. So he's got skills."

"What?" Michael said. "Why would he turn to drug dealing?"

"Hard to walk away from large amounts of money streaming in," James replied. "He thought he'd found his pot of gold."

"He moved to L.A. and became a dealer using millennials to do his evil deeds," Beckman said. "Wasn't easy bringing him in." He bit into the apple and crunched.

I stood and stepped closer. "Why would you assign a new D.A. to take a case against a big drug dealer?"

"Because I'm capable—" James said.

Beckman put up a hand to silence James. "To show Nappy we thought so little of him, we sent in a nobody." Beckman bit into the apple again and caught James' scowl.

"You what?" James spoke low and slow.

"Relax, I know what you're capable of, but Nappy didn't." Beckman crunched. "You were our secret weapon."

Something was off here. Way off. Facts raced through my mind like starving cheetahs chasing gazelles. "You couldn't know the outcome of the trial—"

"Who says?" Beckman tossed the apple behind him, missing the trash receptacle by three feet. The half-eaten apple slammed against the wall and rolled onto the carpet, scattering leftover bits and pieces. He pointed to James. "I made sure he was fully prepared. There was no way he would lose."

My stare cut to James. His brows dropped and his lips turned inward.

"Our team will remain in the building until Nappy's man is caught," Beckman said.

"Why here?" Michael asked. "Doesn't seem safe to me."

Beckman turned to Michael. "This entire floor is like one big safe room. We will stay locked up until we catch the hired gun."

"And if the building's being watched by Nappy's people, someone will notice James never left." I took a step closer to James.

Beckman shook his head. "It can't be closely watched. Too many exits. James could be smuggled out in a car that's leaving. He could be disguised as a little old lady from our victim witness program."

I stared at James. Turning him into a little old lady was like stuffing a bear into a clam shell.

"Don't worry, we'll be safe here," Beckman said. "No one will find us. Personally, I think this guy is done. The loser can't even shoot straight. Ask my butt."

I shot him a dirty look. "Seriously?"

"You…" James turned to Beckman. "…need me out there to bring the gunman into the open…"

"We're making too many assumptions. We don't know that Nappy even hired last night's shooter. Or do we?" I asked Beckman.

"It's the obvious conclusion," he said. "He could easily have put out a hit."

"So he knew he'd get a guilty verdict, and he prepared days, maybe weeks, in advance to take you and James out, just in case," I said. "At that particular restaurant. We need the facts, straight up."

"I'd gladly give you full disclosure," Beckman said. "Except no can do. You're not with our office or any department or agency we work with. Ta-ta." He strolled toward the door.

"Sir, you can give them full disclosure." James stood and took a few steps forward.

Beckman did an about face and lifted his chin. "What?"

"I've hired Corrie as a consultant on the case. My budget allows for that since it's on a temporary basis," James said.

Beckman narrowed his eyes. "What budget?"

"When I first took this case, I asked for a special budget to hire assistance, as needed. You signed off on it. I need that extra help now. She'll be with us for five days, or less, if we catch the shooter. So will her assistants." James tossed his chin toward Michael. "One's here already."

Beckman grunted. "Don't be ridiculous. You have no approval for that."

James strutted over to his desk and pulled a piece of paper out of a drawer. "It's right here in an email exchange between us."

"Let me see that." Beckman marched over to James and grabbed the paper. Squinting, he read it to himself, lips moving. He finished and shifted his squint to James. "Must've caught me in a weak moment. I need to confirm this." He stormed out of the office.

"How about the full disclosure?" I called after him.

"He doesn't even know what that means." James folded himself into his desk chair.

I dropped the files on the floor and stepped over to James' desk. I grabbed a notepad. I drew a rough sketch of the table from last night and positioned everyone in their respective chairs. "Beckman was on your left, James," I said. "He was leaning down, hands on the table between you and Ramsey. The bullet scraped his left buttock, landing in the wall behind him. Michael and I sat on the opposite side, but I wasn't at the table." I looked at James.

"Unless he was a terrible shot, he was aiming for Beckman, which makes the most sense." He was obnoxious and adept at ticking off quite a few people, felons and otherwise…

"Ramsey was the most visible target," Michael said. "But maybe Beckman was first on his hit list. Beckman was blocking James from view. So the shooter went after James later. He was number two on the list."

"Could Ramsey be the next target?" I turned to James. "What do you think?"

James picked up his cell phone. "Time we had a little chat with Ramsey. Let's put him on the grill and turn up the heat."

Chapter Fifteen: Footloose and Ramsey Free

The door to an office down the hall crashed open and banged shut. Ramsey popped into the office seconds later. He squeezed a stress ball in the shape of a mini globe, pulsing it in his hand.

"I'm not in the mood for whatever you've got cooking." He focused on Michael and me.

Yet he'd raced right over. He pulsed the ball a little faster.

"What's this about?" he asked.

"You're the investigator, Ramsey," James said. "Don't you know?"

His beady eyes flashed to James. He scratched his elbow without missing a squeeze. "I'm not psychic. But it's about last night, obviously."

"See," James said. "I knew you'd figure it out."

"Cut the sarcasm," Ramsey said. "I didn't expect to see these two again so soon."

"You're welcome to communicate with us directly," I said. "I'm wearing my kid gloves today."

"Ha, ha," Ramsey said.

Michael put out his hand. "We weren't officially introduced last night. Michael Parris. I'm the dean of—"

"I know who you are. You're the geek."

Michael frowned. "I prefer 'nerd', thank you, but I'm so much more than just another computer nerd. I can dominate a dance floor, belt out a Broadway tune, and whip up a gourmet pizza like you've never tasted before."

"True story." I was so ready for a pizza.

"Not to mention I get a high level of service when I go into an electronics superstore," Michael said.

"I couldn't have wrapped my last three investigations without him," I said.

"All I know is he won't be of any use to the D.A.'s office," Ramsey told James.

Michael turned to James. "Are D.A. investigators supposed to jump to conclusions like that?"

"Only when they're trying to avoid getting asked any questions about themselves," James said.

"Now's the time for your investigative powers to kick-in," I told Ramsey. "Looks like Beckman's entire team is being targeted. Any idea who and why?"

"Of course I have ideas." He puffed out his chest and practically pawed the floor with his saddle shoes.

"What's your theory?" I asked.

Ramsey cracked a crooked grin. "I know about your work. I'm a fan."

"Can we stick to the subject?" Michael asked. "We're all Corrie's fans."

"I'm not talking to you, geek." He shot Michael a dirty look. Ramsey drifted closer toward me.

I held up my palm. "Do not speak to Michael that way. Now's the time to share your ideas."

Ramsey squeezed his globe at triple time. "You should do your research. I've made a bunch of criminals angry by handing the D.A.'s office the evidence to convict." He cocked his head. "About the cases you worked with your father...I always wondered how—"

James lodged himself between us with a scowl and faced Ramsey. "You know how I feel about wasting time. There's a strong likelihood the killer will come after you next. Narrow down the candidates."

Good thing James stepped up. I was about to shove Ramsey against the wall so he'd see me in a whole new light. Once he came to, that is.

Ramsey stopped pulsing the globe and straightened. He tipped his head back and stared James squarely in the eyes. "Maybe you don't know enough about my work with the D.A.'s office to respect my knowledge and ability. I've got a vast database inside my head." He leaned sideways and returned his stare to me. "I really do respect your body…"

James put out an arm to keep me from pressing forward.

"…of work," Ramsey finished.

"Who's the man behind the gun?" I asked.

"Personally, I think the target was Beckman." Ramsey straightened and turned to James. "His coming to your place was his way of making a statement. That he wasn't finished with the D.A.'s office. I studied the shooting from different angles and that was my conclusion."

"What kind of angles?" Michael asked.

"Ramsey's a math whiz. His approach to each case is mathematical." James grunted.

"You're a math nerd?" Michael asked.

"That's right. I mean, no. I'm not a nerd. I study relevant statistics as well as physical placement—"

"What were the odds of all of you dining together at Big Sam's last night?" I asked. "I heard you originally planned to order Chinese and stay in. How could the shooter know where you'd be?"

"Don't you know?" Ramsey let loose a lopsided, close-mouthed smirk. "We go there nearly every Tuesday. And I'm beginning to think the gunman has an inside man or woman."

Someone popped open a can of soda in the office next door. That's how quiet it was.

"Inside the D.A.'s office?" Michael asked.

"That's what I said." Ramsey lowered his chin and narrowed his beady eyes. "Mister Genius A. Geek."

James raised his arm to hold me back again. "Any theories on the insider?"

"Not yet." Ramsey inched toward the folders I'd dropped on the floor near James' desk. He squinted at them. "When you called…" He knelt and opened a file. "…I was on my way to see you, to look at your files and compare them to mine. The answer lies within one of these."

"We figured that much out," I said. "But you have more expertise than we do." Ramsey looked like he did more than his fair share of nosing around, and he'd been around the D.A.'s office for a while.

The crooked grin resurfaced, as did the squeezing of the globe. "You, of all people, understand the thrill of hunting down and collecting evidence. It's such a high."

It was hard to disagree with him on that one.

Ramsey dropped his gaze back to the folders strewn on the carpet. Moments later, he picked up a file and tossed it onto James' desk. "The answer's in this one."

"Answer to what?" Michael asked.

Ramsey headed for the doorway and turned around. "The identity of the shooter."

Chapter Sixteen: Won't Back Down

One thing was certain: Ramsey's ego could fill every seat in Dodger Stadium and spill over into the Rose Bowl a few miles away. The file selection had to be random, unless Ramsey really was psychic. James stared down at the folder. I slid over to his shoulder.

"Are you thinking what I'm thinking?" I asked.

"If you're thinking of popping open a bottle of beer," James said, "the answer is yes."

"I'm thinking…" I lowered my voice. "…Ramsey's wasting our time. So he can investigate his own angle." I whirled around. "Isn't that true?" Ramsey was MIA.

Michael and James flipped around.

"The bum," James said.

"Why would he leave now? We're here to help," Michael said. "And work together."

"How's he lasted with the D.A.'s office this long?" I asked.

James blew out a huff. "He comes through. Even if he's not a team player."

"We don't have room for him on the A-team, anyway," Michael said.

"We wouldn't need him if we had a real lead. That's a hint, you two," James said.

Michael picked up the file that Ramsey had been playing with and opened it. "It's Tulep's file."

"Of course it is," I said. "It sat on the top. A simple matter of deduction."

"You two have a go at it." James stomped toward the door.

"Where are you headed?" Michael asked.

"To talk over insiders with Ramsey," he replied over his shoulder and left.

"What does Ramsey know about Tulep that he's not sharing?" Michael asked.

"Could be Ramsey's a poser, pretending he knows something when he knows nothing." I turned and looked back at the file. "Nappy's the obvious candidate, but Tulep's got my attention. We need to learn everything we can about these two."

"That's where I come in," Michael said. "I'll do a deep search."

I walked over to him and planted a kiss on his lips. "I love your attitude, among other things."

"Did I tell you I feel the same?"

"Not today." We kissed again and I sidestepped to the computer. "You tackle Nappy." I had a feeling Tulep was like a landmine. I wanted to handle him myself. "He happened to be sentenced hours before the shooting. And I'll bet he's got a lot of baggage."

"And I'm the baggage handler. Works fine and dandy."

Meanwhile, I searched the Internet for more photos of Tulep.

Michael sat cross-legged on the floor and scanned the Nappy file. "Edgar Nappy moved to L.A. three years ago to go to engineering school, then dropped out and ran a drug ring. His crew claimed they didn't know he was selling counterfeit prescription drugs laced with fentanyl. He sold drugs on the dark net." He shook his head. "A fellow nerd gone over to the dark side." He thumbed through the file and held up a photo of a clean-cut guy with sandy hair and wide-set eyes.

"Last night's shooter was tall, lean and middle-aged." Murky details were getting clearer. "Angular face, sunken-in cheeks, athletic. Check out Nappy's dad or some older flunky that could've stepped in after his conviction." That wouldn't help if he'd hired an outside hitman.

"There's a newspaper photo of his dad," Michael said. "Let's just say the only sport he might excel at is lawn bowling, which, by the way, was a big pastime for Shakespeare and George Washington."

"Any more photos in the folder?"

Michael took one out. "A few of Nappy."

I scooted over and extracted the pictures. I stared at Nappy's profile. This guy had a thin, pointed nose.

"Did you find anything on Tulep?" Michael asked.

"Just what we know already. He got out and disappeared."

"Do we think he's behind the shooting?" Michael asked.

I shook my head. "Last night's guy took a huge risk. If Tulep's lying low, he'd be focused on hiding out, like we said. He wouldn't take a chance on hiring a gunman that could lead back to him."

"But a professional—"

"Doesn't miss," I said.

James marched through the door. "We've got a break in last night's shooting."

"The bullet?" It was a little too soon to get ballistic results, but it was possible. Michael was on his feet.

"Ramsey found video footage," James replied. "Taken near the corner where you last saw him."

"And?" Michael asked.

"We've got the make and model of the car."

"Plate number?" I asked.

James shook his head. "No plate. But there's a bumper sticker, *US Army, Retired.*"

"So he is former military," I said.

"Anything stand out about the car?" Michael asked.

"An older American black sedan. Looks to be a Ford."

"That's the car I saw," Michael said.

I turned to James. "Where did Ramsey get the tape?"

"From an office building across the street. There's a camera pointing out over the entry."

"No other cameras in between?" I asked.

"None yet. Residential area around the corner," James said. "A grammar school down the street. There's a gas station nearby that we're checking."

"Can I view the tape?" I asked.

"I'll stay and read through the files," Michael said. "I'll keep looking until I find something incriminating." He pulled a bag out of his coat pocket. "I brought my own cheese puffs, so I'm good to go."

"Follow me," James said.

I shadowed him out the door and into the hallway, in the opposite direction I'd taken before. The drabness continued down the corridor, but with James sauntering in front of me, the view was a whole lot better. He barely rounded a corner when a man's voice called out from behind us.

"Where are you two going?"

We turned around to face Beckman, as unsmiling and cold as ever.

"To view the tape again," James said.

"Listen." Beckman shuffled toward us. "You're going about this all wrong. Something rattled the guy when he was about to shoot. The crowd, the noisy diners, anything could have thrown off his aim." Beckman pointed his index finger at James. "Want my updated theory? The bullet wasn't meant for any of us. He was aiming for someone else. If he wanted me dead, I would be."

"Then why did he follow James home?" I asked.

His beady brown eyes shifted to mine and his jaw tightened. "The advanced criminal mind often twists facts." He spoke slowly like he was explaining simple math to a five-year-old. "To throw off the scent of who he's really after. He followed James, so you'd call the cops. He didn't count on you lying in wait for him. Who does that?"

He let the question hang in the air for a few seconds like a spray of light cologne. Come on. I couldn't be the only suspicious minded female who happened to have an arsenal on hand.

"His plan was to throw everyone off so he could go after his real targets," Beckman said. "That's why he followed James. I've studied the behavior of many seasoned felons. Odds are a criminal will attack a police officer before a D.A., isn't that right, James?"

I mentally zipped my mouth. All odds were off when it came to lunatics with a weapon.

James gave a nod and squeezed his lips together.

I pulled open my zipper. "He could've missed for several reasons. He wasn't a great shot. The target moved, or he changed his mind, last second. He didn't see me coming. I was on the floor behind him. Besides…"

Beckman put up his hand. His face turned the color of a ripe pomegranate. He turned to James. "Go back to your office, gather up the other members of your amateur team and escort them to the door, so we professionals can focus on our jobs."

"But we have—" I started.

"Will do," James said. "We'll leave it to law enforcement to handle." He shot me a look that made me swallow my words, giving me instant heartburn. He spun around, back toward his office.

"Odds don't apply to the criminal mind," I said. "Nearly sixty percent of homicides go unsolved in California. Why is that?" I blew out a huff as my heels clicked along the dull linoleum. I glanced behind me. Beckman smirked and stepped back into his office. I took slow breaths and caught up to James. "I hope he doesn't lean against any sharp objects," I whispered. "He's so full of hot air, he just might pop."

"Beckman knows we're the targets," James said. "He just wants you out of his hair."

"I wouldn't be in his hair if he cooperated with us." I took a deep breath. "What did Ramsey have to say about the inside man?" I exhaled.

"He's betting it's a security guard in this building."

"Doesn't anyone have any hard evidence?"

A whistle interrupted my breathing exercise. Michael stood by James' office waving a folder over his head.

"You should see this," he said.

James bolted over and Michael handed him the folder. We followed James inside and I closed the door.

"This could be the dude Corrie saw last night," Michael said. "And he's missing fingers."

James opened the file. "Manny Frederick?"

"He worked with Tulep, but Frederick was arrested first," Michael said.

I leaned in close to the folder. "Six feet two inches, check." I caught my breath. "Thirty-nine. Check. And he's missing part of his first two fingers."

James flipped to the next page. "Released over thirty days ago. He was a middle man that brought customers to Tulep. I didn't work on this case."

"This is the second guy with part of fingers missing," Michael said. "Is that an occupational hazard of drug dealing?"

"Usually, it's the whole finger," James said. "If an underling's caught stealing drugs for themselves, off goes a finger. The bigger the drug lord, the bigger the missing appendage."

"That's the wrong line of business if you value your fingers." He wiggled his fingers. "I'd have to get a customized keyboard." His stare swung between James and me. "Just trying to lighten things up. Beckman put him away?"

"That's right," James said.

"If he's the man with the gun, you're not the target, bro. That's great news."

"It's not him," James said. "Remember the guy at my place last night?"

"He could—"

"Frederick's locked up. Arrested again last week. Didn't post bail." James' cellphone vibrated. He pulled it out of his pants pocket and looked at the screen. "Ramsey." He placed the phone to his ear. "Yeah?" A few moments ticked by and James disconnected. "They found the car."

"The Ford Focus?" Michael asked.

"Where?" I asked.

In two strides James faced the window and pointed outside. Michael and I flanked him. We peered toward the street. A small group of cops and police vehicles surrounded an old black sedan.

Chapter Seventeen: Fools' Gold

"That's crazy," Michael said. "Who parks the escape vehicle in plain sight?"

"Not to mention in front of the D.A.'s office," I said.

"They're feeding us clues so we don't bother looking for our own," James said.

I turned to James. "How did Ramsey know the car was parked here?"

"An anonymous tip came in ten minutes ago," James said. "Ramsey said materials located inside the vehicle confirm it belonged to last night's gunman."

"Like what?" Michael asked. "A signed confession? An autographed photo of the shooter behind the wheel?"

"How about we reserve judgment until after we view the materials?" James said.

"You can't go out there," Michael said. "Maybe that's exactly what he wants. You'll be like a sitting duck, waiting to be picked off—"

"Hey, nobody's picking me off," James said. "I'm flying too high to be shot."

"That's not what I meant," Michael said. "It's just that we—"

I grabbed his hand. "Stick with me and we'll keep James safe. Let's take a look."

When we got to the lobby, I stuck out my arm, blocking James' path. "Wait inside, and we'll report back as soon as we have something."

"I'm not a thumb twiddler in case you haven't noticed," James said and pushed past my arm.

I hurried to keep up with him. "You won't be twiddling. You'll be…observing from afar. You'll see things we might miss. Besides, maybe Michael's right and this is a trap to draw you out. Then you really will be a sitting duck."

"We can handle this," Michael said.

James slowed down and finally came to a stop. He scanned the lawn leading up to the street.

"Personally," Michael said. "I'd use a bicycle as my escape transport. I wouldn't have to worry about getting a driver, getting stuck in traffic or losing the keys. Plus, it's harder to ID a bike and easy to abandon."

We turned to stare at Michael.

"What? It's not like I've given this a lot of thought or anything," he said. "I'm just sayin'."

James gave up a sigh. "Not much I can do out there, anyway." He turned back to the building. "Be quick. I'm not the most patient person."

Michael and I bumped fists and scurried toward the car. The battered black sedan was parked in the red. We hopped onto the sidewalk and near the group poking around the car. The vehicle was patterned with dings and dents.

"Why is a member of the military here?" Michael asked.

A man in an army green combat helmet kneeled next to an open car door, talking to a cop. He was dressed in fatigues, with a hand grenade strapped to his belt. He wore boots to go with his get-up. He waved cheerily at us, while pulsing a small globe in one hand.

"Is that Ramsey?" Michael said.

"Looks like he shops in military surplus stores," I said.

We edged closer.

"That poor sedan," Michael said. "Why would anyone treat their ride that way? It deserves respect."

His concern for cars was the sort reserved for the elderly, infants and rare stamps. He believed they should be handled lovingly and with great care.

"I was right about the first-generation part," Michael said.

"The what part?" I asked.

"It's a 1998 Focus. A star performer for Ford Motor Company in its day.

Not that much different from European models. But look at it now." He shook his head.

I squeezed Michael's hand. "Criminals don't usually care about anything, except their own hides. Let's get up close and personal."

We stopped by the crime scene tape surrounding the sedan.

"Wait here." I stepped sideways and hurried toward the opposite end. I slipped past a couple of cops and didn't stop until I was a foot away from Ramsey. A uniform appeared next to me.

"You need to leave, miss," the cop told me.

I pointed to Ramsey. "I'm with him."

Ramsey's eyes rounded and he grinned more crookedly than ever. "That's right." He moved closer until our shoulders nearly touched. I stiffened.

The cop strode away and I stepped back. Ramsey wiped off the grin and leaned his wiry torso my way.

"I really did study your cases. You may be good, but so am I. We can solve this faster together. I can help things sail along more smoothly, like you just witnessed." He cut his hand slowly through the air near his soft waistline.

I threw him a look that would have pickled an egg, but quickly changed my tune. I'd better play nicely. "There might be a grain of truth to that."

The crooked grin bounced back.

"How did you confirm the car belonged to the shooter?" I asked.

He cleared his throat and whispered, "An anonymous tip came through reception—"

"Asking for you by name?"

"Asking for someone who knew about last night's shooting. I was the first to respond. Items found in this particular vehicle are linked to last night's events."

"Like?" I had a gut feeling it was another set-up, just like Michael said. I stared around at the neighboring buildings.

"A menu from Big Sam's Diner."

"That's not obvious." The sarcasm flowed like rain down a water slide.

He shot me a squinty gaze and added, "There's also a notepad with the address to this office. It's better than the motel receipt that geek found."

"You don't mean Michael, do you?" What did he have against him? "Was the caller male or female?"

"A woman with a British accent. That's what the receptionist said."

Gordon Joshua jumped to mind. Was the caller related to him? Of course, an accent could be faked, but we needed to consider every angle. "I need a criminal background check. Can you do that?"

"You know I can." Ramsey pushed back his shoulders. "Who is it?"

"Gordon Joshua, celebrity chef."

Ramsey raised his brows. "I thought you said the shooter was tall and lean. Gordon looks like a tree stump."

"Humor me," I said.

"You're not trying to create a time-wasting diversion for me while you go out and find the shooter, are you?"

"Now you've hurt my feelings," I said.

He squeezed his stress ball faster. "I'm not your errand boy." He tossed his head and turned away.

"You're right. You've got more important things to do. I'll ask James to run the search." I turned to leave, but Ramsey grabbed my arm. I yanked my arm free and faced him. "I don't like being touched by just anyone."

"I'll run a search on the chef. Because I want our partnership to work."

I fought back the urge to put him in a headlock. Just because I could. I focused on the fake grenade around his belt. "Nice touch." I pointed to the grenade and flicked my gaze back to him. "Any owner ID laying around in the vehicle?"

He made a face and laughed. "Like a pink slip? Insurance certificate? Or did you mean a driver's license? For a smart woman, that was a dumb question."

In one quick move, I snatched the stress ball out of his hand and stomped away. It was a milder reaction than the headlock. I gave myself a mental back pat.

"You can borrow it," he called after me. "I've got a lot of balls."

I threw him a glance. I wasn't going to touch that one.

"I mean, spare globes."

I picked up the pace.

Michael raced over, motioning me to hurry after him. "He's on the loose." He pointed to the entrance. "He won't listen."

James and Beckman stood on a patch of grass, in front of the building.

"Of all the dumb…James!" I called out. A jet roared overhead, drowning out my voice. His back was to me. I called out again, louder. He didn't budge so I pitched the globe at him. It brushed against his shoulder, bounced off and landed in some shrubs. James' arms shot up to his head and he ducked, just as a loud crack ripped through the air. Heart pounding, I crouched and scuttled toward him.

Chapter Eighteen: Driven to Distraction

Two things I knew for certain. No one was hurt. And if I was herded into the D.A.'s building along with the rest of the gang, I'd lose the chance to nab intel on the shooter's ID. That's why while the police rounded up everyone, I made a break for it. The shot rang out from across the street. Either from the church or the office building next door to it.

I'd nearly made it to the curb when a cop blocked my path. I slumped onto the concrete, a limp mass. Going limp would make it harder to lift me up. If that didn't work, Plan B involved hugging my knees. Dragging me inside in that position would be quite a chore, in case he had the nerve to try.

"Don't move," the cop said and jogged over to the sedan. A few people had taken shelter in the car.

I stared back at the building. Beckman had bolted inside ahead of everyone else. I never saw a man of his stature haul butt so fast. Meanwhile, I shot up and rocketed past the sedan, tumbling onto the lawn of the gothic church. I kept on tumbling until I landed behind a large statue of a solemn looking, holy figure, lantern in one hand and Bible pressed against his chest. He stood on a marble pedestal, four feet tall. I prayed he was Saint Owen, the patron saint of escape artists. I pressed my back against the marble and waited.

Only one shot had been fired. Sniper style. Except snipers made the one-shot count. If he was after both Beckman and James, why didn't he try again? And what about Ramsey? Maybe the combat disguise had worked.

Snipers fire, move, and fire again.

So my father used to say. He handled an ex-sniper in the days before I tagged along on his cases. By handled, I mean he pointed the FBI in the sniper's direction. Okay, so our shooter was no sniper. What was he?

I studied the buildings around me. The shot might have erupted from the church. But not at ground level. He'd be too easily spotted running off. Unless he was still hanging around here. The surrounding bushes were sparse and the trees had narrow trunks. The windows in the church were closed.

I peeked around the corner of the marble block and jerked back. Two cops stomped in my direction. Not a problem. I relaxed my shoulders. I'd tell them I was scared and ran for cover…all the way across the street and across the lawn to the statue. I'd explain it had something to do with my religious upbringing. What kind of church was this, anyhow?

Their voices grew louder. The cops were discussing the shooter. I debated turning myself in when a yell interrupted them. Footsteps padded quickly away. I peeked out. Another small crowd had gathered, this time in front of the D.A.'s building. No bodies on the ground, no medics, so I figured no one was hurt. Meanwhile, I scanned the top half of the church. The gothic style structure hosted a three-story tower, positioned directly across from where James and Beckman had been standing. The shot could have come from a high vantage point, but the tower was too narrow to maneuver in and out of easily. Stained glass windows were propped open, but none faced the street. I mentally crossed the church off the list of hiding places. The two-story office building next door featured flat windows in front, and a flat roof. Did the building offer easy roof access?

As I made a dash for the building, a cop shouted, "Stop right where you are."

I froze just short of the pathway leading to the sidewalk and pressed my palm against a tree trunk. It felt rough and had no give, kind of like my current situation. Officer Fisher joined me, panting.

"If I have to throw you over my shoulder and carry you back inside the D.A.'s office, I will. It's dangerous out here." He eyed the area behind me.

"I noticed."

"See anything that could lead to our man?"

I shook my head. "I kept getting interrupted. But..." I stole a look behind the trunk. "Bet he's hiding in there." I flicked my thumb toward the two-story office building next to the church. A vertical strip of beige bricks ran down the center of a building painted the color of a milky latte. The windows were dark. A red and white sign stuck on the stucco read:

For Lease.

What caught my eye was a second-floor window at the far right, mostly hidden by tree branches. It was the only window recessed into the wall.

"The building is vacant, by the looks of it," Fisher said.

Shooters value concealment like shoppers value discounts. "The roof would be the best spot to hide out," I said.

I quick-stepped toward the front of the building. Fisher kept up with me, eyeing the top of the structure. If I had shooting tendencies, I'd head for the roof.

He turned his baby blues back to me. "Looks like a parapet roof wall, two feet or so."

I slowed and my gaze roamed over the building. The roof was looking less appealing. The parapet wall wouldn't work, unless he drilled a hole through it, big enough for the rifle's muzzle. No time for that. And escape from the top would take too long. "On second thought," I said, "he wasn't on the roof."

"What?" he asked. "It's the perfect place to fire a clear shot."

"It's also the perfect place to be spotted, leaning the rifle over the wall. And it's where we'd expect him to be." Moments later, we stood beneath an upper level window. The one that was recessed. I tilted my head back and stared. "What do you see?"

He lifted his chin and peered. His eyes widened. "I'd better call this in." He picked up his radio.

The slider window was cracked open just enough to poke a child's fist through...and a rifle muzzle. It was the only window missing a screen. If he fired from inside the office, in the back of the room, a muzzle flash couldn't be seen and the shot would be muffled. He could exit out a back door. "Is there a parking lot behind this building?"

"I think so," he said. "But we need to go. My first obligation is to get you to a safe place."

"What? That's a bunch of…" I bit my tongue. "You've got to get in there now."

"Come on," he said and shooed me toward the D.A.'s office.

I'd never witnessed such a laid-back cop. I dragged a few steps behind him and dug my heels in the ground. "I'm not going anywhere. Not until you get someone inside that building." I wrapped my arms around the trunk of a small tree.

"I'll do that, but you're a civilian and I need to ensure—"

"Call first," I said. "Please."

He grabbed his radio and called Abby and disconnected.

"You don't scare easily, do you?"

"As long as I'm on dry land, I'm fine," I said.

"Not into swimming?"

I moved through water like a large rock. "I manage."

A cop came running from a squad car parked across the street. Another showed up from around the corner.

"Take a look inside that end unit," Fisher told them. "Check out the parking lot and roof, too." He looked at me. "Just in case."

They sprinted toward the entry while Fisher escorted me back at a slow jog. I glanced over my shoulder. "Hope they're not too late."

As we approached the front entry to the D.A.'s building, I forged ahead. A small group of law enforcement mulled near the bushes lining the front. I made a beeline for the section of the building closest to the entrance and grinded to a halt. A blue US mailbox rested to one side of the front doors, shaded by a large, leafy tree. I moved closer and knelt. It was standard blue issue…except for the roundish black hole ripped in its side, near the bottom. I shifted my stare to the place where James and Beckman stood minutes ago. About fifteen feet away from the mailbox. If the shooter was aiming for James, he'd ducked in the nick, and the bullet found a different target. My heartbeat quickened.

"What's going on?" The familiar voice came from behind me.

I spun around and met Detective Abby Rosewater head on. Gone was any trace of friendliness. Fisher stood next to her.

"I want to know," she said to Fisher, her hand landing squarely on her hip. "Why this civilian is on the exterior of the building when she should be inside."

"It's not his fault," I said.

Abby's lips pressed together. No air could seep through.

"Let's go in. You need to follow the detective's orders," Fisher said to me.

"I know," I said. "But I—"

"Officer Fisher has better things to do than babysit you," she said and turned to him. She lowered her voice, "Get going. I'll take her inside myself."

He shot off and Abby focused on me. She leaned forward and whispered, "Sorry if I sounded a little harsh, but one of the guys complained that I was too nice to be a detective. Can you believe it? That's a great dress, by the way."

"Thanks." I mentally shook my head. "Did you see that?" I pointed to the mailbox.

She strode closer and knelt to take a look, shifting her gaze from the hole to the window in the office building across the street, and finally back to me. "Who was he aiming for?"

"Either me or one of my team," a deep voice boomed behind us.

We turned to face Beckman.

"It's clear that we're the target. Do you mind? I need to speak to my consultant," he told Abby and nodded toward me.

That was an abrupt turnaround.

"I'm in the middle of interrogating her," Abby said.

"Finish up later." Beckman strode forward, pushing me along beside him. He aimed us toward the entry to the building.

"Alrighty then," I said.

James joined us, Michael at his heels. Abby's walkie talkie crackled.

"What is it?" Abby barked into it.

Beckman retraced his steps back to Abby. So did the rest of us. Fisher spoke at the other end,

"The rooftop search was a bust, but a fold-out chair and disposable gloves were left, unconcealed, in the office. It's the only unit missing a screen on the window. Appears to be where the gunman was stationed."

"The crime scene team should be there shortly." Abby nodded toward a nearby cop. "Any civilians in the building?"

"No, ma'am," Fisher replied.

"Any ideas on where he exited?" she asked.

"Not yet," Fisher said. "He could've had a car waiting nearby."

"Check for witnesses. I'll join in shortly." She handed the walkie-talkie to another cop and turned toward me. "We need to talk." She turned to Beckman. "Give us some space."

"Not on your life," he said. "She's our consultant."

"Then Miss Locke can give you a full report when I'm finished."

He stepped away. This was a first. It seemed surreal having a D.A. and a police detective battling over me, in a good way.

Beckman turned and trekked off, Michael trailing behind him, but James held his ground until Abby gave him a stern look. He retreated, as well.

"I don't want the guys to think I'm ever soft, but you and me…" Her index finger pointed between us. "We know better. We're ten times tougher than the toughest of these tough guys. I'd like to request your services as a consultant with us as well."

"I really—"

"But I can't," she said, setting her sights on the office building. "I'm too junior to get approval." She turned back to me. "I want you to know…we're going to do this together, but informally. And under wraps."

"So no one will know that we're working together, except you and I?" I asked.

"That's right." She leaned back. "Because if the head detective finds out, I'll be demoted or worse, and you…" She shrugged. "…won't have access to what could be very useful information. If everything works out, we'll catch the guy together."

Team Corrie seemed pretty popular these days. My only objective was to take him down before he caused any real damage. But could I trust Abby? Maybe she was using me for a promotion. I'd play it cool. "Deal." I was quite the dealmaker lately.

"Can I trust you to report everything you find to me, including any evidence discovered through your consulting work with the D.A.?"

"Just to be clear," I said. "I report to the D.A.'s office, and to you?" I didn't add that I'd report only as I deemed necessary. That would be my little secret. "Except no one will know that I report to you."

"If Beckman finds out, he'll tell my boss and he'll cut us out fast. This way, you get information from both sides in the name of bringing the suspect in. I've heard that your methods can be unconventional. I don't do unconventional." She stared at me long and hard. "Or get caught doing it, anyway."

I stared back at her. There was a certain sincerity about her.

"Can you fill me in on what you know about the black sedan?" Abby asked.

"It's a plant," I said. "The cops and the D.A. found exactly what the shooter wanted to be found and nothing else. Another handy distraction so he could do what he needed."

"I get it." She narrowed her eyes. "He's playing us like an accordion. I'll ask the department psychologist to do a criminal profile." She pulled out her phone.

"No need," I said.

"Why not?"

"Because I'll give you an on the spot profile." I pushed back my shoulders and stared across the street. "He's middle-aged. Possibly retired military, now working a desk job requiring some degree of analytics, as evidenced by his organizational skills. Lives modestly, but has a good amount packed away, along with artillery and supplies stockpiled for Armageddon."

"And you know all this how?" She pulled out a small pad and jotted a few notes.

"There's more." I eyed the sedan. "His initial plan was to kill his target. He wavered last minute because he's not a murderer, yet. Meanwhile, he's doing his utmost to keep us on our toes about his next move while he makes his decision."

Her gaze met mine. "What decision?"

"To kill or not to kill," I said. "That is the question. And he likes to eat steel cut oatmeal every morning, with blueberries, while doing sudoku puzzles." I almost blew on my knuckles and rubbed them against my chest even though I made up the last part for fun. It had been years since I'd profiled anyone. Dad made me do profiles over and over after studying a subject's actions, expressions and demeanor. Then we'd compare it to the real thing. I'd come close many times to being accurate. Fairly accurate, that is.

"I'm speechless," she said. "Our trained staff doesn't even provide that much detail. Where'd you learn to do that?" She continued taking notes.

"Dad. He was good at it. Any ballistics on the bullet yet?" I asked.

"No, but don't hold your breath. Expectations are low," she said quietly. She shoved the pad in her back pocket.

Officer Fisher ran up to us.

"Sorry to interrupt," he said. "We found a witness."

Chapter Nineteen: Can't Be Sure

I texted an update to James and Michael about the triggerman being stationed in the office building, and the witness mentioned by Officer Fisher. Then I hustled away to catch up to Abby and Fisher as they raced toward the church.

When I caught up, Abby eyed me and turned to Fisher. "Let me get this straight. A church volunteer saw a female exit the sedan and walk toward Washington Boulevard?"

"That's right," Fisher replied.

"Description?" Abby asked.

"'Short and stiff,'" Fisher said. "Those were the witness's words."

"What does that mean?" Abby asked.

"That she didn't have a soft spot on her body," he said. "Said she looked like she was part of the turtle family. Also her words."

"Oh." Abby chewed on his words for a beat. "Did she seem like a reliable witness?"

"She provided her name, address, date of birth and phone number fine. Also told me she once played an extra in *Mutiny on the Bounty.* The Brando version."

"Anything else about the woman in the car?"

He pulled out a small notebook. "Dark, thick hair down to her chin, wearing a brown dress. And some kind of bonnet."

"Like a baby bonnet?" Abby wanted to know.

"She didn't specify, ma'am. Sounded like a straw hat."

I had to find the witness. "This witness works in the church?"

"She's part of the 'senior citizen brigade' that keeps the church looking 'spic and span'. Her words again." Fisher spoke over his shoulder.

"Name?" I asked.

Abby turned to look at me. "You know we can't give you that."

My phone vibrated. It was Veera. I stepped back and answered. "What's new?"

"You mean besides the fact that I'm about to knock Big Sam's block clear off if he continues with his overblown, feeble attempts at flirtation? That man doesn't even have an ounce of natural charm."

"Charm is overrated," I said. And in short supply, these days.

"I know it. Big Sam's turning me into the stereotypical angry black woman. And you know I'm no stereotype. Hold-up while I go outside," Veera whispered. A door creaked open and the sound of car engines poured in from her end. "I might have something, but then again, I might not."

"Go on."

"I watched that first tape again." Veera spoke louder. "The possible suspect's sitting at a table alone. It's a table close to the hostess stand. One week before, I found another tape with the same guy, same table, flying solo again. Never once does he face the camera. But get this." She lowered her voice. "Both times, there's this lady sitting on a bench on the other side of the hostess stand. Same lady each time."

"Did you show her to Big Sam? Maybe she's a regular."

"He's said he'd never seen her before. Neither has anyone else here."

"Is she waiting for a table?"

"On the first tape, she gets up after a while and walks away. She passes the guy and keeps going. I watched the whole tape of that night. She didn't come back. She could've slipped out the back door. On the second tape, she sits on the bench and takes off a minute after our possible shooter leaves. Both go out the front."

Maybe there was a connection. "Anything unusual about her?"

"Hard to say, but I'm willing to bet her hair's fake. She's wearing one ugly wig."

"How do you know it's a wig?"

"My neighbor wears the same kind. She's an orthodox Jewish lady. It's this thick, dark bob with bangs that never move. Makes her look ten years older. It's what you put on to turn a guy off real fast. Maybe I should wear one. I'll call it the Big Sam special."

"Veera, your observation skills are top-notch."

"I learned from the best," Veera said. "What's going down over there?"

I told her about the sedan and the shooting.

"Damn, this gunman's got nerve. Lucky he missed again. Maybe he's just a terrible shot."

"Or his heart's not in it."

"If he's aiming a gun at innocent people, he's got no heart," Veera said. "Gotta let him know he can't mess with us."

"We're plenty good at doing that ourselves," I mumbled. Then spoke louder. "If you're done at Big Sam's, please go to the studio. Catch up on anything we missed today." That should take all of ten minutes.

"Oh, alright. I'll watch a few more tapes and get going. But hurry up, will you? I can only do so much organizing in Lacy's office."

We were expecting our new boss to arrive soon. We'd barely started working for her when she took off for India. Lacy Halloway was an old-time actress-producer with a lucrative movie deal at Ameripictures, which gave her a large suite and matching budget. She shared a little of the budget with Veera and me by hiring us away from the children's motion picture division. I couldn't kiss my former boss goodbye fast enough. I should say 'kick' not kiss, because no lips of mine were ever touching him.

"Wait, Veera," I said. "If you owned an old American car that might need servicing, where would you go?"

Veera drove a VW bug from the sixties. All sorts of mechanics had serviced her VW, so she knew a lot of car people. She was also an expert at making useful connections wherever she went.

"You think he had that car sittin' in his garage?" she asked.

"It had a bumper sticker that seemed to fit his profile," I said. "Retired Army."

"I'll contact a few of my car guys to see what they know."

"Thanks." Of course, we could be way off base. He may have paid someone off the street for the car. I disconnected and looked around for the detective. She and Fisher skipped down the church steps and walked toward the vacant office building at a fast clip. I rocketed after them.

"What's the hurry?" I asked.

"The shooter left something behind," she said. "Again."

Chapter Twenty: Under Pressure

I followed Abby and Fisher into the two-story office building and a gloomy lobby. Dark wood covered the walls. Frosted glass windows faded out any hint of natural lighting. We shot up a wooden staircase and into a stuffy hallway. A quick right led into a small space buzzing with law enforcement. Crime scene tape crisscrossed the entry, but Abby and Fisher stepped right through. I did the same. A mesh window screen rested against one wall, next to a fold-out chair. The window faced the D.A.'s building.

"Where is it?" Abby asked a guy in a blue shirt kneeling by the screen.

He pointed his finger to the corner where a small rectangular shaped item sat in a plastic bag. Abby and I got there at the same time. She held up the bag.

"A calculator?" I said.

She turned to me and crinkled her nose. "Why would he need one?"

And more importantly, why leave it behind? "Is there a number on the screen?"

Abby cocked her head and stared at the small screen. "It's blank."

"Maybe it's another false clue," I said. Or a real one. Hard to tell which was which. "Anything else?"

"Yes. You need to leave," she spoke loudly, then dropped her voice. "I'm going to chat with the crime scene investigator. Bye." Her gaze landed on the man in the blue shirt.

I exited, brushing past Fisher who waited near the threshold.

"Anything new?" He turned and walked down the stairs with me.

"Nope."

"I have a feeling this is going to be one of those cases that drag on and on," he said. "Maybe we could help each other, you know, solve it sooner."

It was a lot of pressure having everyone's hopes hitched onto my skirt. "You'd better check with Abby on that." I knew what her answer would be.

We landed at the bottom of the stairs. "Abby'll need you upstairs. This being her first case…I'll show myself out."

"Right," Fisher said. "See you later." He took the steps up, two at a time.

Meanwhile, I hurried outside and zipped along a narrow exterior passage leading to the back section. I landed in a parking lot shared by the office building and a few shops on the street. One thing I knew for certain: the shooter couldn't have parked his car here. The lot was under construction. The asphalt was uneven and broken up in spots. My insides grew so wild with frustration, my toes were curling. Did he have another car parked nearby? Of course he did. With his wheelwoman waiting.

I swiveled around toward the street, kicking pine cones off my path. "Sooner or later you're going to make a mistake. I'll be waiting." My eyes shot upward. "Please make it sooner." Next time we might not be so lucky. A cold shiver ran down my spine.

*⁎⁎

I texted Michael and asked him to meet me by the black sedan. Alone.

A minute later, I hovered near the Ford. CSI team members lingered in and out of the car, dusting and measuring and photographing. Michael rushed toward me.

"There you are." He slid closer and moved his mouth near to my ear. "We need to talk."

"What's wrong?"

"I have my own theory about what's going on," he whispered, pulling back and staring down at me. "About time, right? Gee, you look pretty."

"Thank you. What's your theory?"

"The shooter is a newbie professional assassin. There isn't much on his resume. That would explain why he missed and why he keeps coming back. He's been paid to finish the job. Which also means we're in over our heads. Especially me."

"If that's true, he must be a bargain basement hit man. He's had enough chances," I said. "He's no assassin."

Michael straightened. "Are you sure?"

"If a professional missed more than once, he'd be ousted or worse. This is a do it yourselfer."

"But next time—"

"We'll get him before there's a next time." I stared at him long and hard, not as my boyfriend slash best friend, but as an asset on my hunting-down-criminals-team. "Question." I took his arm and led him away to a large magnolia tree near the building. "He leaves us a motel receipt, deposits a car in front of the D.A.'s office building—"

"While he sneaks into a vacant building," Michael said. "And takes another shot."

"And leaves a calculator in the room where he took the latest shot."

"A motel receipt, a car and a calculator." Michael squeezed his stubbly chin between a thumb and forefinger. "You don't just leave a calculator behind. Why have one in the first place?"

"The jokes on us," I said. "And it's a joke only he understands."

"Or he's an eccentric," Michael said. "Eccentrics can be found in all walks of life. Even the killer walk. I once read…"

"He's trying to tell us something," I said. "Sending a message." Something logical. But my brain was all fuzzy.

"He's leaving breadcrumbs," Michael said. "Just like in *Hansel and Gretel.*"

"But instead of leading us into a very large oven, he's pushing us deeper into a hole," I said. "And out of his way."

Michael's brows dipped and his mouth hung open a moment before the words tumbled out. "I'd say we're about chest-high in the hole. If James hadn't ducked…"

"He'd be toast, I know," I said.

Michael ran a hand through his dark waves. "We should do something."

He straightened and stared at me.

"I'm listening," I said.

"What? No, this is the part where you say, here's what we do." His gaze was stuck on mine.

"Okay." I squeezed shut my eyes, willing a plan to pop into my head. "We'll spread the word that we're transporting the three targets."

"To lure the gunman out?" he said.

"We don't really take them anywhere, but we say we will."

"Back to the baiting game. I like that," Michael said. "We can get police officers to play the D.A. roles. We pretend to drive them to a widely disclosed location, then we wait and catch him when he comes after them."

Sounded iffy to me. Too many moving parts. The detective and Fisher were talking and crossing the street at a brisk pace, headed in our direction. "Speaking of our friends in blue." I hurried over to Abby. "We want to run something by you.

"Not now." She pushed past me.

I caught up to her. "Why the rush?"

She stared at me for a few beats. "You didn't hear?"

"Hear what?"

"Someone's missing."

My heart dropped. "Who?"

She pointed to the building. "A D.A. team member."

Chapter Twenty-One: Take it on the Run

Minutes later, Michael and I waited outside Ramsey's office. Fisher stood by the elevator. The hallway was eerily quiet except for Abby and a cop stirring around inside the office, both wearing gloves and peering into everything.

"Where's James?" I asked Fisher. "Have you seen him?"

"He and D.A. Beckman are in an office upstairs with a member of the force."

"And no one's seen Ramsey?" Michael asked.

"No sign of him," Abby replied from the interior.

"He might've wandered away on his own," I whispered to Michael. "To get out from under the thumb of law enforcement."

"He needs to be located." Abby paused at the threshold. "Now, if you'll excuse me, I have work to do." She retreated back into Ramsey's office.

"Think he's roaming around, doing his own investigation?" Michael whispered, as we moved toward the elevator.

"It's possible. Let's dig deeper." We flipped a U-ey and stood by the entry to Ramsey's office. "You think the gunman got to him?" I asked Abby.

She pointed to a paperback book sitting on Ramsey's desk. It was propped up on a wooden book stand. I slid closer, leaning my torso forward. The book cover displayed two men on what looked like a pirate ship, one with a sword and the other with a pistol. The title was bold. Michael slid next to me.

"Beckman said that book wasn't there before," Abby told us.

"*Kidnapped* by Robert Louis Stevenson," Michael read the title out loud.

"The unabridged edition," I said. "The triggerman, now possibly a kidnapper as well, is a reader who took time to prop up this book. Thoughtful." A slew of classic books lined two shelves of a small bookcase in the office.

"It's a clue," Abby said. "This time he's letting us know what he did."

"Ramsey's got good taste in books," Michael said.

"Fits the shooter's M.O.," Abby said. "Most of law enforcement was either by the sedan or in the empty building across the street," Abby said. "A good time to make his way inside through a back door. Just where we didn't expect him to be."

"Any sign of a struggle?" I asked.

Abby looked at the officer.

"No, ma'am," the officer said.

"Any one review the surveillance camera downstairs?" I said.

The cop shot me a dirty look and said, "We've got someone on it."

"The victim," I said, "is an investigator. He wouldn't go quietly…unless he had a gun pointing at him and no way to defend himself." I walked around the room and stopped by a metal filing cabinet. An open folder sat on top. I caught my breath.

"Agreed." Abby stepped around the office. "Probably won't find any prints."

I pointed to the door. "Any sign of a forced entry?"

Abby and the officer headed for the door. I grabbed the top folder. It was Ramsey's very own Tulep file. I glanced at the first few pages. Michael's eyes rounded as he watched me. I stuffed the top pages into my purse and turned to a taller filing cabinet against the wall. I opened the top drawer. More files.

"Uh, Ramsey was the type that would've been prepped for someone coming after him, don't you think?" Michael made a dash toward the door and stepped outside so Abby and the cop faced him.

"Not necessarily," Abby replied. "He might've been taken by surprise." They were about to turn toward me.

"Unless…" Michael raised his voice and craned his neck to meet their gazes. "…it was someone he knew."

I rummaged around the bottom drawer's contents. Just as I suspected. Fake beards, wigs, glasses, even a French beret and a matching scarf. Ramsey liked disguises. I strolled around the perimeter of the office and circled back to the desk while Michael babbled on.

"Those are all possibilities," Abby said, whirling back into the office. The cop trailed her inside.

Another cop joined us. "No video footage showing any intruders, ma'am. And Ramsey's car is missing. But…"

"Yes?" Abby scooted closer.

"The back-door video shows someone leaving within the past hour. No one seems to recognize her. Female, Caucasian, brown hair, sunglasses. Carrying a large handbag. She left alone."

"Are you saying she smuggled Ramsey out in her purse?" Abby grinned my way, before facing the cop again. "See, detectives do have a sense of humor."

"No sign of him or anyone exiting with her," the cop said.

"Check out the garage video."

The cop turned on his heel and left.

Abby addressed me. "What do you think?"

"I think we'd better find Ramsey fast."

***

"Ramsey's into disguises," I told Michael. "He had a drawer full of them. He could've worn one when he left the building."

"So you really think he staged his own kidnapping?" Michael asked.

The two of us sat around James' desk. I pulled out the Tulep paperwork I'd borrowed from Ramsey's file and spread it on the desktop. "I'm saying it's very possible."

"Since he's not a team player…"

"This gives him freedom to conduct his own investigation," I said. "Just like we like to do."

115

"Yeah, but we don't have a gun pointing at us," Michael said.

"Ramsey can handle it." I scanned the papers and took a picture with my smart phone camera. "Looks like he had a pretty good informant on the Tulep case."

Michael peered over my shoulder. "Do you know the snitch?"

Dad had plenty of his own resources. "Ramsey calls him 'Fly Boy'. Doesn't ring a bell." I slid the Ramsey papers inside James' Tulep file and turned to Michael. "The informant says Ramsey was spotted at his old shop in Beverly Hills."

"What old shop?" Michael asked.

"We'll need to find out," I said. "Let's go track down the church witness."

Chapter Twenty-Two: Into the Groove

Michael and I skipped down the stairwell. I wanted to know what the church volunteer witnessed.

"Maybe someone else there saw something important," Michael said.

We landed on the first floor of the D.A.'s building and Michael yanked the door open.

"I've got good news." Abby stood facing us.

"You haven't found Ramsey yet." That would be good for Ramsey if he was hiding out. And if he'd been kidnapped—

"That's right, but I'm talking about the shell casing entry. The commander of criminal investigations pushed it through as a priority." She bounced her shoulders up and down. "We should know the make and model of the gun any minute." She pushed back her shoulders. "Where're you headed?"

"To my lawyer gig." I wasn't up for sharing. I continued walking outside and around the corner of the building. Abby kept pace.

"Two officers will be in this building twenty-four-seven, watching Beckman and Zachary until we capture our man."

"That's a relief," Michael told her.

"It may be more than one person behind this," I said.

We hurried toward the street, Abby nipping at our heels.

"You're talking about the female that parked the car here?" Abby asked. "It's odd that no other witnesses on the church property saw her."

Or came forward. "A tape from Big Sam's Diner confirms a possible female accomplice sitting near a guy resembling the triggerman. She was present both times he came into the restaurant. We watched tapes that went back a few weeks."

"Does the woman match the description the church witness provided? Never mind. I'll confirm that myself." Abby pulled out a phone and asked an underling to review the diner's tapes again. She disconnected. "I'm not holding my breath. So far I've got a bunch of mismatched leads." She blew enough air through her mouth to flutter her lips like a horse. "I expect to be pulled off the case any day now."

"It's not a bad thing to be underestimated. It paves the way to charge ahead, uninterrupted." I thrived on being underestimated. "You'll dig up something worthwhile. Meanwhile…" I slowed. "…you've got some footwork to do."

"Footwork?" she asked.

Michael headed for the black sedan. Abby and I stopped on the patchy lawn in front of the building. She wore a worried frown.

"He planted the car here to draw the target out so he could try again," I said.

"I know that much."

"So he does and misses." I headed toward the black sedan, which was still being scoured by the CSI team. "He's angry…"

"And that's why he kidnapped Investigator Ramsey," Abby said.

"When you're angry, you're bound to slip up again. You need to be ready to pounce on his mistake." That would keep her occupied. Meanwhile, I pulled out my phone and texted James to ask if Gordon Joshua had a record. Abby was texting, too.

"It's going to be another hour before we get the ballistics report." She finished texting and looked at me. "Can I ask you something? Do you have any resources? Someone who gives you tips? Because everyone seems to have at least one tipster except me."

"Nope." I fixed my gaze on Michael. He was checking out the car's front grille. Of course, I planned to take advantage of Ramsey's snitch.

"I never expected another shooting here today," Abby said. "Or a missing D.A. investigator."

"Crime's like the weather," I said. "Hard to predict with accuracy."

A TV crew had arrived and parked in front.

"Looks like you'll have company soon," I said.

Abby dropped her head and hustled back to the building. I wound my way to Michael. He was poking around the car's back bumper.

"Isn't it great?" he whispered. "I flash my D.A. badge and the crime scene tape disappears. I could get used to this star treatment."

"Anything else unique about the car?" I asked.

"It's got a ton of mileage." He circled the sedan. "There's a little rust, but otherwise, the interior's in good shape."

"Think it was recently sold?"

"The polish on the seat is super fresh. I doubt he cleaned it up before taking his next shot," he said. "Unless, he's the Martha Stewart of hitmen and car care. Kind of like someone you know. The car care part, anyway." He grinned.

I knew too well. Michael's car was hand washed and waxed at least once a week. Sometimes he showed up at my place and glammed up my car, too. The gunner could share that trait with Michael.

I pulled out my phone. "I'll text the make and model to Veera. She's on the lookout for the car's sales and repair history. Maybe we can trace it back."

James texted me first,

Nothing on Gordon Joshua. A DUI five years ago.

"I've got the VIN number," Michael said. "Give it to Veera. Have her do a Carfax VIN search." He held out his phone. "It could lead back to someone who knows something."

"My favorite kind of people." I texted Veera the number. "The knowledgeable kind."

"We've gotta keep James in the loop," Michael said. "Or he might strike out on his own. Like Ramsey. We don't want that to happen."

"Wish we could tie him up and lock him up somewhere, until this blows over," I said. "Think he'll fit in my trunk?"

"Not a good idea," Michael said. "He's pretty irritated. And interior trunk dents are hard to get out."

Fisher jogged up and paused in front of me with a small smile. "I'm on my way to let Detective Rosewater know I talked to the church witness again. Sorry, I can't share."

Abby stood near the D.A.'s building talking to another officer. "Has the detective been with the department long?"

Fisher shot her a quick glance. "She's a recent transfer from Vegas P.D. The senior detective gives her a rough time, but that'll change once he realizes she's smart and easy to work with. And she's no coward. Kind of like you. See you." He jogged back toward Abby.

"We'll check out the church witness later." I didn't think I could squeeze any more information out of her today. I turned back to Michael. "Think we can get into James' office without him?"

Michael shoved a hand into his pants pocket and yanked out a key. "I know we can. James thought you'd need this."

That man could read me like a traffic sign. "Perfect. There's something about one of those folders that's been bugging me."

"That makes two of us," Michael said.

Chapter Twenty-Three: Connecting the Dots

"Are you hungry or is it just me?" Michael sat on the floor, leaning against the wall, a thick folder laid open across his knees. He was reading the Nappy file. I sat behind James' desk paging through the Tulep folder.

"Didn't you just eat?" I asked.

"That was ages ago," he replied. "Got any snacks?"

I shuffled over to a small bowl and picked up a green apple. I held it up.

He stuck the wrists of his hands together and cupped them, ready to play catch. "I'll take it if you don't mind my being hungry three minutes after I'm done."

I tossed him the apple and he caught it. He sunk his teeth in with a crunch.

"Anything more substantial?" he asked after he swallowed his first bite.

"Like a leg of mutton?"

"Never tried that before. I'm game."

I reached in and rummaged around my handbag. "How about this?" I held up a small bag of trail mix and tossed it to him.

He took it. "Just what the doctor ordered." He ripped the bag open.

After a minute of crunching and skimming the file, he said, "Woah, baby."

"What'd you find?" I asked.

"Nappy's assets were all frozen. How would he pay for a hit?"

"They've always got a stash hidden somewhere." I thumbed through Tulep's file. He preyed on teen athletes, selling counterfeit prescription painkillers. "Wait one minute."

"What?"

"There was an attempted murder charge against Tulep," I said. "A sixteen-year-old John Doe fell into a coma after buying drugs from him. The name's been redacted." I read some more. "Tulep sold prescription painkillers laced with fentanyl, an opioid that causes almost certain death if there's enough in it."

"That's like peddling poison. What a scumbag," Michael said. "Hope the John Doe is okay."

Something was brewing in my head, only it was murky again. I stared at four photos in the back of Tulep's file. The first was a mugshot of him wearing a *don't mess with me* kind of look. Unruly black hair, bulging eyes and a thick beard, his head was tilted back like he dared the photographer to take the photo. But the rest were candid shots, snapped on the sly. He stood on a sidewalk, two thugs behind him. All three stared off to one side. He walked down a sidewalk in the next shot, head down.

"Tulep's one gnarly looking dude," Michael said, peering over my shoulder.

The last one showed a close-up of his face, staring into the lens. Tulep's pale blue stare was so hard, it nearly knocked me off my feet. A scar snaked across his chin. I was about to look away when the background caught my attention. I held the photo up closer.

The door to the office flew open and James sauntered in. His wild gaze roved over us and lingered on me. He wore his trademark scowl. "Well? Did you wrap this up yet?"

"I'll need a few minutes more," I said.

"I thought you were somewhere safe, with a police officer," Michael said.

"We have the right to float around, as long as we don't leave this floor. Cops are stationed at the exits."

"That's great news," Michael said.

"A teen's in a coma, thanks to Tulep. Does that ring a bell?" I asked James.

"Enough to fill every church tower across the country. What about him?"

"Is he still in a coma?" I strolled over to James and held out the file. He snatched it away and turned his back to us. "Do you have a name?"

"Don't know and no."

"What happened?" Michael stood. "You were cool, bro, when you left us."

James loosened his tie, yanked it off and threw it to one side. "That was before I was told I'm suspended."

In the past, he'd helped me on my somewhat shady cases, under the wire, where if he'd been caught, he would've been a whole lot more than suspended. His legal career would've been over. As would mine. Half of me was relieved the suspension wasn't my fault, but the other half welled with sympathy. James was a workhorse that thrived on kicking the daylights out of criminals. Kind of like me.

"What about Beckman?" I asked.

James tossed the file onto his desk and sank in the chair, leaning forward. His fingers locked together. "We're on leave until this guy's caught." He raised his gaze to mine. "Which means you'd better hurry and find him before I go stir crazy."

"So you don't know the teen's name?"

"Too many kids were affected," he replied. "There are no names in any of the reports."

"Turn to the back of the file," I said. "Look at the last photo."

James opened the file to a pocket in the back. He removed the photos and took turns inspecting each one. "So? I've seen these before."

"The building in the background." I pointed. "What do you know about it?"

Part of a structure was visible on Tulep's left. The bricks were painted white. A red and white striped awning hung over a tinted window.

"It was a front he used. An ice cream parlor in Beverly Hills." He lowered his voice. "Easy access for students wanting to get high as a kite without having to fly one." He closed the folder. "About six months ago, the place was sold."

Ramsey's snitch might be on to something. "What's there now?" I asked.

"A beauty salon or barbershop, maybe."

Michael swapped glances with me. "Who owns it?"

James turned to his computer screen. Michael and I joined him. Michael hunched over and peered over his shoulder; I perched on the corner of his desk. James glanced at my swinging legs, and I pulled my skirt over my knees.

Michael caught his breath. "Do you think…?"

I hopped down and peered at the screen. I wrote down the address. "Dyno Barbershop on Gregory in Beverly Hills. Owned by VV Investments. Think it's connected to Tulep?"

"I'll have to do some digging," James said. He opened another screen page and typed out the address.

I headed for the door. "Come on." I waved to Michael.

James shot to his feet. "Where to?"

"Michael's beard needs trimming." His beard was so closely trimmed, it looked painted on.

"Hey, now, don't attack a man's beard. I trim it every morning," he said, running his hand along his stubbles. "Is it getting scraggly already?" He caught my stare and raised his brows. "Oh, right. I'm the guinea pig. We'll check out Tulep's former digs in case he's hanging out."

"He's disappeared off the face of Southern California." James stared at his computer screen. "Hasn't been seen since he was released. What makes you think he'd be there?" he asked me.

"I'll tell you when we come back." I zipped through the open door with Michael at my heels.

Michael whispered, "Do you think we'll find him in the barbershop?"

"No." I skipped down the stairs. "There's a chance, a small one, Tulep is still around and lying low. Something or someone near that shop may give us a clue so we can roust him out." Fingers crossed.

Chapter Twenty-Four: If This Is It

The barbershop was located south of Wilshire in Beverly Hills' less ritzy, paparazzi-free zone, meaning celebrity sightings were fewer in this neck of the woods. It was mostly locals strolling the sidewalks. Luxurious mansions had moved aside for single and multi-family homes, which gave the place a down-homey, upscale vibe.

We motored along South Beverly Drive, surrounded by high end boutiques, compact cafes and small businesses, all with cheerful hued awnings hanging over the entryways. We hung a right onto Gregory, a manicured, tree-lined side street loaded with homes that boasted state of the art security systems and expert gardeners. We ambled past a tiny barbershop on our right, squeezed between a Burger Joint and Jasmine's beauty supply store. We parked up the block and hit the pavement.

"Let's meet back here in fifteen," I told Michael. "You know what to do."

"See you soon." Michael squeezed my hand.

We exchanged a quick kiss, and he made a beeline for the burger place. I inspected Dyno Barbershop from across the street. The doorway was indented and the windows darkly tinted. I jay-walked to the other side and focused on the shop. No exterior security cameras. I looked both ways and behind me before pressing my face against the glass. Judging by the few furnishings inside and a stack of local newspapers outside, it had been closed a while. I stepped back and examined the door. The lock was old school, easy to pick. I scrambled over to my next stop: Jasmine's next door.

Displays of sunglasses, hats and hair accoutrements crowded around the entry. I glided inside to the tune of chiming bells announcing my presence.

At the end of an aisle packed with lotions and hair products, a woman lurked behind the counter, eyes all over me. Her jaw moved from side-to-side as she chewed a wad of gum. I smiled, picked up my pace and a hair clip along the way.

"Hello," I said.

The woman blew a bubble so thin, I could see right through it. I dropped the clip on the counter.

"Will that be all?" She spoke about as enthusiastically as if she'd found a fly in her coffee.

"Actually, no. My boyfriend was planning to get a haircut next door. Do you know when they open?"

"How should I know?" She snapped her gum.

"Uh, because you're next door." I was willing to bet she came into her shop daily. "You must know their hours."

"They've been closed for months. Their cuts are no good. My uncle's got a barbershop in Westwood—"

"We have a soft spot for this one. Besides…" I leaned forward. "We were big fans of the old ice cream place, if you know what I mean."

Her cold expression belonged on a Roman statue.

"I like to take trips without going anywhere," I said. "Get it?"

A brow raised and her glossy pink lips rolled back when she spoke. "Twenty-eight eleven."

"What?" That was a lot of dough for a hair clip.

"You're not from around here, are you?"

Why would she say that? I couldn't be the first to object to the high price. She stared without blinking. I stared right back. Which is what I was doing when two bells chimed behind me. I glanced over my shoulder. Michael's head appeared over the tops of the aisles.

"Hello?" he said.

"Over here." I waved my arm above my head.

Michael strolled over. He held a paper bag in one hand and looked around. "This place is so nice. Everything you could ever want to make yourself beautiful. Not that you need to because you're already beautiful." He bent down, kissed me and held up a French fry. "Chili cheese fries. Want one?"

"No food in the store," Jasmine said to him.

"Sorry." He dropped the fry into the bag.

I pulled out my credit card. "Jasmine..." I was willing to bet she never left the register without locking the doors first, which would make her an owner. "...was just telling me the barbershop has been closed for a while."

She leaned forward and told Michael, "You don't look like you need a haircut."

"Actually, I wanted my beard trimmed." He fingered his chin.

"Your beard looks like it was trimmed this morning. You trim it daily, do you not?"

Michael fingered his beard. "I guess so, but I wasn't going to trim it tomorrow if I could get it done today. Hey, wasn't the ice cream parlor great? I was hoping the new owner could tell me where I could buy the...stuff."

She tilted her head sideways while she ran my card. "The owner was arrested and sent to prison."

"I heard he was released." Michael lowered his voice and leaned in closer. "Think he'll come back?"

"For what?"

"Someone at Burger Joint said they saw him a few days ago," Michael told her.

Sounded like one of my lines.

The woman shoved my bag and receipt toward me and stepped back. "I wouldn't know." She crossed her arms over her chest.

"Thanks." I slid my business card across the counter. "In case he shows up again. There'll be a little something in it for you, if you call me." I had no idea what that something would be, but she needed some enticement, I could tell.

We headed for the door. I'd barely stepped outside when I tossed a lingering gaze over my shoulder. Jasmine was staring at my card. She pulled out her cell phone a moment later. I caught her eye and scurried out to join Michael.

"She's obviously lying." He chomped on some fries and held the bag out to me, as we walked away. "Tulep came back and she knows it."

"Maybe." I took a fry. It was still warm.

"You don't think so?" he asked.

We paused in front of the barbershop.

"Did someone at the burger place see Tulep?" I asked.

"Someone saw a guy that sort of fit his description, but I thought it might be a good way to get her to verify it."

Did that count as telling a lie? Or was it a conversation starter? I'd ponder that later. "Take a peek through the window and tell me what you see," I said.

He stepped into the indented space and pressed his face against the glass. "Two barber's chairs, a shelf along the wall with clippers, scissors and razors. Another shelf higher up with framed pictures. There's a hat and coat rack, a stereo sitting on a crate and a closet. Looks very vintage." Michael turned to me and pulled out another French fry.

"Jasmine's seems deeper or wider or something." I was thinking out loud.

Michael stopped chomping. "You're right. There must be a back room. This is why you're the brains and I'm the…what am I again?"

"The computer whiz."

"Oh yeah," he said. "I'm the asset. For all things technical in your sleuthing world."

"We need to get inside this shop."

Michael's hands dropped and he spilled a few fries. "I was afraid you were going to say that."

We stepped back onto the sidewalk and turned our heads to Jasmine's. She was peering at us through the front glass, arms hugging her chest.

"Do you suppose there's a back entrance to the barbershop?" Michael asked.

"Uh-huh." Contrary to what Jasmine thought, this was not my first trip to this section of Beverly Hills. "There's an alley running behind these stores, and a small, shared parking lot, which means back doors for everyone."

Michael leaned away and narrowed his gaze past me and the beauty supply shop. "I spy the alley." He turned back to the barbershop and slid up to the glass door. He pressed his nose to the surface, turning his head to the left so he could see the outer edge of the shop. "There's a hallway. On the far left." He lifted his head and looked at me. "Must lead to the back." Using the sleeve of his shirt, he wiped his face print off.

"Maybe Tulep didn't sell this place. Or if he did, it was a sham sale. We'll come back tomorrow night and check it out." I threw a little wave at Jasmine. She was furiously snapping her gum. "Let's go."

Chapter Twenty-Five: Court Marshall

The next morning, I dropped Michael off at the D.A.'s office and headed for Ameripictures with eighties tunes blaring on the radio. Since Michael was on summer break from L.A. Tech, he had a few weeks before school started up again, which meant he had free time. Unlike me. I had a day job where I needed to show my face now and then, in case anyone noticed. Which was unlikely with the boss a couple of continents away. Lacy gave me carte blanche while she was directing her documentary, but she was the moody type, and I didn't want to take any chances. I was awaiting orders, but until she arrived, finding the triggerman was my main job.

Meanwhile, I kept Lacy's parking spot warm until her return. I'd just pulled in when Michael rang. I turned off the radio and answered.

"I was thinking," he said. "We D.A. staff members should stick together."

"We're D.A. staff members now?" I asked. "Does that mean we get our own cubicle?"

"I should've tagged along with you."

"Are you saying I can't take care of myself?"

"What? No. I would never—"

"No one has the guts to use me for target practice." That was two parts false bravado and one-part truth. I wielded all sorts of weaponry, legal and otherwise. My firing aim was sharp, thanks to Dad. And I always carried my weapon of choice; my Japanese throwing star was tucked into a zipped pocket of my purse, when it wasn't in my belt.

"I want you to feel at ease with me watching your back," Michael was saying. "Like you're in a safe place all the time. I can't do that if I'm not with you."

"Did my mother put you up to this?" Mom's eyes were usually super-glued to my back, but she might've made Michael her back-up for when she wasn't around.

"I'm serious, Corrie. I like watching your back better than watching anything else."

"No one's ever said that to me before. That's sweet. But it's not my back that needs watching. This shooter's doing his best to confuse us so we don't focus on his next move."

"Which is?"

"Not sure yet," I said.

"Just don't do anything I wouldn't do," Michael said.

"That would wipe out ninety percent of my playbook."

"See you soon."

"Wait," I said, locking the door of my car. "Can you zip across the street and see if you can figure out who the witness was that saw the female accomplice exit the sedan?"

"On my way," he said. "I'll find out her name and set up a secret rendezvous. We'll interrogate her together. I'll be your second set of eyes and ears. If you want, that is."

"I'd love that." I headed past the sound stages toward the back of the studio lot. "Don't tell James we're going to the barbershop tonight."

"Oh, uh, well..."

"You already did?" I asked.

"I wanted him to know we're on it, but don't worry. He didn't say anything about coming with us."

He didn't have to. "Make sure he knows he'll put us in danger if he decides to join our stake-out."

"Roger that," Michael said.

I disconnected and picked up my pace. James didn't want to jeopardize his friends, of that I was fairly to pretty damn sure. How tight a leash did Beckman have on him? My mind drifted back to the shooter. Did he have poor aim or suffer cold feet before pulling the trigger? Or was it something else?

I moseyed down the main studio walkway with questions swirling around in my head and my skirt swirling around my thighs. The wind lifted the bottom half of my blue silk wraparound dress, left over from Mom's days of working in the fashion industry. I wore a slip beneath so no free peeks.

I aimed for an art deco style, three-story structure, the Otis building, named after one of the founders of Ameripictures Studios. I swiped my key card, stepped inside, waved hello to the aging security guard and took the steps two at a time to Lacy's suite.

Veera lounged on a white leather recliner in a mini-screening room. She stared up at the oversized TV screen hanging against the wall. A half-eaten bowl of popcorn rested on her lap.

"Is that Perry Mason?" I asked. She was watching an original black & white episode. I was all about old movies and TV, thanks to my parents.

"It's *The Case of the Restless Redhead* where this glamorous jewel thief is claiming she was chased by a hooded man who ends up dead, and she's the prime suspect because she happened to be carrying around a loaded pistol that someone had planted in her apartment." Veera took a breath. "Let's hope your hooded guy doesn't end up dead with you holding the smoking gun."

"No need to carry around someone else's gun." I had plenty of my own. I headed into my office, a compact room with high ceilings and plenty of natural light. Everything was white and pristine to make up for Lacy's dark and not exactly sparkling personality.

"I was thinking…" Veera followed me inside with her popcorn.

"Find something new?" I asked her.

"I watched more videos at Big Sam's yesterday." She plopped onto a small loveseat. "The gunman only showed up those two times in the last three months. That's how far back I went."

"Which means he'd been planning everything over the past two weeks." About the time when Tulep was released. I sat on the edge of my desk. "Think, Veera. Anything identifiable about him?"

"He wore a hat each time and dark sunglasses, and never once looked directly at the camera—"

"Yet he knew where the security cameras were located." My mind was racing. "Because he had been there before but in a different disguise."

"Or his female partner-in-crime scoped out security. Holy heck!" Veera slapped her knee. "What kind of PI-in-the-making am I? I only looked for the lady in the spots where the shooter was in the video." She stood and kicked an imaginary ball. "At least I called a few car guys about the sedan. They're on the lookout for any word on the owner of the Ford Focus. And the VIN number belonged to a Chevy Impala. He must've messed with the numbers somehow. That's all I got. You find anything noteworthy?"

I brought her up to speed and onto her feet. I told her about the trip to Beverly Hills.

"I missed all that?" she said. "We need to get into that phony barbershop. Sounds real suspicious."

"My thoughts exactly." Veera wasn't as hesitant as Michael.

"Should we go now?" she asked.

"Later." If there was illicit activity, it was likely at night.

Veera rubbed her hands together. "I'm ready."

"One of us will have to keep watch."

"I can do that, but I'd rather get in on the action. I need constructive activity, something bad." Her cell phone vibrated and she grabbed it. She stared at the screen. "It's a car guy I texted about the Ford." She pressed the phone to her ear. "How you doin', G-Man?" She put the phone on mute and turned to me. "This guy stands on the corner of Venice and Bagley and waves people into his shop for an engine check and body work. I figured he might've seen that old Ford Focus drivin' by." She unmuted and put him on speaker.

"Ferraris, Lambos—" he was saying.

"Those rides would be easy to spot," Veera said. "I'm looking for the needle in the haystack. A black, beat-up Ford Focus sedan, with way too many dings and dents. I'm figurin' it's a local car. From 1998."

"I don't notice average vehicles. I'm into high end rides like Bentleys,

Rolls', Buga—"

"I get it. If I ever need help with one of those, I'll call you back. Thanks, anyway." Veera disconnected. "Man's got a one-track mind."

She stood and planted her hands on her hips. She looked around the room. "I feel kind of guilty doing nothing around here. I straightened up everything I could, returned two calls, followed up on a few emails. Now what? I almost miss working for Marshall."

"Me, too," I said. "Like I'd miss sitting on a rattlesnake." I slapped my leg and laughed.

Veera's eyes turned round as she stared past me and into the reception area. I slowly pivoted. Marshall hovered just inside the doorway, wearing his usual mushroom colored suit and thick graying hair. His complexion was sallow, his handshake weak, and his thirst for power incorrigible. I wanted to ask what he was doing here, but all I said was, "Do you want something?" like he was lost and needed to be pointed back toward his own office.

"Thought I'd come by and see how you're doing," he said in a low, slow drawl. His gaze dropped to the bowl of popcorn. A large manila envelope was squeezed under his armpit.

"Is that for us?" I asked. He was still in charge of drafting contracts for Lacy on behalf of the children's motion picture division. I held out my hand.

He dropped the envelope onto a chair. "How are you getting along with Lacy?"

"Surprisingly well," I said. Especially since she wasn't around. She was like a thorn on a rose. She was fine as long as I kept my distance.

"I have information you might be interested in."

He let that hang in the air for a few seconds. I stifled the urge to yell at him.

"The studio's cutting back on new production deals." He waited for that to sink in. "Anything not already in the works isn't moving forward."

Lacy had a two-picture deal. One was in the works. I swapped glances with Veera. She stepped forward. "You're saying our jobs are on the line?"

He shrugged his narrow shoulders. "I'm saying you'll be the first to go."

He shuffled out without another word.

I was about to step forward and slam the door behind him, but Veera put out her arm, blocking my path.

"Hold up," she said to me and hurried out the door. "Thanks for the visit. Don't be a stranger," she yelled after Marshall. She closed the door and turned to me. "Now is not the time to make enemies. We gotta make him think he's on our good side, in case we need him in the future."

I needed him like I needed a pet hyena. "The man's a—"

"A motivator," Veera said. "That's what he is. If they eliminate our jobs, we'll have to go out and open up our own private investigation agency."

Veera had been pining for a career change since we'd started working for the studio six months ago.

"You wouldn't like being a full-time P.I.," I said.

"Who says?" she asked.

"Me, that's who. You're a good person, Veera, and I want you to stay that way. " I was already seeing my bad influence on her. She was always on the up and up before she met me. "The line between right and wrong gets blurry when you're doing P.I. work. You become a liar and a snoop. Which'll keep you from ever feeling good about yourself."

"That's B.S. and you know it." Veera threw her manicured hand at me. "You're talking about old school P.I.s. We are the organically grown, new school crop, the up and coming female force. We're out to bring justice, the best way we know how, while setting good examples every which way we turn."

"You make us sound like volunteer firefighters."

"Our hearts are real and in the right place." Veera shook her head. "I'm sick and tired of sittin' around here waitin' on the concrete hearted Marshalls of the entertainment world."

"While collecting a steady paycheck." I perched on the arm of the loveseat.

"It's not about the money, although I can't pay rent or buy these stylish clothes without it." She ran a hand along the side of her pink sheath dress with flared sleeves that ran just past her elbows. "I'm talkin' about the need to do important work. Something that uses our brains and talents to help people. Not just rich studio people with major attitude."

"You know what? You're—" My ringing cell phone interrupted my next words. I dug my hand inside my purse and pulled out my phone. It was a local number, one I didn't recognize. "Corrie Locke," I answered.

"It's me." The male voice was quiet and muffled, like his lips were pasted to the phone. "Can you talk?"

"Who's this?" I asked.

"Dirk."

Did I know a Dirk? "I don't know any Dirks."

"Ramsey, Dirk Ramsey, D.A. investigator."

Chapter Twenty-Six: Livin' On a Prayer

"Where are you?" I asked.

"In the trunk," he whispered.

"Really?" It was all too neat and tidy. "A tree trunk? An elephant's trunk? Or maybe an antique trunk?"

"Ha, ha." He spoke at normal pitch. "How did you know?"

"Never mind that. Where are you, really?"

"Not in the D.A.'s office, that's for sure. It was getting claustrophobic in there. Don't you want to know why I called?"

"Because you missed us already?"

He huffed. "Don't you get it? This is our chance to work together. We team up and drag that sucker in."

I liked flattery. I really did. But I needed to be able to trust the people working with me. I trusted Ramsey like I trusted a leaky boat.

"When you've got some useful information," I told Ramsey, "call me." I disconnected.

"Who's in the trunk?" Veera asked.

"The trunk is empty," I said. "Meanwhile, let's pay a visit to a D.A. we know."

***

A half hour later, Veera and I walked into James' office. He stood behind his desk, his back to us, reading through a file in his hands. Michael sat cross-legged on the floor, leaning against the wall, balancing an open laptop across his thighs. His gaze flicked over to me. A wide smile broke out and he jumped up. He gave me a big hug.

"Hey, you two! I am so glad to see you." He held me out at arm's length. "How long has it been? Like two whole hours?" He hugged me again.

"Nothing like a happy reunion to warm the spirit," Veera said.

James glanced up, nodded at Veera and flashed a quick grin. "Find anything?"

"We sure did," Veera said. "We might be out of our studio jobs real soon, so we're looking for office space to set up shop."

"A legal office?" James asked.

"Heck no," Veera said. "A P.I. agency. What do you think of The C.V. Agency? Or how about Private Eyes R Us? Or P.I. in the Sky? Maybe even Sweetie P.I.s."

"Uh…" he said.

"That's a good one," Michael said.

"I can even get behind Esquire Investigations, Inc. since Corrie's an esquire and I'm almost one," Veera said.

She batted agency names past James while I enjoyed entwining with Michael. I could've stayed there longer, but I gently pulled away and moved toward James before he showed Veera the door. "Any news about Ramsey?"

"Like what?" James spun toward me.

"Did he call?" I asked.

"Call how?" Michael asked.

"With a phone," I said. "He went MIA so he can continue investigating, uninterrupted. He called me."

Veera lit up. "Investigations, Uninterrupted."

"The sneak." James edged closer to me.

"I picked up a little something from Ramsey's office during his absence." I handed the Tulep file to him. "Take a look at the first few pages."

James opened the file and speed read. "He knew Tulep was spotted in Beverly Hills? He should've shared what the informant uncovered."

"Does he usually tell you?" Michael asked.

"No, but we don't have guns at our backs every day," James said and turned my way. "Do you know a Fly Boy?"

"Informants change names for different clients," I said. "I might know him."

"You're slowing down, Locke," James said to me.

Now he was rubbing alcohol in my wound. "Michael and I—"

"He told me." James stony stare was probably very effective in the courtroom to make criminals talk, but it had no effect on me. "You're going back to the barbershop tonight. Do you really expect to find anything?"

"I do," I said. "We're closing in—"

"We're going to get some answers tonight," Veera said. "I just know it."

"Guys, I don't want to rain on our parade, but hasn't Tulep been busted in that same shop before?" Michael asked. "Wouldn't he want to pick a new hangout?"

"Criminals are like the rest of us in one way. They find comfort in familiarity," James said. "And he's a free man, thanks to the technicality. Why not go back? If he's clean, he won't get arrested."

"If he's clean," I said, "then I'm a first-rate private investigator."

"But you are, Corrie," Michael said. "And a whole lot more."

The man believed I was whatever I wanted to be. A top notch P.I. with integrity and enough smarts to bring a criminal in fast. I hated to let him down.

I flashed Michael a grin and turned to James. "We'll report back." I held my elbow out to Michael. "Shall we? All this talk of criminals and I'm famished."

"Does the same to me." Veera headed for the door.

Michael took my arm. "I'll text you updates, bro."

I waited until we got into the elevator to reveal the plan. "We'll grab a bite and wait it out."

"Wait what out?" Michael asked. "We're not breaking into the barbershop, are we?"

"We've got to pick our moves carefully," I said. "We're D.A. consultants now."

"What does that mean?" Veera asked.

"The fashionable and friendly lead detective is going to get us in legitimately."

Michael grabbed my hand and kissed it. "I've been dreaming of this day for a long, long time."

Chapter Twenty-Seven: Girls Just Want to Have Fun

"Did you visit the church today?" I asked Michael.

"Oh yeah," he said. "But I might as well have skipped it."

We were on the way to my car, which happened to be parked near the holy statue I hid behind yesterday.

"Nothing to report?" I asked.

"The lady that talked to Officer Fisher won't be in until..." He checked his watch. "...noon."

It was nearly noon. "Let's take a detour and see what we can find out." I switched direction and so did my posse. I pitched my chin toward the rose garden. A man in white coveralls was spraying weed killer. "Michael, find out what he knows."

"Should I do a mild interrogation or the kind where I need surgical gloves and a tooth extractor?" he asked.

"I like your attitude," I replied. "Use your discretion."

"Let him have it if he clams up," Veera said.

"Okay," Michael said. He strolled over to the opposite end of the lawn.

"Veera, please go across the street." An old school looking beauty parlor sat on the corner of Vinton and Jack Street. I could see a couple of vintage helmet style hair dryers. The type you'd lower over Granny's hair rollers and that could sizzle her scalp if she sat beneath them too long. A small cafe and a gym took up the rest of the short block. Single and multi-family housing popped up around the businesses. "See what you can find out from the surrounding stores. Maybe someone saw something."

"I will snoop the living daylights out of them," she said, smiling from ear-to-ear.

"We'll meet-up on this corner in twenty minutes."

***

I pointed my pumps toward the church entry and pulled out my phone. I called Abby.

"Tell me you have a lead," she said. "I'm floundering over here."

"I might." I slowed my pace so she wouldn't hear me panting. "With a little help from you."

"Anything. Almost…" She lowered her voice, "…because there's a chance…" She hiccupped. "…I'll be off the case sooner than I thought. I overheard my boss saying he's taking it over in twenty-four hours. If I don't hand him something, I'll be cooked."

"What can you tell me about the witness in the church who saw the woman get out of the sedan?"

"I really can't talk about it." She spoke at warp speed. "Fisher said she's in charge of the rose garden. She was outside and saw it all happen."

"Name?"

"Don't press your luck," Abby replied. "But it starts with an M and ends in an E or an I or maybe a Y or some other vowel sound. She's small with gray hair. Let me know what you find." She disconnected.

Abby narrowed it down some. But even if I did find the witness, what were the odds she'd talk to me?

You could make a rock talk with the right mindset.

Dad's words buzzed through my ears. "Here goes," I whispered.

A wide set of stairs led to tall entry doors. I skipped my way up, heaved one side open and slipped into the hushed foyer. Thick walls shut out all outside noise. A woman stood in a dim corner, leaning over a table brimming with pamphlets. Long white hair snaked down her back in a ponytail. Not the witness I was seeking. She disappeared into a spacious meeting hall. I grabbed the door handle before it shut and peered inside. Neatly attired seniors scattered around in front of the pews. Almost all were female, petite, and with short gray hair. How was I going to find the witness in this crowd?

"Looking for somebody?"

I jumped and whirled around. An older lady stared at me through oversized glasses that magnified her close-set eyes to the size of a quarter. Her snowy hair was skinned back in a tight bun, her chin was small and rounded. Her gray cardigan hung over a navy-blue dress. I never heard her rubber soles coming.

She looked me up and down and pulled her wicker handbag closer to her. "The confessionals are around the corner."

"I'm not here to confess," I said. "Not that I need to." Oh brother. "I'm here for information."

"Don't move a muscle. I'll be right back." She turned her back to me and shuffled toward the pamphlet table. She lifted her glasses and read the back of a pamphlet.

I slid over. "Not that kind of information."

"Geez." She jumped and slapped a hand over her heart. "Why'd you sneak up on me? You nearly sent me to an early grave. Not that I don't like a little excitement now and then, but you should clear your throat or cough before you scare the hell out of someone. Especially in church."

Like she hadn't done the same to me a minute ago. I pegged her at a hair or two over eighty, so I'd say an early grave wasn't an option. "I'm here for—"

"The cupcake meeting?" she asked.

I debated making up a story. "No." Maybe it was the holiness in the air or the renewed desire to stay off Liar's Lane.

She rolled her eyes over me, ambled closer and lifted her chin. "I'm Alma. You in some kind of trouble?"

"What? No." Not today, anyway. "I work with the D.A.'s office across the street, as a consultant. My...D.A. friend was nearly killed yesterday."

"Heard all about it. In fact..." She leaned in, looking around to make sure there were no eavesdroppers. "I did more than hear."

A priest strode past and Alma buttoned her lips.

"I'm looking…" I said after he disappeared down the hall, "…for the witness that talked to the police."

"What for?"

"To see if there's something she neglected to mention."

She bunched up her lips and leaned back. "My turn to do meal prep." Alma disappeared down a narrow hallway.

"What was that about?" I threw up my hands. I turned toward the meeting hall and pulled open the door. Singing voices drifted past me. I stepped back into the foyer.

How much can these seniors recall anyway? Crime unfolds fast. They get distracted, plus it's hard to recall facts accurately when the brain slows down with age. Older adults remember fewer details, and were more open to suggestions, which changed their story from fact to fiction. "I'm out of here."

I stomped through the entry and down the steps. Roses in full bloom scented the air. I padded to the grassy lawn where the garden fanned out in a large half circle. Where was Michael?

"Pssst."

I froze. There was no one in the garden but me and the saintly statue. I stared up at the holy figure. His lips weren't moving.

"Over here."

I swung around. "Where?"

A clang came from somewhere close by.

"Look down."

The voice came from near my feet. I crouched and crept toward the building. A rectangular window ran across the bottom of an exterior wall, half hidden beneath a leggy shrub. The lower half of the window was propped open enough for me to see a grainy face through the screen, peering up in oversized glasses.

"It's me. Alma. In the kitchen, making soup." She glanced over her shoulder. "I saw her first."

"Saw who?" I knelt by the window.

"The broad leaving the black car yesterday."

"What? Did you tell the police?"

"That wasn't an option."

"Why not?" She didn't strike me as a person who'd hold back or be easily intimidated.

"There's a warrant out for my arrest."

That was unexpected. "What's the charge?"

"What's it to you?"

"Maybe I can help. I'm a lawyer."

"Oh." She raised her brows and pulled back her torso. There was no sign of her for a few beats. Then she reappeared, staring straight into my eyes. "It was March of 2014. I ran a stop sign on the corner of Stoner and Idaho Avenue in West Los Angeles."

"So? People run stop signs."

"Yeah, but a cop pulled me over."

"And you didn't pay your ticket?" I asked.

"I never got one."

"You got off with a warning?" Wish I'd gotten that treatment. I'd had more than my share of tickets.

"I didn't get a ticket because I left."

"Define 'left'."

"I took off while he wrote me up."

"Wow."

"Why do you think I help out at church? I'm repenting," she said. "Can you clear my record or what?"

"I know someone who can help." James might be able to pull a few strings. "If you have information that could help him. What exactly did you see yesterday?"

She tossed a look over her shoulder. "Can't talk here. Be right up."

She joined me ten minutes later. We monopolized a concrete garden bench and she spilled the beans.

"I was in the kitchen chopping celery when I heard voices from above."

"Wait. Above where?" Heavenly voices?

She waved her hands in front of her. "Out here in the street. Geez, the kitchen's in the basement, okay?" She clicked her tongue and shook her head. "I came out and I saw police swarming everywhere. It was like a raid. Not that I know anything about raids."

"Go on."

"Next thing, this looker in a uniform comes up to Maisie, asking if anybody saw the driver of the sedan." She waved her arms around again. "That's when she started talkin'. Little did the cop know, I saw more than she did."

If I was a Hail Mary person now would've been the time. Instead I said a mental thank you and promised to tell the truth from now on.

"Help me to find the woman driver," I said. "Any details?"

"I'm gettin' there," Alma said. "I'm in the kitchen looking out the window like I always do and I see this beat up looking sedan parallel park. It took her forever. Then I see the driver slide to the passenger side and come out. Who does that?" She waited for my reply.

I obliged her. "Someone sneaky."

"Someone up to no good. I got a sixth sense for these things."

"Did you notice where she was headed?"

"Does pastrami taste better on rye? Of course, I noticed. I took off my apron and raced up and out the door. That's when I saw her walking. Up the next block."

"Yes?"

"Crap." She cradled her chin.

"What happened?"

"You think I should've told the cops all this? They could've cut me a deal."

"So far, you've got no new information."

"Oh yeah? How about this?" She leaned toward me. "She got into another car on the passenger side. The engine was running. You know what that means?"

Who was the daughter of a private investigator? "It was her getaway car."

"You catch on quick. But this time she wasn't the driver."

My heart beat faster. "Someone else was driving?"

"Windows were tinted so I couldn't see, but it pulled out too fast for her to slide behind the wheel."

"Did you notice the make or the model?"

"It was a pick-up car."

"A pick-up truck?" I asked.

"Did I say 'truck'?" Alma replied. "It was a car."

"Cars don't have pick-ups. You mean a station wagon?"

"Did I say station wagon?" She craned her neck toward me. "Read my lips. A regular car. Except without a trunk. Get it? The back was open air."

I debated hightailing it away from her. "Was it newer?"

"Brand-spanking new. Right off the showroom floor. No dings, dents or scratches. Except…"

"Yes?"

"It wasn't new. It was the kind of pick-up that was big in the sixties. No, the seventies. Could've been the eighties. Decades blend together, you know?"

Can't say that I did.

"And it was either a Ford. Or a Chevy. Maybe a Dodge or a Pontiac. All American cars look the same to me."

"How do you know it was American?"

"Because it had no gimmicks, no hype, and I know roll-up windows when I see them."

"What color?"

"Silver, and running under the passenger door, it was black at the bottom. Like a fancy schmancy trim."

A professional killer wouldn't be seen in such a unique car. Even if he was waiting nearly two blocks away. "Feel like taking a stroll?"

***

Alma and I shuffled along the sidewalk. Tall, thick shade trees waved their branches above us. After a few minutes, she slowed and pointed to an empty spot. I had to admit it was the perfect place to park and wait for your cohort in crime. I studied the neighboring apartments. Thick trunks and foliage from the trees prevented a clear view of the parked cars.

"Anything unusual about the way she looked?" I asked.

"Hair the color of brown shoe polish. Coarse and thick. Pasty skin. Wearing Jackie O sunglasses."

Nothing new there. "Sounds like a disguise. Any idea how old she was?"

"Fifty, maybe. On the frumpy side."

A few beats passed as I pictured the woman.

"Come on, come on," Alma said. "Ask me more questions. I've got the attention span of a honey bee."

"No more questions."

"It was a two door. Did I already say that?" Alma asked.

I shook my head.

"Okay, let's go." She turned on her rubber soles and shuffled back toward the church.

I kept pace, slowing to stay by her side. "Where are we going?"

"You have to meet Julio."

"He's a priest?" Was she still trying to get me to confess?

"No. He's the guy the lady nearly hit."

Chapter Twenty-Eight: Run to You

Ten minutes later, Michael and Veera joined us outside the church steps. Alma told us about Julio, gave directions to his place and a copy of a newspaper clipping showing him tending the rose garden.

"He didn't show up today, so you'll have to go find him," Alma said. "Should be at home. He's a little guy with big muscles. That's how he got out of her way so fast or he would've been dead meat. You get me? Roadkill." Alma climbed back up the stairs and through the church doors. A second later, she stuck her head out. "Tell him I said he's sharp." She disappeared.

I turned to Michael. "Navigate, please."

"I like the way Alma defies stereotypes. That is no ordinary sweet old lady," Veera said.

"How do we know she's not chasing windmills?" Michael asked.

"My gut feeling," I said. Since my gut was pretty empty right now there was plenty of room for feelings, including the one telling me Alma was on the ball.

"Let me get this straight," Veera said. "The shooter's lady friend was in such a hurry to get to the D.A.'s office to park the car, she nearly wiped out Julio, the church landscaper?"

"That's right," I said.

"How could Julio not see a car speeding straight at him?" she asked.

"He was walking to work while eating a breakfast burrito," I said.

"Wait. Did he go to the food truck up the street, Burritos Por Favor?" Veera asked. "Was he eating the bacon breakfast burrito with green salsa?

'Cause I wouldn't mind being plowed over while I was eating one of those. I'd go to heaven mucho happier."

"I'll second that," Michael said.

We spent a moment of silence to fill our empty bellies with visions of burritos.

Twenty minutes and six burritos later, we left Burritos Por Favor and continued our journey toward Julio's place.

"That explains why the gardener I talked to didn't know anything," Michael said. "He was filling in for Julio."

"I got nowhere with the beauty salon people," Veera said. "Although I did get a sample of coconut mango hydrating shampoo and a coupon for a mani-pedi."

"I've got Julio's address mapped out," Michael said, heading toward Venice Boulevard. "A right, a left and two more rights plus a quick turn into an alley."

"I'm not going down any alleys," Veera said. "That's where shifty people hang out."

"It's also the back entrance into Julio's apartment," Michael said. "In case we're being followed." He stared over his shoulder.

"I'm so proud of you two." I swelled up like a mother hen watching her chicks dig up their first worm. "You're thinking like true private investigators. Watching out for shady types and on the lookout for ways to sneak in."

"How about Lacy's Angels?" Veera asked. "If we name our P.I. agency after our boss, I bet she'd invest in our business. I've got a Jaclyn Smith wig I've been dying to wear."

I'd watched my share of *Charlie's Angels* reruns. I wouldn't mind being decked out in enviable clothes and having good hair days…all of the time. "Lacy'll never go for it."

"Why not?" Veera asked.

"Because it wasn't her idea."

"Truth," she said.

Above us, the summer sky hosted a whole lotta blue with a few streams of white jet trails zig-zagging across each other. We hustled past a row of mom and pop stores on Venice Boulevard. I told them about the getaway car Alma described.

"What has a pick-up, but isn't a truck?" Michael stroked his barely there beard. "This is a riddle I can solve."

"I'm going to ask Lacy when she comes back," Veera said. "About our agency name."

If she comes back.

The next block gave way to upscale yoga shops, bistros and coffee bars. Art Deco buildings of yesteryear now housed cutting edge art galleries and boutiques.

"Why didn't Julio step up and let the police know what happened?" Veera asked.

"He might have a problem with the law, too," I said.

Both went silent.

"I'm not talking about my problems with the law," I said. "It's Alma." I told them about her long ago encounter with a cop. "That's why she didn't step forward."

"That would explain the shortage of witnesses when you need one," Veera said.

"James texted me. He's checked out Jasmine. She's clean," Michael said. "In fact, she'd called Beverly Hills P.D. a bunch of times to report noises next door. She probably had nothing to do with Tulep's operation."

"I had such high hopes," I said, like I do for everyone connected with the case.

"Police never found anything when they investigated," Michael said. "That's where we come in."

We threw out our anchor behind a faded green apartment building trimmed in white. Patches of lawn and a row of scrawny cypress trees made up the landscaping.

Before I finished rapping on the apartment door, a woman cracked it open and peeked through. A chain latching the door ran across her forehead.

"Yes?" she said.

"We're here to see Julio," I said.

She shook her head. "He's not home." She started to close the door and Michael's hand shot out, bracing it open.

"Do you know where he is?" he said. "It's important."

I shot a glance at Michael. There was the unexpected side of his again. Where he rises to the occasion.

"You are policía?" she asked timidly.

Before I could open my mouth, Michael said, "No. We just have a few questions that could lead us to catching a criminal."

My sidekick had taken the lead. Veera stuck her hand on her hip and fought a grin.

"We believe he was almost hit by a car yesterday. The driver is a suspect involved in a shooting," Michael said. "No one's been hurt. We want to make sure she doesn't try again."

The woman closed the door and we looked at each other.

"I should've let you handle things, Corrie." Michael's shoulders drooped. "I'm no good at this—"

The door opened wide. "Come in." A petite, stout senior wearing a nursing uniform and sensible clogs waved us inside. Michael perked up and waved us forward.

We walked past an empty bathroom into a small studio apartment. There was no sign of anyone besides the woman. A closet door sat open, jammed with clothes and shoes and home goods.

"Do you know where he is?" I asked.

"Gone to pick up the laundry and to go to some other places."

"Whereabout?" I asked.

"Around the corner of Venice and Danfield."

"Thanks." I gave her my card. "If you see him, please ask him to call."

I headed outside with Michael and Veera close behind. We took off toward Danfield.

"We'll divide up," I said when we arrived. "He could be on his way back. You take that side of the street, Michael. Veera and I'll take this one."

Michael hurried to the crosswalk and dashed to the other side. Veera jogged to the opposite end of the block. I canvassed each storefront until Veera and I met up mid-way.

"No sign of him," Veera said. "Must've gone somewhere else."

I scoured the faces inside a coffee bar when Michael bellowed out.

"Wait! I just want to talk."

I turned in time to see a guy in a white T-shirt and jeans take off at a run and Michael sprinting after him.

Chapter Twenty-Nine: How Will I Know?

I cut across the street, jogging between cars and nearly tripping in front of a lumbering utility truck. Michael was hot on the heels of the running man. They turned the corner, racing toward Venice. I rounded the same corner and slammed on the brakes. Michael grasped the guy's arm and was talking to him behind a bus stop. Veera caught up.

"Tienes que…no." Julio panted between words.

"Why did you run?" I asked.

"They're with me." Michael pointed to Veera and I. "Ella es mi amigas."

Julio's gaze darted between us. "Yo creo que…maybe you…" He pointed to Michael. "…with the conductor femenino."

"Julio says the woman driving the old Ford nearly killed him," Michael said. "He thought I was with her. I told him we talked to Alma." He turned back to Julio. "Por favor, señor." Michael stepped forward.

We'd both taken Spanish in high school. Most of mine fell off my tongue and landed with a thud in a crevice right after I'd graduated, but Michael seemed to have held onto more than I did.

"La señora, como she look like? Besides the glasses and el sombrero." Michael circled his hands. "Did she…" He turned to me. "I don't think he realizes how important it is that we find the woman. How do we convince him that next time someone could get killed?"

"Okay," Julio said. "I'm convinced. That lady shouldn't be loose on the streets. Next time could be serious."

"Well, well," Veera said.

Julio spoke like an Angeleno. Michael and I exchanged a grin. I turned to Julio. "Tell us something we don't know. Besides brown hair, shades…"

He rapped his knuckles against his chin and stared at the cracked pavement. Julio couldn't have seen much. It was so unexpected, and he was eating a delicious burrito. The whole episode lasted seconds.

"I left the food truck and finished the last bite of my breakfast when I crossed the street…inside the crosswalk lines. She nearly ran me over."

"Who would do something like that?" Veera asked.

Practically every other driver in L.A.

Julio shook his head. "I was headed to the church. The crazy driver got so close I could've banged my fist on the trunk. I yelled. But she kept driving. If I'd known she parked so close by, I would've gone after her."

"Dazzle us with detail, okay?" I asked. "Alma said you were sharp."

"That's right, I am." Julio lifted his gaze to meet mine. "Are you interested in trash?"

"You mean like gossip?" Michael said. "No. We want the straight scoop, buddy."

"I mean like something that belongs in a garbage truck," Julio said. "She nearly kills me, then throws litter out the car window. I noticed 'cause I was shaking my fist at her for a long time."

"Many violent criminals started out as litterbugs," Veera said.

We turned to stare at her.

"It's one of those things I don't have statistics for, but I know it's true."

We nodded in agreement. I turned to Julio.

"What kind of trash?" I asked.

"A list or piece of paper with stuff on it," Julio told us.

"Can you show us where she tossed it?" I wasn't holding my breath, but…

"Sure," Julio said.

While we wound our way back toward the church, Michael told him about the pick-up car the driver got into before she disappeared. "Any idea of what kind of car that could be?"

"A low-rider mini truck?" Julio said.

"That would be unique." Michael turned to me. "The shooter's an American car enthusiast. Alma said the pick-up car was ding-free. How many old cars are dingless? The Ford Focus was thrashed so this one must've meant something special to him."

Michael's previous model BMW looked like it had just rolled off the showroom floor. He would know.

"Or the black one belonged to the crazy lady driver," Julio said.

"Good point," Veera said.

"Can't see how anyone with that kind of respect for cars could turn into a killer," Michael told me.

"Listen, Dr. Freud," I said. "There's no logic when it comes to murder."

Michael turned back to Julio. "The car was silver except for a strip of black running along the bottom on each side."

"Like an old Cadillac, maybe," Julio said.

"Or a VW Bus," Veera added.

"Good one," I said. "But that's not an American car."

"When is a pick-up not a truck?" Michael mumbled.

The conversation continued amid honking horns, revving engines and sirens whizzing by. Michael eyed cars driving past for something resembling a pick-up car.

"Are we close to where it happened?" I asked Julio.

"Almost."

We followed him into a residential neighborhood near the church. Tidy homes held their own next to shabby apartment buildings. An abundance of native flora and fauna popped up everywhere.

"There's the crosswalk." Julio stared straight ahead.

We walked to a spot where the apartments took a hike and cozy bungalows dominated the quiet street. He stopped near a telephone pole.

"Here," he said.

"Where'd she throw out the trash?" I asked.

He took a few steps forward. His index finger pointed to a spot between the church and the crosswalk.

I quick-stepped down the curb and scoured the asphalt. The road bore its share of litter. Veera and Julio followed while Michael stood behind us, keeping an eye out for cars.

"I don't see it," Julio said.

I knelt near the sidewalk. A cigarette butt lay along the curb, reddish-brown and shimmery tinted at one end, it was long like the smoker only took a few whiffs before trashing it.

"She's a smoker." Julio appeared behind me.

"How do you know?" I asked.

"When she rolled down the window, smoke came out," Julio said.

"Michael, call James and see if the sedan smelled—"

"It did," he said. "I sat inside."

"I'm not sure how far that'll get us…" I picked up the butt with a napkin and dropped it in a little plastic bag I carried in my purse. "Wait a minute…" A nearby gutter gaped up at me. A rumply piece of paper stuck out at one end. I reached out and grabbed it. Veera joined me.

"What do you think?" I held out a receipt.

She stared at it. "Arnold Dentistry, dated yesterday. Forty-nine dollars. That's a great price. Since when does a dentist charge forty-nine dollars to do anything?"

"That's what she threw out the window," Julio said.

I stared at him. It was hard to tell whether he was showing off some imagined attribute of sharpness or whether he actually saw her litter. But the date on the receipt won me over.

"Look at the address. The office is only a few blocks away," Michael said, peering over my shoulder.

"That's her garbage," Julio said, pointing to the paper. "And so is the cigarette."

"You never mentioned the cigarette," I said.

"I'm remembering better now," Julio said.

Talk about an unreliable witness.

"She threw out two things," he said. "It would be just like her."

"What do you mean?" Michael asked.

"A careless driver would be more likely to be a litterbug," I said.

"What she said," Julio agreed.

I pushed a few buttons and stared at my phone screen. I looked up at Julio. "How are your teeth?"

"I have a cavity that hurts. My dentist wants to do a filling, but it's too much money…"

"It'll get worse, if you don't go," Michael said.

"The pain," Julio said.

"They'll give you a shot and—" Veera said.

"We'll take you to the dentist," I told Julio. "Act like it's an emergency."

"I can't go," Julio said. "Besides, I need to weed the church."

"We'll be quick," I said. "Maybe they can help find the driver. We need you to make that happen."

"How will I know what to do?" Julio asked.

"Pick up the pace and I'll tell you," I said.

Chapter Thirty: Hold On Loosely

Fifteen minutes later, we stood in front of Arnold Dentistry, a modern looking office front pressed into the center of a single-story building. Julio had been given instructions on what to say and, with any luck, we wouldn't get kicked out before we got answers.

Veera stood guard at the entrance so there'd be no intrusions. The rest of us waltzed into a bright reception area with pale yellow walls and a library quiet vibe. Magazines flooded the table-tops. The receptionist stared up at us from behind her desk. Julio didn't budge from the doorway. I grabbed his sleeve and yanked him forward. He stumbled, and I gripped his arm to straighten him up.

"I...I need..." He turned around and Michael blocked his path.

"He's in pain and he's scared of dentists," I told the receptionist. "Can we make an appointment?" I stepped back and gave Julio a little push.

The receptionist wore a green smock, light pink nails and a nice set of pearly whites. Her badge said Eva.

"Welcome." Eva slapped a clipboard on the counter with an information sheet attached. "Please complete this form and we'll take care of you."

Julio shook his head. "Not before I'm sure this is the right place."

Her smile faded. "If you need a dentist, this is the right place."

"I want to know if the lady who sent me here is a patient." He turned his face away. "This might be the wrong dental office. Maybe I should go to the one down the street."

"What's the lady's name?" Eva asked.

"I do landscape work for her." He held out a hand, shoulder high. "I call her Missus. Dark brown hair, this long." Julio brought his hand just past his chin. "Yesterday, she wore big sunglasses and came here for a cleaning, very early."

"What time?"

Julio turned his face to mine. Michael and I stood near the entry.

"Eight," I mouthed.

"Eight o'clock." Julio faced her again. "She said it was a good cleaning."

Eva frowned. "Our first cleaning appointment came in at nine."

Julio turned to me again. I stepped forward.

"Are you sure?" I asked. The receipt was printed out at ten to eight.

The receptionist clicked her tongue. "The only person who got her teeth worked on early yesterday was a hygienist. She got in at seven-fifteen and was finished before eight." She turned to Julio. "I don't know who the other dentist is, but Doc Arnold is better."

"Does the hygienist fit his description?" I asked.

"Are you with the police?" she asked.

My sweat glands opened for business. "Yes, I am." So much for my holy experience in church today. But I was sort of working with Abby, so this counted as police work in order to capture a criminal. I popped the tiny bubble of guilt sitting on my shoulder. Michael appeared next to me.

"I'm an undercover traffic cop," I said. "The woman in question is a terribly dangerous driver. We witnessed her nearly plow someone down yesterday. This civilian…" I turned to Julio. "…came close to being a victim."

"Nearly flattened like a tortilla," he said.

Eva's mouth dropped open. "Do you arrest people who text when they're waiting at traffic lights? Because technically those people aren't driving."

"We have an organized sting operation just to catch texters. But we're not interested as much in stop-light texters. Right now our focus is on this female driver."

Eva took turns gazing at each of us. "Okay, you didn't hear it from me, but she is the absolute, worst driver ever. She ran over a delivery guy's packages on the sidewalk in front of this office. And she nearly hit a dog that was sniffing a fire hydrant. The hydrant wasn't so lucky. Who knows what else she's done? She needs to be locked up."

"Amen, sister." Julio put up his palm and Eva gave him a high five.

She leaned in closer to me. "If I get busted for texting, can I call you?"

"Call Culver P.D. and ask for Detective Rosewater," I said. "She'll take care of you." My tongue was itching. Better than my nose growing.

Michael pulled out his phone and took notes. "Name please?"

"Eva Montoya," she said. "Single, smart and fun."

"He means the hygienist's name." I pushed my way in between her and Michael.

"Bianca," she whispered after stealing a glance behind her.

"We'll be discreet so she doesn't lose her job," I said.

"Are you kidding me? She's married to the boss. She's not going anywhere."

"She's Doctor Arnold's wife?" I asked.

"Yes, and he never lets her drive, no surprise there. She must've snuck behind the wheel."

"What kind of car does she drive?" Michael asked from behind me.

"This old black four-door that she's always banging around."

Michael and I swapped looks.

"Is she here now?" Michael asked.

"She didn't come back after the cleaning yesterday," she replied.

"Can we speak to the doctor?" I asked.

"He's with a patient."

"Is the doctor a good driver?" Michael asked.

"Very," she replied.

"Do you have a number or address for Bianca?" I asked.

"I'll have to ask first…" She picked up the receiver.

Michael stepped forward. "No. That'll ruin our operation. This is top secret. Very few know about this team. If word gets out, you may have to be relocated."

Eva's mouth dropped open. "Seriously?"

"We are covertly working to penalize drivers that consistently pose a hazard to other motorists," I said.

"What about his tooth?" she asked, pointing to Julio.

"I'll come back later." Julio headed for the door, with Michael and I close behind.

It was all I could do to prevent myself from doing cartwheels once we got outside. We had our first clue. I told Veera all about it.

"See," Veera said, "looking under every stone, and even into a gutter, really helps."

"Shouldn't we confirm Bianca's the right person?" Michael asked. "Maybe there's a photograph."

The cartwheel turned into a belly flop. "Follow me."

Moments later, the three of us tripped back into the office. We stared at Eva straightening out the magazines.

"One more question," I said. "We need to confirm Bianca is the person that nearly hit Julio yesterday. Do you have a photo? And one of Doc Arnold."

"Stay right there." Eva disappeared through a side door. Her footsteps padded along a hallway and grew faint for a minute before she padded back. She opened the door and held out a framed photo. "That's her."

We crowded around the picture of a woman with thick dark brows and brooding eyes. A felt beret covered the top half of her bob. She wore a tight smile and was all decked out in gold chains, bracelets and rings.

"That's her," Julio said.

"How can you be sure?" I asked.

"She looks crazy," Julio replied.

"This was taken on her birthday," Eva added. "We'd just finished singing and opening presents. Meet the Doc." Eva held out a framed photo of a short, hairless man holding a trophy of a big gold tooth. "That's from when he got his first Gentle Dental award."

"How tall is Doctor Arnold?" I asked.

"About your height."

The shooter wasn't five foot seven. I took a picture of the photo with my smartphone to compare it to Big Sam's video.

"Why do you need to know Doc's height?" Eva asked.

"We're looking for Bianca's accomplice in another traffic violation." I felt like a poker player, bluffing my way to a win with a not so great hand.

"Could've been one of her brothers," Eva said.

"Names?" I asked.

"Was a man driving?" Eva asked. "Because if it wasn't a man, that's not relevant."

She had me there.

"I'm not getting them in trouble. They're nice guys." She handed me a business card. "Let me know when she's arrested. Then I can drive in peace again."

"Sure." I headed for the door. "Does Bianca wear a wig?"

"Never seen her without it," Eva said. "She has a problem with pulling out her hair when she's stressed. Which is nearly all the time."

We stepped back outside and I updated Veera again. She looked at Bianca's photo on my phone.

"I want to say yes, that's her in Big Sam's video," she said. "But I can't be sure."

"Julio," I said. "We need you to make a statement to the police."

He shook his head and backed away. "No. I'll deny everything."

"Why?" Veera asked. "Don't you want her off the street?"

"That's why I came," he replied. "But you gotta find someone else for the statement." He turned and walked away.

We caught up with him moments later.

"Do you have a criminal record?" I asked. Wasn't anybody clean anymore? "We know a district attorney who can grant you immunity."

Julio broke into a slow run. "No one can help me. The church doesn't know or I'll lose my job. I'm not legal in this country."

"That's okay," I said. "We'll help fix that."

"No, you can't," he panted. "I have a DUI from ten years ago."

And with that last remark, we parted ways.

"What can we do?" Michael asked.

"Put him on the back burner for now," I said. "We'll have to find another witness."

We took off toward the D.A.'s office.

"You're calling the detective, right?" Michael asked. "To get a background check on Bianca."

"She could be a jewel thief. All those bracelets and necklaces. I'll bet she has a secret chest filled with expensive jewelry," Veera said. "You just don't turn to a life of crime overnight."

"Let's stick with what we know," I said. We had enough trouble with the facts, let alone making stuff up. "I'm calling James first. Maybe he can establish a connection to Tulep." If there was one. I pulled out my phone. It rang in my hand before I could place the call. It was James. "We've got news," I answered.

"So do I." He spoke low. "Come back to the office now."

Chapter Thirty-One: Don't You (Forget About Me)

Twenty minutes later, we hung out in James' office. He sat behind his desk gathering intel on Bianca Arnold. We huddled around his broad shoulders and stared at the computer screen.

"No police record," he finally said.

"Plenty of criminals don't have a record," I said. "She will soon enough though."

"Can we get a search warrant based on Big Sam's video footage?" Veera asked. "I believe she's harboring incriminating evidence."

"I'll second that belief," Michael said.

"You have zero evidence for such an accusation," I reminded them.

"If we can get into her place, we'll find something," Veera said. "She's a law violator, I can tell. Then she'll be in custody and that'll slow the shooter down. And our favorite D.A. here will be safe. Win-win." Veera did a fist pump.

"I like the way you think," I said. "But Abby'll want something more for a warrant."

"There's always tax evasion," Michael said. "It worked for Al Capone."

James, being the only rational one in the room, ignored us and found Bianca on LinkedIn.

"She's been a hygienist," he said, "at Arnold Dental for three years. Before that, she was a bank teller. She married Arnold a few years ago."

"If only we could bring her in on a possible attempted vehicular manslaughter charge." I'd only just thought of that.

James turned his gaze to me. "Where'd that come from?"

"We found a witness who says she nearly ran him over," Veera said.

"Why didn't you bring him in for questioning?" James asked.

"There was a slight obstacle." I told him about Julio and his immigration problem.

James tapped his fingers on his desk. "Can't blame him. We could help, but there are no guarantees he wouldn't be deported, especially since he's got a criminal record."

We spent the next few hours poring over files and ping-ponging theories between us, most of which made little sense and worked up quite an appetite. We ordered an extra-large New York style pizza that could've fed a dozen starving soccer players. Not a morsel was left ten minutes later.

"Mama mia, that was delicious," Michael said.

"Amen to that, and amen to us going in with officers of the law to find that trigger happy maniac tonight," Veera said. "I don't want to be the first Bankhead to end up in jail."

My phone was on speaker and I was on hold, waiting to chat with Detective Abby Rosewater. She'd answered, asked who was calling and made me wait. I disconnected ten minutes later. This was why I didn't go to law enforcement when I had a lead.

"What happened?" Michael asked me.

"Nothing." I sat on the floor and leaned against a wall. "That's the problem."

"Maybe you should text her. Make it all juicy, so she'll have to call back." Veera said. She pulled out a small mirror and reapplied her berry hued lip gloss.

"That's a great idea." Michael shifted his chair closer to me. He stared down at the phone in my hands. "A possible suspect was seen in the vicinity of his former business. Could be the gunman. Based on a new lead, we have reason to believe he'll be there again tonight." Michael caught my gaze. "How's that?"

"That should get her going." Veera peered into a compact mirror and smacked her lips.

I wrote this text:

Shooter seen in front of former business, south of the tracks in Beverly Hills. Informant states suspect will be there tonight.

I looked up at Michael. His hazel eyes grew wide and he rose to his feet.

"That's not exactly true," he said.

"Let me have a look." Veera took Michael's chair and read the text. "It could be true. Or we might've heard wrong." She looked like she was fighting a grin.

"Detectives are busy people, Michael," I said. "We've got to nab her attention or she won't be interested. Isn't that right, James?"

He stood next to the lone window in the room, staring out. "Can't argue with that."

"But, if she—" Michael started.

"Something's going on in that barbershop that warrants a closer look. Jasmine was nervous when we mentioned the place. Which means we can't waste time. Of course..." I moseyed up to Michael and lifted my chin. He wore his melt-me-into-a-puddle smile. "We could go in under the radar."

"Don't forget what Lacy said to you just before she shoved off for India." Veera walked over to us. She'd switched to serious mode.

Michael snapped his fingers. "She said to watch out for sharks."

"And that's why I'm sending this off..." I pressed the send button. "...to Detective Rosewater. To make sure she's with us. I heard she's some kind of shark repellant."

I cast a glance at James. He was lost in thought. I knew what he was thinking. He wanted to join us tonight. He had a hyperactive sense of responsibility...and justice. And he wasn't afraid of being taken out. Not that anyone could take him down. The man was permanent. He threw me a mild grin and sat behind his desk.

My phone rang a minute later.

"Hello, Detective." I plopped down on a chair. I put her on speaker.

"Where are you getting your information?" Abby spoke quietly into the phone.

"The lead came from D.A. Investigator Ramsey before he disappeared..."

I rolled my eyes skyward. "… as well as a nearby shop owner." Sort of true. Jasmine saw something. I just didn't know what. "I was told that activity usually takes place much later, like after midnight." Details always helped move a lie a little further along.

"What's the address?" she asked.

"Hold on." I pressed hold. If I gave her the address, she might go without me. She already said her boss didn't want me involved. I had to handle this with care.

"Be sure to give her the right address," Michael whispered.

The man was a mind reader. He and Veera stood over me, like two prison guards watching me write my confession.

I returned to Abby. "9465 Gregory Way." The truth would set me free, right? Free to get there before the Detective, so I wouldn't miss anything. "See you at midnight." I disconnected.

"I'm proud of you," Michael said. "That wasn't so hard, was it?"

"She's been on a truth streak for a while now," Veera added with a big smile. "Nearly a whole month."

Little did she know. I was a liar with a few dry spells now and then.

"But…" Veera said, "in P.I. work, we can't always go with the truth. Like Confucius says, lying is acceptable if it's done to preserve the good of humanity."

"Confucius never said that." Michael fell for it.

"Check it out," Veera said. "I'm studying Imperial China in my international law class."

Either Veera was a better liar than me or her night law school classes were teaching courses I'd never heard of.

"Well," he said. "The legal system in Imperial China developed from—"

"People," I said. This was not the time to discuss historical foreign philosophy. "We're leaving in ten minutes."

"Where to?" Michael asked.

"Our stakeout." I grabbed my purse.

"I'll get some snacks." Veera headed for the door. "I noticed a kitchen down the hall." She disappeared.

"We can't rely on law enforcement to clue us in. They're planning to check out the place without us, most likely. I want to get there first to watch and wait."

"I get it. We need to be a few steps ahead." Michael grabbed some water bottles from one of James' cabinets. "You'd think Detective Rosewater would realize by now what an asset you are."

"Thank you." I headed for the entry. "I'll do my best to convince her tonight." I turned to James. "Don't leave the building. We'll text you reports."

He crumpled up a piece of paper and aimed for a trash can a few feet away.

Michael shot up and walked over to him. "You're not going anywhere, right?"

"Beckman expects me to stay here. Just like you do," James said. He tossed the paper and down it went, into the can. "I never disappoint."

That's what I was afraid of.

Chapter Thirty-Two: Karma Chameleons

Nearly an hour later, I'd parked up the street and around the corner from the barbershop. Abby would be arriving soon, if she wasn't lurking nearby already. She'd want her players in place well before midnight. Michael, Veera and I exited the car and landed on the sidewalk.

"Hotel Beverly's on Gregory, across from the barbershop," I told Veera and Michael. "We'll blend into the scene and wait."

"We'll be like chameleons," Michael said. "Karma, karma, karma chameleons."

His grin stretched from Honolulu to Trenton. New Jersey, that is.

Veera stared down at her pink sheath. "Wish we had some time so I could've changed. This is not appropriate clandestine activity wear."

"You practically glow in the dark." Michael wore his megawatt grin and stared down at his black T-shirt and olive-green chinos. "Looks like I made the cut. I'd better take the lead on this one. What do you think?" He turned to me.

I leaned forward. "All yours." I'd always watch Michael's back. "But first, there are two small details we have to take care of."

"Like what?" Michael wiped the grin off his face.

"First, we need a couple of modifications." I turned to Veera. "Remember the last time we practiced at the shooting range?"

Veera's smile lit up the street. Or maybe it was her dress.

"I forgot about that," she said.

We zipped over to my trunk and I popped open the lid. I yanked out two large vinyl bags. Inside we'd stored black sweats and T-shirts plus matching Nikes.

"You're quick-change artists," Michael said. "Impressive."

Veera reached back to pull down the zipper on her dress.

"Wait, I know it's dark, but…" Michael put up a hand. "You can't—"

"Just foolin' with you," Veera said and turned to me. "Where's the nearest dressing room?"

I looked at my car. It would work, but I had a better idea. "The hotel ladies' room is spacious."

"I'm all about spacious," Veera said.

"What's the second small detail you mentioned?" Michael asked me.

"You'll see," I said.

We strolled along the sidewalk beneath a row of young magnolia trees, to the part where the residential area faded and the retail shops jumped in.

We hightailed it inside the hotel lobby. It had a comfortable European appeal with velvet sofas, large potted plants and a sparkling crystal chandelier as the ceiling's centerpiece. Veera and I scooted into the marbled restrooms and emerged decked out in black hoodies and drawstring jogger pants. If only we had matching face paint. We'd completely disappear into the night. Of course, we'd also attract some unwelcome attention.

"Veera," I said. "Go into Jasmine's and distract her, so she's not facing the street. Michael and I will wait a minute and follow. We'll pay a visit to the barbershop."

"Why are we…" Michael started.

"I'll explain later. We'll have to work fast," I said.

"Meaning we have to do something possibly illegal before the detective arrives." Michael's eyes widened.

"On my way." Veera quick-stepped down the sidewalk.

"Meet us in the hotel bar when you're done," I called after her.

She gave me a thumbs up. We gave her a two-minute head-start and took off.

"One small recurring question," Michael said. "Our next move. Would James approve of it?"

"We don't need his approval."

"I know. Hypothetically speaking, if we were just making casual conversation, would he?"

"He sure would, hypothetically." James broke laws now and then. Especially when he was with me. "Don't worry. We're not breaking any laws." As long as we weren't caught in the act.

"Okay, cool."

A touch of guilt prickled up and down my arms. Michael trusted me, and there was a chance I'd let him down. "We'll play it safe. I promise." I needed to get back on track. The do the right thing and don't lie so much track.

We hustled through the hotel and emerged onto Beverly. I grabbed a neighborhood newspaper and handed it to Michael. We kept our heads down and headed for the barbershop.

"When we stop," I whispered. "Stand in front of me and open the paper. Hold it up, blocking me from the street view, but look like you're reading it."

"Because you don't want—"

"Hurry."

We stopped by the doorway and he held up the paper, pinching the middle edges of each side. His gaze peered over the top of the paper and into the night.

"I'll let you know if I spot any police officers," he whispered. "Or any other law enforcement agency that's spottable. Or anyone who…"

He continued mumbling while I flipped around and stepped into the shadows. Michael talked a lot when he got nervous. I focused on the doorknob and bent over it. The lock would be easy to pick, and from what I could see, there was no alarm. I pulled out a bump key from my purse. I'd found it in a goodie bag packed with other breaking and entering tools inherited from Dad. Locksmiths used bump keys to get through a locked door, with a little help from a hammer or a screwdriver. I pulled out a screwdriver.

"Corrie, should we—"

"One minute, please."

I stuck the bump key into the lock, rammed it in with the butt of the screwdriver and turned the knob. In less than ten seconds, I briefly opened the door and closed it again. I straightened and shoved the goods into my handbag. Hoodlums didn't usually go out of their way to install high security. They had plenty of weaponry to take you out once you broke in. "Let's go," I told Michael and paused. The pile of papers was gone. Someone had been here. Could've been Jasmine, a cleaning crew or practically anyone.

We trekked across the street without a word. I glanced over my shoulder. Veera exited the shop just as we entered the hotel. Michael and I headed into an art deco era watering hole, populated by after-work schmoozers and neighborhood regulars.

"Did you—" Michael started.

"We'll chat about it later, okay?" I didn't want Michael to know anything, just in case I was busted. He was an innocent bystander, and I wanted him to stay that way. Anyway, bump keys weren't exactly illegal unless I had felonious intent. Which I didn't. That's what I'd tell the judge.

We sunk onto a comfy loveseat and stared out of a row of tall arched windows facing Gregory. Veera arrived minutes later and snagged the sofa across from us.

"Jasmine knows a lot about applying lip gloss," Veera said. "She had this primer I'd never even heard of before." She pulled a small tube out of her purse. "I highly recommend it." She shoved it back in and said, "You get the job done? Whatever that job was."

"All good," I said.

"My time was spent reading the events page of the local paper," Michael said. "There's an art show this weekend featuring South of the Border artists."

We whiled away the next hour munching on chips and salsa and tea-infused cocktails, light on the liquor. We needed to stay sharp.

"On to our next move." I turned to Michael. "Find a spot behind the alley where you can watch the back entry to the barbershop and Jasmine's place." Michael darted out and into the lobby. I shifted to Veera. "Sit right here and keep watch." I stood so Veera could take my seat.

"Who am I watching?"

"Anyone going into, coming out of or loitering near the barbershop," I said.

"Piece of cake, which I wouldn't mind eating right now. Where are you going?"

"Into Burger Joint. I need questions answered."

We parted ways, and I strolled into a sleek yellow and chrome eatery, filled with the mouthwatering scent of French fries. It's not like I was hungry, but still. I inhaled the sweet and salty, crave-inducing aromas. All the vinyl seats were spoken for. I singled out the manager and told him I was doing a story for the *Daily Bruin*, UCLA's student newspaper. Since I was a former Bruin, it was no real stretch to add reporter to my resume.

"I'm looking for stories on ex-cons now running legitimate businesses." I focused on his name-tag. "Do you know of any, Hector?"

He chuckled. "You've picked the wrong spot. Been here five years and the Burger Joint owner's legitimate. He owns a bunch of burger places in Southern California. But…" Hector leaned in. "Next door, people come and go."

"How do you mean?"

"The place is closed, most of the time, but people still go inside."

"Define people," I said.

"Night crawlers," Hector said.

"Like partygoers?" I asked.

"Males. Always men. Dressed in jeans and stuff. Nothing fancy."

"How often do ladies frequent barbershops?" I asked.

"Noted. The previous owner was arrested," Hector said. "It was an ice cream shop before."

"Who's the new owner?" I watched a guy in cheap sunglasses pick up an order at the counter. His Hawaiian shirt was loose and untucked. His crew-cut was tight.

"One night I was putting out the trash and I saw him park in the alley. From the back, he looked like the same guy who owned the ice cream store."

The man at the counter slapped a ten spot on the counter and grabbed the white food bag with his left hand. His right hand never left his side.

"That's kind of vague," I muttered.

"Maybe. But why do his customers come at night?" Hector asked. "Who gets their hair cut at nine p.m.?"

"People who work during the day for a living?" The boots on the guy at the counter grabbed my attention. Black leather, law enforcement grade.

"Got any more questions?" Hector asked me.

"Uh, no." I faced him. "Thanks."

I headed for the counter just as the guy in the Hawaiian shirt turned around. I blocked his path.

"Mind grabbing a menu from the counter for me, please?" I asked sweetly.

In one quick motion, he dropped the white bag on a nearby table, turned, grabbed a menu off the counter and handed it to me, all with his left hand. His right elbow was bent and pressed into his side.

"Thanks," I said.

He snatched up the bag with his left hand and took off. Just as I suspected. A plainclothes cop. I was willing to bet he wore a Velcro belt and holster underneath his shirt, which explained why he kept his right hand free. I watched him loop around the corner and take a seat outside, the seat closest to the barbershop. It was only nine-thirty, but Abby's players were taking their places. Had he seen Michael and me in front of the shop?

I stepped out to the tune of traffic when my cell phone vibrated.

"I've got company," Michael whispered into the phone.

"Is someone else watching the back door?" I made a left to avoid the cop outside the burger place. The alley was my next stop, but the block stretched out a distance before I could get there. Trendy boutiques and well-stocked cafes brimmed beside me. I needed a shortcut.

"Officer Fisher," Michael was saying. "He showed up minutes after I did. He looked right at me so I opened the nearest garbage bin and stuck my head inside."

"Seriously?" That didn't sound like Michael. He was Mister Clean.

"I stopped at Jasmine's before taking my post. She was just closing up. I bought a pair of dishwashing gloves and a beanie. Best purchase ever."

"Smart move."

"I figured the beanie would change-up my look, and I'd use the gloves to rummage through the garbage. I had it all planned out. If anyone asked, I was an artist searching for rubbish to create my art."

"Sounds smelly, but creative." I hung a sharp left into a small vegan cafe. "Hold on," I told Michael and turned to a server. "Is there a back door?"

He nodded and pointed to the kitchen. I took a few steps and flipped a U-ey. I retraced my steps and eyed the occupants of the cafe. For a moment, I had an odd sensation I'd been followed. No sign of the Hawaiian shirt guy or anyone that looked suspect. My paranoia reared its suspicious head. I shook it off and hotfooted past the clatter of the bustling cooks.

"Go on." I spoke into the phone and pushed open a door leading to the alley. Cool air swept over me.

"I didn't recognize Fisher at first," Michael said. "He was talking on his cell phone when he turned into the alley. But I peered around the lid and it was him."

I stopped at the corner of the building next door and stared into the part of the alley where Michael was stationed. I spotted him about forty paces away, peering into a metal dumpster. One hand held his cell, and the other held up the lid. He craned his neck out toward the back entry of the barbershop. I hurried forward and paused next to another building that jutted out just enough to block me from being seen. I peeked around the corner. Officer Fisher leaned against the metal handrail of the building next door to Burger Joint. He had a broad view of the back entry to the barbershop; one black boot pressed against the bottom of the rail. His head swayed back and forth between the alley and the shop. He turned back and eyed Michael.

"Michael, stop what you're doing," I said.

He froze and straightened up. "Okay."

"I'm going to call Fisher. As soon as you see him on the phone, count to five, then turn and walk in the opposite direction, slowly. Change your gait. Hobble or something. You'll find me next to a white stucco building to your right. It says Urban Bee Cafe."

I disconnected and pulled Fisher's card out of my handbag. He answered on the first ring.

"Yes?" He spoke quietly and muffled, like the phone was pressed against his lips.

"It's me, Corrie Locke. I'm near the front of the barbershop. Can you come?"

"Are you in danger?"

"I think I'm being followed." That could be true, which made it a half-lie, which was better than a whole one.

"Where's your exact location?" Fisher asked.

"I'm at an exterior table outside Burger Joint."

He disconnected and I gazed out. Fisher hurried toward the street while Michael slowly limped toward me, head down. I pressed my back against the wall of the building.

"Pssst," I said as Michael passed by.

He took a quick glance over his shoulder and slid over to me.

My cell phone rang. It was Fisher. I knew this was coming.

"Who is it?" Michael whispered.

"Hello?" I answered.

"Where are you?" Fisher asked.

"I had to run. I saw someone suspicious sitting outside. In a Hawaiian shirt. Talk later." I disconnected. That should hold him off for now. That plain clothes cop did look suspicious.

"Is that Fisher? Would it be a bad thing if he saw us?" Michael asked.

"If he thinks I'm taking matters into my own hands, he'll tattle. We need to appear cooperative."

"That didn't sound cooperative to me. Maybe I should go and keep an eye on him, while you do whatever you need. That way I can see what he's up to."

I peeked around the corner. Fisher was fast-walking back to his original spot, head pivoting in all directions. I turned to Michael.

"We'll lie low, for now. Let's take the scenic route to the hotel and join Veera."

"Wait. Abby's team members might be in there, too."

"The bar's dim. We'll blend in. Besides, we'll just be hanging in a bar. No harm in that."

Ten minutes later, we'd joined Veera in the hotel bar and polished off a basket of sweet and spicy chicken wings. Rose colored lighting seeped out from beneath brass ceiling fixtures giving the room a dim glow. If there were undercover cops, they stayed hidden. Meanwhile, Burger Joint was lit up enough to spot from the moon. The guy in the Hawaiian shirt still sat at the same table.

"I've been keeping my eye on that guy," Veera said, glaring at the plainclothes cop.

"He's law enforcement," I said.

"I knew it," she said. "They gotta be watched, too."

Nearly an hour later, the plainclothes cop walked away and into Burger Joint. Minutes later, I jumped to my feet.

"What is it?" Veera asked. She and Michael joined me.

I squinted toward the barbershop, shifting closer to the large window facing Gregory Street.

"Michael? Do you remember the left interior side of the shop?" I spoke quietly.

"Sure. There was a hallway. A narrow one, going somewhere in the back."

"I think…there it is again." A light flickered briefly from somewhere inside the shop.

"I don't see anything." Veera's neck stuck out toward the window.

"Me neither." Michael stepped closer to me.

We waited a few more minutes but all remained dark.

I grabbed my cell phone.

"Who are you texting?" Michael asked.

"The detective." I sent a quick text, telling Abby I saw something. I turned back to Michael and Veera. "We can't wait for her. Let's go."

Chapter Thirty-Three: I Can't Go for That

Officer Fisher was ready and waiting by the time we got to the front of the barbershop. The Hawaiian shirt guy had disappeared. Abby arrived minutes later.

"Any ideas about what's going on?" she asked me. "Fisher's been here for hours and had nothing to report, except for your call."

I waited a beat or two, expecting her to ask why I'd called, but she didn't. "I saw a flash of light from inside the barbershop. Twice."

"As in a flashlight? What are we talking about here?" she asked.

"Like the kind of light you see in a dark room when firing a gun," I said. "Muzzle flash."

"Oh." Abby looked around. "Officer Fisher, did you hear or see anything in the past..." she looked at me.

"Ten minutes?" I asked.

"Like what?" he said.

"A gunshot? Maybe two," I said. Maybe it wasn't muzzle flash. It could've been from a camera flash.

"Well, Officer?" Abby turned to Fisher.

He stared at me with his puppy dog, blue-eyed gaze. "Hard to be sure. There was an old truck parked in the alley that backfired a few times. Could've drowned out anything else if the timing was right."

"Where were you the last ten minutes?" I asked.

"Behind the shop," he replied. "Didn't see anyone suspicious in the back."

My gaze shifted to the entry. "We need to look inside."

"We can't," Abby said. "Without probable cause."

I stepped toward the door and inspected the doorknob. Would anyone notice my handiwork? "I think it's unlocked."

I moved aside and Abby drew closer. She put on a glove and grabbed the doorknob. She turned it and the door yawned open. I glanced over my shoulder.

Veera caught her breath. Michael's eyes grew wide.

Abby pushed her way forward and snapped on a light switch. The tiny shop lit up. All was quiet.

"You unlocked the door," Michael whispered in my ear. "So we'd have no trouble getting in. Genius."

I gulped. Glad that part was over with.

I followed Fisher inside while Michael and Veera lingered by the doorway. I reached into a pocket of my purse and slipped into a pair of disposable gloves. With a gloved hand, I lifted a bottle of shaving foam. It felt full. The hairbrushes looked new. I picked one up and smelled it. No odor. But there was another odor. One I knew well. Like a hundred matches had been lit.

"A gun's been fired here recently," I said.

Abby inched her way down the hallway. I caught up as she reached a back door leading to the alley. Beretta drawn, she pulled open the door, hesitated a moment, then stepped outside. I peered into the night. A hodgepodge of food smells drifted through. The guy in the Hawaiian shirt stood nearby. I retreated inside. Fisher was examining the contents of the cabinets. I studied the hallway. The place didn't seem as wide as the adjacent structures, just like I'd thought. Why was that? I patted my hands along the inside wall.

Abby stomped down the hallway. "Nothing out there. Looks like the place's been empty for a while." She stopped next to me. "Your information was wrong."

I knocked on the wall next to us. It sounded pretty solid to me. "What's back here?"

She cocked her head. "The burger place next door. I studied the blueprints before coming down here tonight. Burger Joint has a room in the back that stretches out. It's a funny shape. So is this shop. And I got a copy of the title report." Abby put away her gun. "A Vegas LLC owns this place. It's been on the market for months. The listing agent said the tenant's been sick and can't work the business. But another barber comes in to give haircuts now and then. I'm not blaming you for wasting our time. It's good to check all leads."

I hurried out behind her. "Wait. What about the flash and the gunshot smell?"

She slowly pivoted around to me. "It's been a long day. My team is dragging and so am I. The flash might have come from a reflection of car headlights in one of these mirrors. And I don't smell anything, besides aftershave." Abby raised her nose and sniffed the air.

Veera and Michael still hovered near the entry. They both lifted their noses and sniffed.

"I smell something that doesn't belong here," Veera said. "Like charcoal."

"She's right." Michael took a few steps inside. "And something else. It's gingerbready. Reminds me of a cigar my uncle smoked."

Abby moved around. "Could've drifted in from a nearby barbecue and someone might have walked by who was smoking a cigar. Not enough to make me stick around."

I stared at the dry-walled ceiling a moment before dropping my gaze to the wood floor. My eyes lingered on a spot near the wall. A heavy brown rug, about the size of a yoga mat, lay behind the barber chairs. Who'd want a thick rug around a barbershop? It was sure to be matted with hair. I stepped closer and toed the rug aside. My heart skipped a beat.

"Maybe this'll make you want to stick around," I said.

Chapter Thirty-Four: Harden My Heart

"Fisher, come with me. The rest of you stand by the door," Abby said and leaned toward me. "I'm responsible for your safety, so stay back until we have a grip on the situation."

"Two minutes?" I mouthed.

"Fine." She sent a text. The guy in the Hawaiian shirt showed up seconds later. "Call for back up," she told him.

He stepped outside and Fisher slid over to Abby. She knelt and shoved the rug away. She touched the floor with her free hand. I moved in closer. Michael hovered at my shoulder. Veera peered out behind him.

"Oh my…" Veera started.

We eyed a trapdoor on the floor. A recessed pull had been built into one end, housing a hinged ring in a fitting attached to the wood. The door lay perfectly flat against the laminated dark wood floor.

Abby flicked her chin up at me. "How'd you know?"

"A wild guess," I replied. "He'd need a place to hide out. I thought there'd be an extra room off the hallway. I was wrong."

Abby straightened up. "Or maybe you'd already been inside here."

"That's ridiculous," I said. She was getting warmer. "If I knew of the trapdoor, I would've taken you straight to it." That was the truth.

"Before or after you did your own investigation?" Abby asked.

It was dark, but I was betting that Abby's face was flushed. She waved her Beretta toward the floor and spoke to Fisher. "Lift it, will you?"

Fisher grabbed the metal pull. The heavy door creaked 'til it came to a stop at a perpendicular angle. Abby's gun and flashlight shone downward on a sturdy wooden ladder converted into makeshift stairs. My ears pricked. So did my nose. The smell of matches grew stronger. If someone was down there, they could be lying in wait. Or sleeping. Or worse.

Fisher pulled his light out from his jacket and shone it down the ladder. "There's blood spatter on the floor, ma'am."

I knew it. It *was* muzzle flash. Someone must've stood at the top of the stairs and shot down, twice.

I dashed forward the moment Fisher finished his downward climb. As soon as they left my line of vision, I scrambled down, pausing midway to scan the floor with my flashlight. Bright red blood pooled at the bottom. Drips and spatters led down a narrow hallway.

"Be careful now," Veera said.

Her head and Michael's bent over the trapdoor.

"Get away from there," a male voice boomed above me. The cop in the Hawaiian shirt had returned.

I looked up in time to see Veera and Michael jerk back their heads. I jumped to the bottom, landing in a crouched position, and hurried down a narrow hallway. I spotted Abby just ahead of me, gun drawn. Fisher stood behind her. Abby stepped through the doorway.

Fisher flashed a light inside the room and followed her.

I joined them a second later. Fisher stood staring down at the floor. A beam of light shone on the face of a large bearded man with wild hair.

Stepping forward, I stared at the body, careful to avoid trampling on possible evidence. Oops. My heel cracked a mechanical pencil in two. I side-stepped closer.

The victim wore a thin green sweater spattered with blood. A gaping hole appeared over the place where his heart had been beating. This time the shot had been precise, meant to be a death wound. A belly band holster wrapped around his waist. No sign of a cigar.

Abby knelt beside the body and turned to me. "The CSI unit will be here in a few minutes. You need to leave."

I rose and she rose with me.

"But first, any information you have to share?" she asked.

I looked around the room. Small padded envelopes, mailing labels, stamps and empty pill bottles spread across a wooden table against the wall. He'd set up shop alright, but not the kind that offered haircuts. "Not yet."

"How did you know Tulep would be killed tonight?" Abby asked.

"I didn't," I said. "He was the defendant in a recent D.A. case, and got out on a technicality right about the time the shooter was first spotted on the security cam in Big Sam's Diner."

"You're saying he's the shooter?" Abby's lower lip stuck out. "And he was killed by one of his flunkies. Or even a competitor. Makes sense, I think."

"Your ballistics should shed some light on that," I said.

"I got the ballistics report on the bullet in the diner," Abby said. "We got nothing out of it."

"Him being the shooter makes the most sense," Fisher said.

I heartily disagreed. He was too hairy, too short and didn't look agile enough to run like the guy I'd chased.

"What doesn't make sense…" Fisher turned to me. "Is that you said you saw a flash of light. The trap door was closed, which means the shooting took place down here. You might've heard something, but you didn't see anything."

"You're holding back vital information," Abby said to me.

I turned on my heel and gingerly made my way to the ladder.

"You have no answer?" Abby followed me.

"Was that even a question?" I replied. "What doesn't make sense is why Officer Fisher has already decided how the kill took place." I stepped forward. "Here's my assessment. The shooter entered the shop."

"That's why the front door to the shop was open," Abby said.

I sent a mental thanks to the Universe and continued. "Or from the back." Made the most sense to me. "He knew about the trap door. He pulled it open and called out to Tulep."

"The shooter was someone he knew?" Abby said.

"Or posing as a customer," I said. "Tulep appeared and was shot. Didn't even have a chance to pull his gun." I was willing to bet Tulep's gun never left the holster sitting around his waist. "He staggered back to that room…"

I pictured the cell phone. "Maybe to grab the phone. But he didn't make it. The shooter pulled the rug over the trapdoor and…" I paused.

"What?" Abby asks. "How did he get out without being seen?"

"That's what I'd like to know." I craned my neck and looked around. "Maybe there's another exit. Who was watching the back?"

"I was," Fisher said. "Until I traded places with Slezak."

Slezak must be the undercover cop in the Hawaiian shirt. "Was there any gap in time?"

"A brief one," Fisher said.

"Any time Slezak was out of your sight?" I asked.

"Oh yeah. Just before I came in here," Fisher said. "He took a spin around the block."

Sirens wailed and Abby turned to Fisher. "Escort Ms. Locke out and bring the CSI team down when they arrive." She faced me. "We'll be in touch."

***

"What's our take-away?" Michael asked.

"Tulep wasn't the triggerman," I said.

He walked behind Veera and me, as we tramped our way back to the car an hour later. More cops had arrived along with the crime scene unit. We stuck around for questioning and were finally released. It was past midnight before we headed out.

"I can't say I'm sorry he was taken out. Selling opioids out of his basement to kids." Veera shook her head.

"How could no one know what was going on?" Michael asked.

"He only operated at night," I said. "Doling out the goods in person and sending counterfeit prescription drugs in the mail to his customers." Which would explain all the envelopes and stamps.

"That's what sent Tulep to prison in the first place," Michael said. "And he didn't stop."

"It's easy money as long as they don't get caught," I said. "I'll bet they find wads of cash in there."

185

"Tulep's dead," Michael said. "And there's a gunman out there. Think he still plans to take out a D.A. Team member?"

That question weighed on all of our minds.

"We have to act as if he is," I said.

A couple strolled between us toward Beverly Drive. A quartet of college aged guys walked across the street, talking loudly and laughing.

"How could Jasmine not know what Tulep was doing?" Michael asked.

"That no good lip gloss primer pusher next door just looked the other way," Veera said.

"Remember, James said she called the cops a few times," I said. "She suspected something, but the timing was off each time the cops arrived."

"Because they didn't know about the trap door," Michael said and turned to me. "What about that gingerbread smell? Did you see any cigars down there?"

I snapped my chin up. "No smell. And no cigar either. It was only upstairs."

"The shooter smokes cigars," Michael said. "But his driver prefers cigarettes."

"I've got a theory," Veera said. "Tulep hired the gunman to eliminate D.A. team members, but he didn't pay up, which made the shooter mad enough to kill Tulep instead."

"That's a good one," Michael said. "Because Tulep only recently got back into business and the taste of making moolah again was too much to share with anyone." They exchanged a high five.

"If that was true," I said. "That means the case is closed and James can go on with business as usual. Anybody feel like celebrating?"

Michael stopped. "We're just batting theories and kidding around. We want this thing wrapped up so we don't need to worry about best friends being targets."

"Life is never neat and tidy, so why would murder be?" I said.

"I didn't mean—"

"Forget it," I said. "Why didn't we see the triggerman coming or going tonight?"

We walked in silence.

"We know he didn't go in the front," Michael said. "We would've seen him."

"Unless he was already inside before we arrived," Veera said. "We need to regroup and recharge to think clearly."

"How about we go back to Corrie's place and talk shop 'til we drop?" Michael said. "Between us, we can figure out a few angles, and maybe a solid plan."

I slowed. A tall figure stood just past my car, in a cone of darkness that had escaped the street lamp. The silhouette leaned against a tree. Veera and Michael tramped ahead of me, discussing the night's events. Michael turned around.

"What's wrong?" He stepped back and took my hand, linking it in his.

I halted in my tracks. "Someone's waiting by the BMW. Don't turn around…"

They both froze mid-turn and faced me again.

"Be cool. Not obvious," I said.

"Who do you think it is?" Veera whispered. "Jasmine? I knew it. She's been hiding out, waiting for us, to find out what we know."

I was afraid of this happening. Some of my paranoia had leaked onto Veera.

"She couldn't have known we'd come this way," Michael whispered back. "Maybe it's the shooter." He turned to me.

"He would've made his move by now." I stared between their heads at the shadowy figure.

"Could one of the detective's people be watching us?" Michael asked.

"Maybe," I said.

"There are three of us and one of him or her," Veera said. "Sneaking around like that. We can take the gangster down right here and now."

"We'll divide up," Michael said. "Veera and I will continue walking up the street, like nothing happened, then double back behind him, just before you get there. You stop and tie your shoe or something."

"We'll tackle him from behind." Veera beamed and they bumped fists.

"He's on the prowl," I said. "Get down." I knelt and peered over the hood of a parked car.

Michael stiffened and crouched. Veera turned her head slightly to steal a look behind her before kneeling behind a car.

"Incoming," I said.

Veera's hand dove into her purse. She rummaged around and pulled out a can of pepper spray. Michael's knife was already in his hand.

Someone crossed the street, heading toward us at a fast clip. My fingers curled around the gun in my purse.

Chapter Thirty-Five: No Stranger

The silhouette was manly and large. The cautious stride looked familiar, as did the slightly cocked head. He strode in and out of a beam of streetlight giving enough time for me to note the black baseball cap covering his head, and the dark waves feathering around his ears. I stood and so did Michael and Veera.

"James," I said.

"Buddy!" Michael said. "You weren't supposed to leave the building."

"Needed my friends to watch my back," James said.

"We will, but you shouldn't be out in the open like this." Michael slid next to him. "You're still a target."

"He's right." I scanned the area around us. Too many people pounded the pavement this time of night.

"What do you mean 'still' a target?" James asked.

Michael nut-shelled tonight's events. James took it all in and was quiet until the end.

"He shot to kill tonight," James said.

"Could've been a different gunman with no relation to the other one. Let's scram." I didn't like standing out in the open. "How'd you get here?" I asked James. We hurried down the block.

"Janitorial crew gave me a lift. Beckman thinks I'm still in my office."

"Good thing you found your bodyguards," Michael said.

I led the way. In two long strides James matched his pace with mine.

"What really went down tonight?" he asked.

"One of our suspects was shot and killed." I swiveled my head around, keeping watch. "That's all I know. Our eyes were glued to the front entry. The cops were watching the back door. Looks like the killer slid in and out without being seen."

"What's your take, bro?" Michael asked from behind us.

"Simple," James replied. "Tulep's the connector to the potshots aimed at the D.A. team."

"Which means…" Michael said.

"There are people," Veera said, "Tulep made so mad, they're coming after everyone who failed to keep him behind bars."

"That's it," I said.

"We're all staying at Corrie's tonight," Michael told James. "You should, too. It's better than a safe house."

All eyes turned to Michael.

"What? She's got everything from slingshots to smoke bombs and surveillance cameras." Michael gave a quick shrug. "And her mom loads her pantry and keeps her fridge stocked. We'll take turns sleeping."

"Tempting," James said. "But Corrie's place is not ideal."

I knew what he was thinking. He still thought there was a possibility, a slim one, that I was the target. I'd had enough dealings in the criminal world to make someone want to wipe me off the face of the earth. But I wasn't the target.

"We already decided," Michael said. "He can't be after Corrie."

"How about y'all come to my place?" Veera asked.

"Do you have ammo, too?" Michael said.

"Let's just say I have a few weapons," Veera said. "We know this maniac isn't after me. I'm not as well-known as C is in criminal circles. Not yet, anyway."

"But then we'd make you more involved," Michael said.

"Like I'm not already? If we're being watched, I'm on the hit list." Veera rubbed her hands together. "Good thing I've been practicing at the shootin' range."

Michael's brows shot up.

"She's good, too." I'd been her instructor the past few weeks.

James eyed Veera like he'd never seen her before. "Where do you live?"

"On the east side of Culver City. It's nothing fancy, but I've got a fenced in front and back, a remodeled bathroom and a working garbage disposal. I'm living the life, thanks to Gran."

"Is it her house?" Michael asked.

"We're roomies. It's her place and I live with her, which makes me one grateful grandkid."

"How would Gran feel with four strangers moving in?" I asked.

"She always sayin' her door's open to everyone, not countin' the bathroom door."

"Appreciate the offer." James stared at Veera. "But she'd be better off if we weren't at her house."

"Well, truth is," Veera said. "She doesn't have the kind of supplies we'll be needing. Stuff to protect us and bring the gunman and his driver in."

"Stuff that makes an impact," Michael said.

"That's what I'm talking about," Veera said.

We crossed over, backtracked to my ancient BMW, and stuffed ourselves inside. Michael rode shotgun, and James and Veera sat in the rear, shoulders and knees almost touching. Surprisingly, James still had an inch of headroom. Veera didn't mind tight squeezes since her usual ride was a VW bug. The steering wheel nearly sat in her lap. She liked it that way.

I pulled onto Olympic Boulevard and motored toward the 405.

James stared at his vibrating phone. "It's Beckman." He pinned the phone to his ear. "James here."

There was a long pause before he spoke again.

"Alright." He disconnected.

Michael turned around and I pulled over in a gas station.

"Well?" Michael asked.

"There was another incident," James said.

Chapter Thirty-Six: Freeze Frame

"Does this latest incident end badly?" Michael asked.

"Does a papercut count?" James said.

"What happened?" I asked.

"An envelope was found against the backdoor of the building, addressed to Beckman," James said. "Security discovered it. In it was a note with letters cut-out from a newspaper."

"We already know the guy's old-school," Veera said.

"What did it say?" Michael asked.

"One down, three to go," James said.

A shiver trickled down my spine. Dead bodies didn't trip me up, but once in a while, I suffered a delayed reaction. This was one of those moments. A wave of nausea swept over me.

"I'm glad you're with us," Michael told James. "We'll keep you safe."

"This plays right up our P.I. alley," Veera said. "There's another name for our agency. P.I. Alley."

"Any security footage?" I asked.

"Being reviewed now," James said.

"I need to see that footage," Veera said. "That's one of my areas of expertise."

I stared at James through the rear-view mirror. "Anyone hear from Ramsey lately?"

"He's not answering my calls," James said. "You?"

"Haven't tried," I said. "I figured he'd call when he was good and ready."

We motored along the boulevard at a steady pace. The silence in the car was louder than any traffic noise. I cut a glance at James through my mirror.

"What's on your mind?" I asked him.

He leaned his head back. "When I worked in the Orange County D.A.'s office…my boss had a case…a misdemeanor drug charge. I had a feeling about it so I looked the case up this afternoon. Tulep was the dealer." He stared down at his hands and dropped his voice. "Everyone thought it would be a slam dunk conviction. Ended up, there wasn't enough evidence to convict. That's when Tulep relocated to L.A. County."

"Why didn't you tell me this earlier?" I asked.

"I had nothing to do with that case," James said. "Which means it wasn't relevant."

"Maybe it had something to do with someone harboring a grudge against the D.A.," I said.

"You're saying an old grudge killed Tulep?" Veera said.

"Another dealer, maybe?" Michael said. "Or someone he double-crossed."

"Someone's out for revenge," I said.

"How do you know that?" Michael asked.

"It's the only motive that makes sense to me," I said. "Revenge for what?" I turned to James. "Can you get me into your office?"

"What for?" he asked.

"To take another look at Tulep," I said. "On paper. Your office is on the way, sort of." Culver City was south a few miles, but still an easy hop onto the freeway. "Tell me how to get in and I'll grab the files."

"I'll get you in," James said.

I made a left onto Overland.

Fifteen minutes later, I'd pulled into the subterranean parking lot reserved for the building's occupants. Michael and I tumbled out and followed James to the office. Veera waited in the lobby.

"I'm going to inspect the surveillance in the building," she said.

We'd barely landed onto the third floor when James paused by Ramsey's office. Light spilled out from beneath it.

"Maybe Beckman's in there," Michael whispered. "Going through files."

I lightly pressed my ear to the door. "Someone's moving around," I whispered. I was about to knock when the door flew open.

Chapter Thirty-Seven: He's Back

"Aha!" Ramsey's red-rimmed eyes gleamed behind his glasses. "I knew you were out here." He stared at James and Michael and sobered. "I'm busy."

"Aren't you supposed to be kidnapped?" Michael asked.

"What game are you playing?" James said. "A staged kidnapping to get the gunman off your back?"

"Wrong," Ramsey said. "That was just a byproduct. It was to free me up to find him so I could save your hide and Beckman's."

"And your own." I pushed past and into his office. He was the type that never took an action unless there was a benefit to him. "A question."

"How did you know I'd be here?" he asked me.

"I meant I had a question." He gave me way too much credit. But a girl's gotta take credit wherever she can when she's on a case. "Trade secret."

"I'm in the same trade, remember?" Ramsey followed me.

"Don't bother," Michael told him. "She's got skills ordinary people will never know about."

"I'm hardly ordinary," Ramsey said. "And I wasn't talking to you."

James and Michael followed me into a compact space littered with a variety of paperwork, from police reports to photographs to witness statements. Caricatures dotted the walls. An open bottle of brandy sat on a filing cabinet, next to a half-filled plastic tumbler.

Ramsey dashed to the door, slammed it and turned the deadbolt. He faced us and crossed his arms over his chest. "Why are you here this time of night?"

Michael peered at the pictures on the walls. "Who's the artist?"

"I'm a cartoonist." Ramsey grinned briefly and turned back to me. "I heard about Tulep."

"Of course, you did," James said. "Beckman knew your kidnapping was staged. You should've told me."

"Why?" Ramsey's upper lip curled. "The fewer people that knew, the less chance of a leak."

"Who killed Tulep?" I asked him.

Ramsey regarded his fingernails, which looked bitten to the core. "Drug dealers have enemies. Plenty of them. You ought to know that."

"That's some coincidence, a random enemy striking on the night the police decided to show up," I said. The stale air was getting to me.

He tipped his head back and shook it slowly, keeping his eyes on me. "You've got a lot to learn, little girl." He stuck his scrawny neck out. "Tips roll in when something big's about to go down. You should—"

"Know that. Right," I said.

"You knew Tulep would be killed?" James stomped over to him, paperwork flying in his wake.

Ramsey bent over to straighten up a pile. "Let's say I had a strong gut feeling."

"I've got a strong gut feeling, too," I said. "How long have you worked for the Culver D.A.?"

"Almost two years. Started out in the biz as a police cadet with L.A.P.D., but before I finished training, I was made an offer I couldn't refuse, by the Chief D.A. herself."

"In L.A.?" I asked.

"In Orange County. I worked there first. What's your gut telling you?"

I swapped glances with James before refocusing on Ramsey. "You worked as a junior D.A. investigator on the Tulep case when he was arrested in Orange County."

"You looked me up?" He grinned broadly.

"Didn't have to. We figured you were involved."

The grin faded. "How could you possibly know?"

"Ramsey wasn't in Orange County when I started." James moved over to me.

"I left," Ramsey said. "Before you came on board."

"At the beginning of Tulep's trial," James said.

"My role was done," Ramsey said. "It was time to set sail for a bigger body of water."

"You must've made people mad," Michael said. "Leaving mid-stream like that."

"Are you deaf?" Ramsey said. "There was nothing left for me to do."

James took a step closer to Ramsey. Ramsey shrunk into James' shadow. "Rumor was the investigator left on bad terms."

"What do you mean?" Michael asked.

"We didn't have enough evidence to win the case," James said. "The former D.A. investigator dropped the ball. It was too late by the time another investigator stepped in."

"Lies," Ramsey said. He marched over to the cabinet, picked up his drink and downed it, wiping his mouth with the back of his sleeve. "I never start a job I can't finish. And I finished it."

I headed for the door and unlocked it. "Let's collect what we came here for." I yanked it open and stepped into the quiet hallway, Michael at my heels.

We stopped about twenty feet away, next to James' office. Meanwhile, James was yelling, full throttle, at Ramsey. Something about a habit of leaving things undone and being an idiot. Moments later, James stepped out, one hand gripping Ramsey's upper arm.

"Oh, you are so getting into trouble, Mister Hotshot." Ramsey scrambled to keep up. "This is an assault right here. There are witnesses, under penalty of perjury. He's manhandling me."

"Doesn't look like manhandling to me," Michael said.

"I've never seen James exhibit such a gentle touch," I added.

"What are you going to do with him?" Michael asked James.

"Ramsey insisted we meet his stoolie to find out where he got his information from about tonight's shooting," James said. "Maybe this informant has more to share."

"I'll need my phone to call him," Ramsey said. "It's on my desk."

"You're resourceful," James spoke through gritted teeth. "You'll figure out a way to call. Better yet. We'll visit him in person."

"Bro, how are we all going to fit in the BMW?" Michael asked.

"It'll be nice and cozy," James said.

We popped into James' office, stuck a few files under our arms and headed downstairs.

Veera waited by the elevator, chatting up a security guard. She hustled over to us when we landed on the first floor. "Did you know this security guard was never informed about the Ramsey kidnapping? How can security help if they don't know what's going on? I aim to find out...what the..." She pointed to Ramsey.

She nearly reared up when she laid eyes on Ramsey.

"What's he doin' here?" she asked.

Chapter Thirty-Eight: Eye of the Tiger

"You know him?" Michael asked Veera. "How?"

"You'd better not be messing with my friends," she told Ramsey. She swayed from foot to foot like she was getting ready to punch him in the kisser.

"What's the big deal?" he asked and passed his stare around. "She and I met once, at a social event."

"That was no event," Veera spit out the last word. "And it wasn't social either."

"We need to find his informant. He's going to make that happen." James stepped back into the elevator. "Get in."

Veera joined us, occupying the opposite corner from Ramsey.

"You know how slippery informants are," Ramsey said. "You never find them where you expect to."

"You'll find this one, Ramsey," James said.

"This is Ramsey?" Veera asked. "The D.A. investigator? Now I know who the shooter is really after."

Ramsey curled his lips. "You don't know squat."

"And you expect him to find our man?" Veera clicked her tongue. "That's like asking a raccoon to barbecue burgers. He doesn't have what it takes."

"Do so," Ramsey said.

"Veera." I grabbed her arm and pulled her out as the elevator door slid open. "Let's go." I lowered my voice as we moved ahead of the others. "Want to talk about this?"

"Heck, no."

"Don't let him get to you. Look at him as a temporary walking stick we need until we firm up our legs."

"I am not going to look at him at all." She shot him dirty looks. "I've seen enough already."

This was intriguing. I couldn't visualize the two of them together in any circumstance, unless…no, he couldn't have been investigating her. What had he done to get her so riled up? Veera dragged her suede sneakers to my car.

"We're going to switch the seating around," I said. "Michael, would you trade places with Veera, please?"

"I can do that," he said, heading for the back door. "You don't mind sitting in my lap, do you, Rams?"

"I'll ride shotgun with her." He pointed to me. "And don't call me that."

"I want you close by," James said. "To finish our chat."

Michael slid into the backseat, and James gave Ramsey a little push to get him going. By the time Veera and I were seat belted in, Ramsey was squished between them, staring straight ahead. I started the engine.

"Where are we going?" Veera asked.

I reversed and motored out of the parking lot.

"Answer her," James told Ramsey.

"Venice and the 405," Ramsey replied.

One of the shoddiest areas in Culver City. Buildings were shabby, worn and faded. Riff-raff occupied the shadowy places and homeless souls lived in cardboard dwellings on the sidewalks.

I turned into a quiet side street and headed for Washington.

"We never meet in person," Ramsey was saying.

"I can see why," Veera said.

I shot her a look and she lifted her chin, staring straight ahead.

"How do you know where he lives?" Michael asked. "If you don't meet in person."

"Because I scrounge around 'til I hit pay dirt." Ramsey sat stiffly.

"Like a rat," Veera said.

Ramsey's beady eyes stared at Veera. Her lips squeezed tight to prevent an outpouring. I admired her self-control. Nastiness wasn't her style, but she'd clobber him in an instant if given the chance. It would be a miracle if we got through the next hour without anyone strangling Ramsey.

"What's at Venice and the 405?" I asked.

"His favorite hangout," Ramsey said.

"He's a night owl?" He'd better not be toying with us.

"He likes to unwind by shooting pool. He'll be at the TLC Billiard Club," he said. "Make a left at the corner."

***

Fifteen minutes later, I parked in a small lot belonging to a bar. Wood beams crisscrossed past the roofline of the single unit building. A weary looking pine tree rose up against a wall and pygmy palms flanked the front walkway. Thick, stained curtains draped over the windows.

"I'm not going in there," Veera said.

"Ramsey and I will go," James said and opened his door.

"I'll stay with Veera," Michael said.

I was already outside, headed for the entry. I wasn't about to miss any action.

Ramsey stumbled out and jogged over to us. His thumb pointed to the door. "He comes here weeknights between midnight and closing."

"Call," James said, "and tell him to meet us outside."

"With what? You didn't let me bring my phone, remember?"

"It's in your shoe."

"That's...how do you know about that?" Ramsey turned to face James.

I'd noticed the thick soles on Ramsey's sneakers, but I didn't connect it to a hidden compartment.

"Make the call," James said

Ramsey trekked behind the car and bent down, out of sight. A minute later, he emerged with a cell phone in his hand. A solid deduction on James' part.

"Fine," Ramsey said.

I caught Veera's eyes. Her smile was back, up and running.

Ramsey placed the call. "I'm at TLC. Meet me outside. What?" He listened and disconnected. "He's not here."

"Where is he?" James asked.

"At another bar, a block away."

"Let's go," James said.

Minutes later, we'd parked the car beside another divey watering hole. A windowless bunker with only a lone neon sign to give it character. Inside carried the same vibe. Small, dark and boozy, the smell of industrial strength cleanser hung over the place like a lampshade. The bar was cash only, but the drinks were cheap like the decor. I muscled my way inside.

"I don't see him," Ramsey mumbled behind me.

"Look closer," James said.

A wide archway led to a couple of pool tables.

"Listen, hotshot." Ramsey turned to face James. "This was a mistake and you know it. Once he sees me with you two, he'll bolt. And after that, he'll stop feeding me information. Beckman won't be happy when my prime source goes dry, no thanks to you."

James caught my gaze.

"You wait here," I told Ramsey. "We'll look around first. Give us a minute and you follow. That way it'll look like you're alone."

"Dumb idea, cupcake," he said.

"What did you call me?" I reared up to him.

"What I meant was, he'll spot you two right away. You look like you stepped out of a fashion shoot. Take a look around."

Besides the bartenders, everyone else looked like a hooker, a salty old timer or a lush. The floor was sticky, and smudge-marks ran across the mirror behind the bar. Customers were either in the midst of crashing from a bender or about to break into a fistfight.

James leaned down toward me and whispered. "He's right. We stick out."

"Stay with him," I told James. I pulled down the zipper of my hoodie, messed up my hair and held out my hand to Ramsey. "Give me your belt."

"Why?" he asked as he unbuckled and pulled it out. "Aren't you carrying any heat?"

"Let me worry about that." I grabbed the belt, wrapped part of it around my wrist and left enough out for me to twirl. It was my best drunken hooker in a jogging outfit imitation. "How will I recognize him?"

"Fly Boy'll be playing pool. Never misses a shot and looks like an old grizzly bear. Talks like one, too."

James scowled at him.

"What?" Ramsey shrugged a narrow shoulder. "He does. You'll see."

I was intrigued. I sashayed and swayed my way toward the pool room, tossing out a hiccup every few steps. I stopped in my tracks.

A gaggle of older men gathered around a green felt topped pool table. I represented all females and persons under thirty. I scanned the faces. Make that forty.

I spotted the informant right away. His back faced me. He sported a medium cut afro, full bristly beard and black and white pajama pants. His flannel shirt belonged on a lumberjack. He wielded the cue stick, and the room grew quiet. Aiming for the far-right corner pocket, the ball dropped in the hole seconds later, with one smooth shot.

He straightened and looked right at me.

"Uh-oh," I whispered.

Chapter Thirty-Nine: Disappearing into the Night

In seconds, I raced after the informant. He shot out the back door moments after we made eye contact. This was a race I wouldn't lose. The guy had over two decades on me and wasn't in great shape. Oh sure, he threw a couple of trash cans in front of my feet, but I leapt over them with ease. I only tripped once, trying to avoid a taxi when I crossed the street, but I caught up to the geezer right away.

He turned into a residential street, and I jumped into light speed, which meant I tackled him around the waist moments later. He dove onto a patch of lawn with me on top of him. I straddled his back and pulled his arms behind him. He was too busy panting to say much.

"Hardly any way to treat an old friend," I said, catching my breath. "Or even the daughter of one."

"You…it's not…I didn't…" was all he squeezed out in his raspy growl.

"It's been a while, Roger." I tightened the belt around his wrists and he groaned. "Or should I call you Fly Boy?" I stumbled onto the sidewalk and sat. The coldness of the hard cement seeped through my pants. Roger kicked out his legs a couple of times and groaned again.

"What would your daddy say about how you're treating me?"

"He'd say your pool playing skills have improved." Dad used to beat him all the time.

"I'm no criminal," he said. "You know it."

James barreled around the corner and put on the brakes when he saw us.

He offered his hand to me. I took it and stood.

Ramsey showed up moments later.

James pulled Roger's arm and helped him to his feet. "Nice cuffs," James said to me with a grin.

"What have you done to him?" Ramsey asked, breathing heavy.

Roger blew out a huff. "Man, I'm gettin' too old to be knocked around."

"That was a very mild knocking," I said. "We just have a few questions and then you can go."

He raised his bushy brows. "Really? Just like that? I was worried that, you know, you wouldn't be like your dad, since you're a lawyer and all."

"I'm not my father," I said. Dad had been a man of few words and little time for me, unless I tagged along on one of his cases. "Tony Tulep was murdered a few hours ago. You knew he was running a drug operation out of a barbershop in Beverly Hills. What else do you know?"

Ramsey quit panting. He slid closer, all ears.

"All I know is the word on the street." Roger stopped and looked at the men with me. Well, the one and a half men. He pitched his chin toward the guys and looked at me. "Can we talk alone?"

"What?" Ramsey said. "You're my informant, not hers."

"I don't belong to you," Roger told him.

"Let's go." James grabbed Ramsey's shoulder and steered him away. He shook off James' hand and stormed off into the darkness, with James strolling behind him.

"The only reason I tell that little weasel anything is so the police and Miss Head District Attorney leave the people in my life the hell alone."

"They pay you for the information?"

"Man's gotta live," he said. "But ain't no one as generous as your daddy was."

I doubted the D.A.'s office paid much. Of course, Roger had his day job.

"You still flying?" I asked.

"I'm at the airport every day," he said. "Me and Hattie Mae."

Roger was a licensed helicopter pilot with his own charter service. Hattie Mae was his chopper, named after his mother. He'd worked as a pilot for years until he saved enough to buy his own. I reached into my memory banks. Dad had me study the backgrounds of all his information sources. It helped to better understand them, put up with them, and anticipate what to expect.

"Still one chopper strong," he said.

"How's your son?"

He nodded. "This has nothing to do with my boy."

"Grandson?" I pulled back on any urge to say more. I guessed his grandson had gotten into trouble with the law. Roger's cooperating with the D.A. was a way of making the trouble go away or, at least, lessening the impact.

"You always did have a knack for seeing things."

"What about Tulep?" I asked. "Any ideas about his murder?"

"I swear I had no idea he'd be snuffed out tonight."

I crossed my arms against my chest.

"Okay, there was a rumor he'd gotten someone mad. Real mad."

"A rival drug dealer?"

He shook his head slowly. "No. A rival's name would've circulated. It's not anyone in the business. I can try to find out, but I would've heard something by now."

I walked a circle around him. "Tell you what. If you find information that's useful, I'll take care of you." I had no idea what I meant by that, but I'd find a way to help him out. My helping hand list was growing long.

"Fair enough." He turned back to me. "Now how about setting me free?"

I placed my index finger and thumb close together and into my mouth. I blew out a whistle so low, it sounded like a puff of air. I had zero whistling skills so I yelled out at the top of my lungs, and James and Ramsey padded over. A few lights went on in the neighboring homes.

"You okay?" James asked me.

"More importantly," Ramsey said. "How's my informant?"

"We're fine." I unbuckled Roger out of the belt and tossed it back to Ramsey. I handed Roger my business card while he rubbed his wrists.

"Let me know if you ever want to fly." He passed me a card. "I'll give you a friends and family discount." He turned his back to us. In a sort of half swagger, he disappeared around a corner.

James and I made our way back to my car with Ramsey trotting behind us.

"Did he say anything?" Ramsey asked me.

"Nope," I replied.

"You'd tell me if he did?" Ramsey said.

"I got nothing."

"Like I believe that. Then why did he want me to leave?" Ramsey wanted to know. "That wasn't fair."

"He wanted to say something about my father," I said. That was almost true. We headed for the bar.

"Oh." Ramsey slowed and caught up to us moments later. "Well, that was a wasted trip," he told James.

I checked my phone. Three missed calls from Michael. I texted him our arrival time.

We headed to the parking lot only to find Michael and Veera weren't alone.

"Quick," I told Ramsey. "Duck!"

Chapter Forty: The Safety Dance

"Why would you be in this part of town this time of night?" Officer Fisher shone the beam of his flashlight on us. "Especially you, D.A. Zachary. You've got a shooter after you. You were supposed to stay in the building."

"A nightcap after a long day," I said. We'd left Ramsey hiding out in the men's room. The cops still thought he was a kidnap victim.

"We travel in packs. There's power in numbers," Michael said.

"What brings you here, Officer?" James asked.

"Someone reported a fight in the bar," Fisher replied. "We broke it up and I found these two hanging out in the parking lot. I didn't see you or Ms. Locke in the bar. Where were you?"

"I'd had enough to drink tonight," I said. "I was…"

"Sobering up," James said.

"That was some scary stuff back in that barbershop," Veera said. "I'm not used to—"

"Violence," Michael added.

"That's right," Veera said.

"Yet," Officer Fisher turned to James and me. Another officer stood in the shadows behind him. "We checked outside the bar and didn't see either of you."

"We went bar-hopping," I said. "To the one down the street. Back and forth between the two. To stay sober."

"They had better drinks," James said.

"Mind if I run a breath test?" Fisher asked.

"You know the answer to that," James said and headed for the backseat sauntering so close to Fisher he had to step back.

Fisher turned to me and smiled. "I know you're competent, but it's really important we work together. I have this feeling you know more about the Tulep murder than you're sharing."

Why did I feel like a first grader accused of lying? "I don't have anything to report yet. When I do, I'll pass it along to Abby."

"Good enough." He flashed a grin and we parted ways.

We drove off and James texted Ramsey.

We waited a while and when he didn't respond, James strolled back into the bar with Michael. They returned empty-handed.

"Probably called an Uber to take him back," Michael said.

"We're done with him for now," James said.

I tried Ramsey's phone. No answer. I filled everyone in on my conversation with Roger.

"Maybe we can start a GoFundMe campaign to pay Roger, assuming he comes through with some information," Michael said.

"That's a great idea," Veera said. "People ask for money for all kinds of things. From building a doghouse to paying for medical bills. Sounds like Roger could use some extra funds. Informant money can't be that consistent, even if it is tax free."

"We can use the GoFundMe money to pay all our informants," Michael said.

"You mean the informants we don't have?" I asked.

"I mean the ones we're going to get," Michael said.

"Then we'll have a head start when we open *P.I. Experts*," Veera said. "PIE for short. Word'll get around and everyone'll be calling us with information."

"Roger owns Beach Hoppers in Santa Monica," I said. "He charters out his helicopter for rides along the coast, but he could always use some extra dough." I'd watched one too many Bogart movies.

"I'll start the GoFundMe tomorrow," Veera said. "Meanwhile, where're we headed?"

"My place," I said. "We need to plan our day tomorrow. I see a visit to Big

Sam in the cards."

"If I were a betting man, I'd say the likelihood that a restaurant rivalry led to the shooting was…" Michael said, "…zero."

"Just investigating all possibilities," I said. "Maybe a D.A. did something to get Gordon Joshua angry."

"I've only been to his restaurant once," James said.

"How did it go?" I asked.

"I ordered a steak and it was served nearly raw. I sent it back and it was served exactly the same again. Except with a fresh piece of parsley."

"Did you get mad?" Veera asked.

"Damn right. I was hungry."

"Good thing it wasn't Corrie. She would've shot him for sure," Michael said. "I mean, she wouldn't shoot to kill. Maybe in the foot or something."

"Sounds kind of like our gunman," Veera said. "Until tonight, that is."

"It's possible…" A clear thought was finally forming in my head. "…he has trouble pulling the trigger when it comes to non-criminals, but has no problem with convicted or almost convicted drug dealers."

"That's a viable theory," Veera said.

"On second thought," Michael said. "I've watched enough of the Cooking Channel to know chefs can be cutthroat."

"If there's money at stake, I'd say that's true," James said. "But not likely in this case."

"Unless it's drug related," Veera said. "Maybe Tulep was Gordon's dealer. Maybe they hung around the same drug parties."

Talk about long shots. "All we know is that Gordon has the weapons. And trouble's brewing between him and Big Sam." Did that spillover into the D.A.'s office?

"Maybe it's two different bad guys we're dealing with," Veera said. "The diner gunman versus the barbershop killer."

"What should we do?" Michael asked me.

"We stick together." No one was getting hurt on my watch. "We are our own best weapons."

"You got enough food in your fridge from your mom for all of us?" Veera asked.

"Plenty," I replied.

"No complaints from me," Veera rubbed her hands together.

My mom was a world class cook and regularly stuffed my refrigerator with gourmet meals so I wouldn't go hungry. She'd gone overboard on healthy snacks, too.

"Why would I want to jeopardize my friends?" James said. "Drop me off in Redondo. There's a hotel near Riviera Village."

"So you have no problem jeopardizing strangers?" I looked behind me. As long as we weren't being tailed, I could sneak James inside without incident. "It's already decided."

"That's right," Veera said. "I'm proud to be doing my part to get this maniac off the streets."

"I've been practicing for this since I was a teenager," Michael said. "This is like playing a real-life video game."

"I have a plan, which I'll unveil after we get some shut-eye," I said. I figured I'd finally have an honest-to-goodness plan in the morning. Fingers crossed.

Chapter Forty-One: Staying Alive

I motored down the Rosecrans exit. My gaze darted between the road ahead and my rear-view mirror. James sat in the backseat, head twisted around to watch the cars behind us. A silver sedan cruised two car lengths back. A sedan that had followed us onto the 405 when we first got on.

"How's the view back there, James?" I asked.

"Haven't decided yet."

I trusted him to know. I merged into the left-hand turn lane and onto the Coast Highway. The sedan made a right. The only car behind us now was an old Porsche.

"All clear," James said.

I relaxed my shoulders and my grip on the steering wheel.

"Thanks. All of you," James said. "For putting yourselves on the line for me."

"We've been bored up to our eyeballs, anyhow," Veera said. "What with our boss incommunicado. We got grit in our veins that doesn't allow us to just sit around. This is the on-the-job-training we need to keep us up-to-speed on criminal catching."

"It's our continuing education class," I said.

"This is beyond fantastic for me," Michael said. "There's nothing I like more than helping my sweetie and her first officer fight crime. And to play a co-starring role in protecting my best pal. Is that a good answer?"

"It's acceptable," James said. "As long as we bring the guy in quickly and no one else gets hurt."

"I like being called first officer," Veera said. "Like Batman and Robin. I always did have a thing for yellow capes."

"I was thinking of Mr. Spock," Michael said.

Her hands shot to her ears.

"It's the struggle between emotion and intellect that reminds me of Spock."

"Oh, okay." Veera lowered her hands. "Yeah, that's me. Always trying to keep my emotions in check while improving my intellect."

I drove the scenic route to my pad in Hermosa Beach, swinging down side streets before winding my way back up to the highway, making sure we stayed tail-free.

When we arrived, I hopped up my staircase to search for traces of intruders. The rest of the Save-James Team sat in the dark, parked near my driveway. My street hosted duplexes and triplexes galore. The attitude was energetic or laid-back, depending on the day of the week. But tonight, late as it was, things were kind of quiet. Lights were off in most of the neighboring units.

I unlocked my front door and slipped in, dead bolting it behind me. My ears sucked in all sounds as I listened for something out of the ordinary. I coasted through my pad, careful to step around trip wires and motion sensors. My place was rigged to make sure unwelcome visitors didn't enter unannounced. Yeah, it was overkill, but it came in handy. I texted Michael a thumb's up emoji and unlocked the door.

Within minutes, they'd hustled inside and joined me. We congregated in my bedroom, lights off, except for a small red night light. James had dragged in the files from his office.

"This is where you'll be sleeping," I told him.

He broke into a silly grin.

"With Michael," I added. "He'll be in here, too." Geez, we might've almost been an item one time, but come on. "Veera and I will take the living room."

"No way. I'm not sleeping in here," Michael said and turned to James. "No offense, bro."

"None taken," James said.

"I'll handle the first shift. I'll stay up to keep watch so nothing slips by us," Michael said.

"Good thinking," Veera said. "We'll take turns, so you can get some sleep time. The second shift's all mine. It'll give me a chance to snack on some goodies."

"I'll take the next shift," James said.

"You're the one we're protecting, remember?" I glided to the window at the top of my bed. I peeked outside.

"Maybe you should bury me in the yard," James said. "Until this is over."

"Good idea," I said. "I'll just stick a straw into your mouth that reaches the surface so you can breathe." I stole a glance over my shoulder. He wasn't smiling.

I pointed to the files. "Take a closer look, but use your penlight." I knew he carried one 'cause we'd used it before when we were creeping around at night. On a case, that is. "Be sure to get some shut-eye. We need to bring our A games tomorrow."

I stepped outside the room and opened a closet. I grabbed a couple of blankets and pillows. That's all I had for bedtime warmth, so I pulled out my coat. That would do for me. I handed the blankets to Veera and Michael. "I'll take the shift after Veera." I turned back to James. "Does anyone know where you are?"

He scratched his head. "Beckman thinks I'm still in my office. Haven't talk to anyone else."

"It's doubtful the shooter's coming after you tonight." That was so not true. The shooter had no timetable. "We should be good until the morning." Nothing was certain when it came to the criminal mind, but I'd be ready for him if he happened to drop in.

Chapter Forty-Two: No Can Do

I woke up to find myself on the floor, face down, nose squished against the back of my hand. I raised my head and blinked in the dimness. Michael sat across from me in my living room, his back against the wall, head lolling forward, eyes closed and breathing heavily.

"Oh no," I whispered. The day's events stampeded into my head. Michael wasn't supposed to be sleeping. I shot up. I'd stretched out near my front door to make sure no one could get in or out without my knowing. Unless they stepped over me. It seemed like a good spot last night.

A loud rumbling filled my ears and I nearly jumped out of my skin. It came from my futon. Veera lay sprawled on her back, deep in snoring slumber land. I debated checking on James. "Nah," I whispered. He should be okay.

I tiptoed to my kitchenette to check the back door. The deadbolt was in place. I shuffled back to the living room. I'd keep watch since I was wide awake. I was about to kneel next to Michael when a thump froze me in place. It came from my bedroom. In four long strides, I stood behind my door. I pressed an ear against the smooth wood surface. All was quiet.

I was about to walk away when there it was again: the thump. I turned the knob and opened the door in slow motion. The room was pitch. James must've taken my night light out. I stepped forward. Within seconds, I was pushed against the wall, but the next move was mine. I head-slammed into a firm surface. I heard a gasp and a solid landing on my bed. I pulled out a penlight just as James was getting to his feet.

"Don't you ever knock?" he said.

"I heard noises and wanted to make sure you were alone in here."

We spoke in fast whispers.

He ran a hand through his hair. "Sorry, I overreacted."

I relaxed my stance and put the penlight away. "Did you get any shut-eye at all?"

"Not with the racket out there."

Veera's snores practically shook the walls. I must've been sleepier than I'd thought. I'd managed to be out through most of her snore fest.

"When I couldn't sleep," James said, "I walked out and found Michael crashed, so I decided I'd do the watching."

"Things didn't go according to plan." I wasn't usually such a deep sleeper.

"They rarely do."

He sat cross legged on the floor and pulled an open file closer. He rested his back against my bed and there was the thump again. It was my bed frame hitting the wall when he leaned against it.

"I came out an hour ago to run something by Michael. I'd rather run it by you." He shoved the Tulep file closer to me. "Let's do a quick replay. Shot number one hit Beckman in the rear. It was a quick shot in a crowded diner."

"Was he aiming for Beckman's butt or did he just miss?" I sat next to him.

"Shot number two never happened, thanks to you, but shot number three could've hit me, if I hadn't ducked, also thanks to you, which could mean—"

"He's done playing around. He's likely to shoot to kill on his next try." My words faded into a shudder.

"Especially if he's behind the barbershop murder," James whispered. "All we've got besides a bare physical description of him and his accomplice is that he has guns. Where do people with guns go?"

"Gun stores and…a shooting range," I replied. Why didn't I think of that?

"He either practices to stay sharp or to learn to be sharp."

"There are about ten ranges in L.A. that I know of." I'd been to most of them. I also needed to stay sharp.

"Pick one."

I got to my feet and paced the floor. "I'd go to Live Oak in Newhall or the Shootster Club on Tujunga Canyon."

"Why those two?" he asked.

James moved in next to me and I stepped away. I couldn't think straight when he was so close. Even in the dark.

"They're close to L.A., but off the beaten trail. Everyone keeps to themselves. Low-key, informal. No instructors. The other ranges keep closer tabs." I looked up at him.

James broke into a slow grin. "Impressive. We'll divide up and pay both a visit tomorrow."

"No need to divide up. They're about twenty minutes apart."

James turned his back to me and lay on the bed. "See you in the morning."

I hesitated. My eyes rested on the Tulep file. Why didn't I see the killer come or go at the barbershop? Was there another hidden door somewhere?

"What is it?"

"Mind if I borrow the file?" I asked.

"You won't find anything." He turned his back to me.

I grabbed the file and turned to leave the room.

"Corrie?" he whispered.

"Yes?" I faced him again. That is, I faced his silhouette. I couldn't see much in the dark.

"Remember the birthday party we planned for Michael?"

"His twenty-first? That was a long time ago." Eons ago.

"Seems like yesterday to me," James said. "If you ever need someone, a friend or to talk—"

"Like we did tonight?"

"No, not like tonight," he said.

I waited, but that's all he had. I debated shining the penlight on his face, but I didn't. "Thanks."

I slipped outside, closing the door behind me. Another reminder that in the past, I might've felt a rush of whirly, mixed-up feelings about him and what he could be thinking. I might have even given in. But that was the old me. The new me had Michael. He was all I've ever wanted.

I tiptoed to the front door and reclaimed my spot. Veera's snoring hadn't let up. I lay back down, facing the front door, and kept the file by my side.

Why weren't we closer to finding the shooter? The guy entered a crowded restaurant with a specific target in mind, and he missed. He made his way to James' place, but didn't have a chance to try again. Then there was the long range shot on the lawn of the DA's office building. You think one of those avenues would've opened up a way to nab him. "Next time, you won't get away," I whispered. I could say that again. "You won't get away."

Chapter Forty-Three: It's Tricky

I hung on for dear life to the top of a wooden utility pole outside my duplex, knees and arms locked together, eyeing the faded strip of lawn below. The pole was taller than the surrounding trees and buildings. How was I going to get down? How had I even climbed up? I opened my mouth to yell, but a swarm of angry bees buzzed around my head. I waved a hand, but the buzzing wouldn't stop. It grew louder and closer.

"Want me to get that?"

My eyelids flew open. I blinked a few times. Veera stood over me, my cell phone in her hand. She'd changed into a gray V-neck T-shirt, black sweatpants and her usual beaming smile. She lifted her nose and sniffed the air.

"Love the smell of bacon in the morning," she said.

Why was I on the floor? I looked up at the battered dartboard on my living room wall. The one I used for shuriken practice. Below the dartboard lay a nicely folded blanket. I shot up.

"Whoa." Veera stepped back. "Don't you want to know who's calling? Your phone's been buzzing."

I really was losing it. I'd never slept through a vibrating phone call before. She held out my smartphone. I grabbed it and found two missed calls from an unknown number, and two voicemails. There was also a missed call from Big Sam. I pressed a few buttons and held the phone next to my ear.

"Been thinking about our talk last night," Roger said. "Your daddy did a lot for me and my boy. I want to make things right. Can we meet? Gotta get some stuff off my chest."

"Who is it?" Veera asked.

"Roger, the informant." Yesterday rushed into my head and rustled around, pushing out all other thoughts. I called him back. "Talk to me."

"Your daddy was good to me, but I don't do freebies, girl," he said.

"I'm not a trust fund child," I said. "Either you spill the beans because it's the right thing to do or forget it." I held my breath and wracked my brain for how to pay him. I was always low on cash. My rent and gas ate up most of my paycheck.

"I'm retired and social security's not—"

"You're going to have to trust me to pay you later." Another idea was brewing in my head. "I hear the owner of the diner where the shooting took place is offering a reward. It's all yours if your tip pans out."

Veera's mouth dropped open. She shut it and whispered, "I'll have to do some major sweet talking to Big Sam. On second thought, I'll get that GoFundMe campaign goin.'" She stepped over to the coffee table and picked up her phone.

A few beats passed.

"Word on the street says Tony Tulep knew the guy that knocked him off," Roger said. "Same guy shot the side mirror off Tulep's car a few days ago while Tulep was behind the wheel."

Maybe the gunman tortured his victims before he took them out. That would explain the shot to Beckman's rear end. "Go on."

"Word also says Tulep was fixing to leave for good after closing up shop last night."

Leaving the triggerman no choice. "What's the word say about the killer's identity?"

"I gave you all I got," Roger said. "If you get the reward, I'd appreciate my share."

"Deal." I disconnected and listened to Big Sam's voicemail.

"Come over, you hear?" he said. "Something bad's happened."

That could be anything from a surprise visit from the Department of Health to the shooter's holding a gun to his head.

"Veera, can you please call Big Sam and see what he wants?" I hurried toward my bedroom. The door was slightly ajar. I pushed it open wider. My bed looked like it had never been slept in. I stepped inside and Veera joined me.

"Michael's been busy," Veera whispered and closed the door. "He and James are whippin' up breakfast. A man's place is in the kitchen. That's what I always say."

"You're in a good mood this morning." I opened my closet.

"That's because Michael never woke me up so I got a real fitful sleep. He kept watch all night."

I was just grateful the night had been incident-free.

"I texted Big Sam and told him he needs to offer incentive to find the shooter, and if he did, it would be positive P.R. that would bring people runnin' back to his diner. He's thinking about it."

"Good," I said. "He'll be doing his part to make the streets of Santa Monica safer. Or at least Ocean Avenue."

"He's supposed to phone me in a few to tell me why he called you."

Minutes later, a green hoodie and matching jogger pants had replaced my black sweats.

"Looks like Big Sam left me a voicemail." Veera stared at her cell phone. She pushed a button and pressed the phone to her ear. "Wants us over at his place. Claims he has a new development to discuss in person. Think it'll be worth our time?"

"Nope."

"But we'll go, right? Because lurking behind that hotheaded exterior could be another clue. His videos were helpful."

"Big Sam's a good cook. He spends most of his time in the kitchen. He might just be your kind of guy."

"I don't care if that man slaves by the stove twenty-four-seven. I want nothing to do with him and his barrel of misbegotten machismo."

"Want to tell me about Ramsey?" I slid closer and spoke low.

Veera wiped off her smile and caught my stare. "We met through an online dating service a year ago. Let's just say he was six inches shorter than I expected, photo editing must be his superpower, and he had the gall to tell me I'd be really hot if I lost ten pounds."

"Oh, no," I said. Sounded just like Ramsey. The man had zero charm. "I hope you landed a solid punch."

"I couldn't. Remember what I said about not wanting to be the first Bankhead hauled into jail?" she said. "I told him I wasn't the one with self-esteem issues since I didn't need to create a phony online profile. And I didn't need to jump on a scale to know I look appealin'. Then I accidentally squished the front of his boat shoe with my stiletto heel when I left. I could still hear him yellin' when I got to my car."

"A heartwarming ending."

We exited my room and stepped into the kitchenette. Michael was flipping an omelet over the pan and James was setting the table. Both men wore grins and the clothes they'd slept in, which looked freshly pressed.

"Good morning, my lovely." Michael's gaze lit up when he saw me. He wrapped me in a hug and planted a kiss on my lips.

"It's about time you woke up," James said to me.

"Why is everyone so chipper?" I asked.

"We've got a whole day ahead of us," James said. "I've got a good feeling something's going to give."

Veera stood next to Michael until he gave her a taste of the omelet and a slice of bacon. "I'm in breakfast heaven," she said. "He's also got pancakes keeping warm in the oven."

Seemed like everyone slept well last night, but me.

"Can't believe I dozed right through my changin' of the guard time," Veera said, licking her fingers.

"Wish I could say I held up the fort." Michael opened the oven door and lifted out a plate filled with pancakes. "But I was out like a log, too. I'm making up for it now, though." He put down the plate and slapped James in the bicep. "Glad you're still with us, despite lack of help from your teammates."

I turned to Michael. "Did you iron your clothes?"

"Does it show?" he said. "Just wanted to look presentable. I made James presentable, too."

I avoided looking at James. "You're a sight for sore eyes," I told Michael. Bleary eyes, in my case.

We downed all the food in ten minutes and slipped inside my car in twenty.

"First stop, Big Sam's," I said.

"Drop me off at my place," James said. "I'll go to the shooting range."

"I'll come with," Michael said. "But we'll go to my crib instead. I'll grab my tranq gun."

"This isn't about target practice," James said. "We're going to find out if the shooter hangs out there."

"I've got a better idea," Michael said. "We'll go to Big Sam's and catch an Uber to my place. We'll take my car."

"Even better," I said. No sense going near James' pad right now.

Thirty minutes later, we arrived at Big Sam's. I parked the car down the block. Michael and James aimed toward Third Street to meet their driver, and Veera and I headed for the diner. Big Sam burst through the kitchen door the moment we arrived.

"Follow me." He stormed out the entrance.

"Good morning to you, too," Veera said to him and whispered to me. "That man has the manners of a mosquito."

We tailed him to the parking lot where he marched up to a Cadillac SUV. He stopped next to the passenger door and stared at us, face crinkled together like he was going to blow his top at any moment.

"Take a look," he said.

"It's a sweet ride," Veera said.

"You have a flat tire," I said, staring at the rear tire.

"Notice anything else?" he asked without budging.

I focused on the tire. A round hole bore into the wheel lip, about a quarter of an inch in diameter. "How long have you been parked here?"

"Nearly six hours," Big Sam said. "I arrive five a.m. sharp every day."

Veera moved in closer. "Looks like a bullet hole. When did you first notice it?"

"About an hour ago, when I came to get my lucky pen."

"Doesn't seem like it was that lucky for you today," she said.

"Oh yes it was. It might have been me that was shot instead of my rim."

I knelt close to the tire. "Not sure it's a bullet hole." I tried to stick my head near the area behind the tire to get a better look. A bullet hole might make a hole or at least a mark on the other side.

"Damn right it's a bullet hole," he shot back. "Think I don't know who's responsible?"

Veera and I swapped glances.

"You going to arrest him, Lawyer?" he looked at me.

"Lawyers don't have the authority to arrest anyone," I reminded him.

"Well, do something!" He shouted so loudly, a baby in a stroller across the street woke up crying. "Go get Gordy, you hear?" He dropped his voice to a whisper. "What are you waiting for?"

Veera slid to my side and we turned our backs to Big Sam.

"Does he sound deranged to you?" Veera asked me.

I stole a glance behind me. Big Sam was circling his neck around, eyes shut tight. I turned back to Veera. "Yep."

"I'd say he was working too hard lately and the loss of business didn't help."

"You could be right," I said. "Stay here and calm him down. I'm going to pay Gordon Joshua a visit, just in case."

"I don't think that's a good idea," Veera said.

"No worries. I'm ready for anything."

"I mean for me to stay." She moved in and whispered. "This man yanks my chain, and you know I don't do well if I'm yanked."

"You shouldn't be wearing a chain," I whispered back. "Focus on our mission, which is finding clues to get the shooter off the street. Find a way for Big Sam to help us with that. I'll do the same. Also…" A thought popped into my head that could be useful. "Can you take a photo of the shooter from Big Sam's video and send it to me?"

"You know I can."

"Thanks."

We turned around and looked at Big Sam.

"I'll squeeze something out of him that'll help," Veera whispered out of the side of her mouth.

I patted her arm. "I'll be back," I told Big Sam.

"That's right." He lifted his arm and pointed his finger in a back and forth dance with each of his words. "Bring that sucker in. I'd go myself except I'll kill the man."

"Someone would've heard the gunshot," Veera said to him. "Let's go ask around. You really should have security cameras in this lot."

"That sucker needs to be arrested."

Big Sam continued on his rant while I wound my way toward the pier. I slowed in Pacific Park first, gray sky overhead and the whisper of rolling waves down the hillside. A car puttered off, a cat edged along the grass, but no sign of the homeless souls I'd spoken to the day before yesterday. I jogged toward the pier.

Passing beneath the arched Santa Monica Pier sign, down the asphalt walkway and onto the wooden planks of the pier, I headed for a pale yellow building. Home to Gordon's restaurant. It was a breezy summer morning, which meant the pier was bustling.

Within minutes, I waited by the hostess stand. Breakfast diners scattered throughout the restaurant. The place did its best not to channel the breezy, beachy vibe of Big Sam's Diner. GJ's was antique-y with a supper club ambiance; white tablecloths, old time Santa Monica photos on the walls and diamond-tufted booths.

"He's in the back," the hostess told me. "I'm surprised Big Sam didn't come."

"Were you expecting him?"

"Yes," she said. "He called about thirty minutes ago and Gordon invited him over."

The rivalry grew stranger by the minute.

"Big Sam sent me instead," I said.

"Why don't you go in the back and let him know?"

"Uh, sure."

"Don't worry. He'll be happy to see you."

Why did I have the feeling I'd be the last person Gordon wanted to see?

Chapter Forty-Four: Fishin' in the Dark

I swept past the servers and the busboys. No sign of Gordon. I made a sharp left down a hallway and stopped in front of a closed door. I expected the security guy who looked like a bouncer to appear, which meant I needed to explain my presence. I was in no mood to explain. I caught my breath. There he was. The muscular bouncer stood at the end of the hall, staring into the dining area. I turned the knob and stepped into Gordon's office.

His back was to me, but he swiveled around moments after my entry. His eyes popped and his brows fell.

"Get out," he said.

"You're going to want to hear what I have to say." I sat in a corner chair to show I meant business.

"Why is that?"

A Bloody Mary waited patiently on his desk. The computer screen was open to a page filled with recipes.

"Big Sam's about to call the cops about another murder attempt, and guess who he's going to blame?"

"You're not very good at playing the role of a private detective."

"That's investigator, and I'm investigating all angles, as a lawyer, that is."

"If you were any good in either capacity, you'd know what was really going on behind the scenes."

I didn't like to admit it, but he was right. Why didn't I investigate the background of these two chefs? My stomach filled with burning cinders.

"My focus isn't on you or Sam," I said. "I'm trying to keep members of a

D.A. team alive. You two are an unwelcome distraction."

"This is no charade. It is a very serious matter." He got to his feet and faced me. I rose a moment later.

There was a hard rap on his door.

"Go away," he said.

Footsteps clipped down the hallway.

"All I did was sabotage Big Sam's supply of eggs, so they were a little less fresh. I know he fooled around with my reservations, but that does not mean I tried to kill him. You think I want to face prison on his account? The man's nothing more than a short order cook. He belongs behind a wiener stand. The fool said my flourless chocolate dream cake tasted like baked pill bugs." He lifted his chin and turned around. "That still hurts."

The wheels in my head turned in rapid motion. "Your restaurant was full the day after the shooting. That was unusual. You set up a triggerman to eliminate the competition." As far-out as that was, I needed to lay it to rest.

"I would never. That's not my style." He leaned his torso toward me. "I live to compete. Competition encourages improvement."

My cell phone buzzed. Michael sent this text,

Ended up going to James' office instead. We called the two gun ranges. No leads yet.

I turned back to Gordon. "Okay, I'll get to the point. Did you shoot out Big Sam's tire today?"

Gordon pulled open the bottom drawer of his desk. He held up a pistol. "This hasn't been shot in over a month. Last shot was at a range. Besides..." He put the gun back. "...I wouldn't waste a bullet on that artery-clogging cook's jalopy," Gordon said. "Why isn't he here, anyway?"

"Did he say he was coming by?" I asked.

He slammed a hand on the desk. "The only reason I gave him the time of day was because the lying sack of rotten potatoes said he owed me an apology." He jumped to his feet and waved his arms. "Get out!"

I stood. "Maybe you should come with me and lay this feud to rest. Big Sam's having a rough time and could use the support of a friend. And..." Here's where I hoped his ego would jump in. "...since you're a gun expert, you can help determine if a bullet made the hole in the rim of his tire."

"Out." He marched toward me and shooed me away. "And don't come back!" He slammed the door.

"Wait!" I rapped on his door. "I have another question about guns." My heartbeat quickened as I texted Veera.

Please send the photo of the shooter from the video cam.

I spoke through the door again. "Only you can answer this particular question." I had no more tricks up my sleeves.

I trekked down the hallway when his door creaked open. I hurried back. "What?" he asked.

"You said you hadn't fired your gun in a month. What shooting range did you go to?"

He opened the door a bit wider. "Why?"

"Because you may be able to point me in the direction of the real shooter." He left the door and sat behind his desk. I slid inside.

"Malibu Tactical Training. It's the only range I use. Very hush-hush and it's by invitation only. Very few people know about it."

"I've heard of MTT. It's off Topanga. How do you get invited?"

"By another member, of course," he said. "I can't tell you who invited me. A big Hollywood name that most people would never associate with guns."

My phone chimed to indicate a text. It was from Veera. I held my phone out to Gordon. "The picture's not great. Any chance you've seen this guy at MTT?"

Gordon took my phone and peered at the image.

"About six foot one, lean," I said. "Hollow cheeks, hooked nose and possibly missing the top joint of his left index finger."

"Good thing it's not the middle finger. That won't help if you're trying to give someone a really effective bird, now will it?" He chuckled a moment and turned serious. "What do you mean 'possibly' missing the joint? Either he is or he isn't."

My temperature was rising. This was going nowhere fast. I stood. "He probably wears a prosthetic, meaning you wouldn't know if—"

"Wrong." Gordon slid my phone across the desk. "This man does not wear a prosthetic when he's shooting a gun."

I froze. "How do you know?"

"It makes sense," he said. "The silicone fingertip gets in his way. That's what he told me, anyhow."

"In whose way?" I stood a foot away from Gordon.

"No clue. The whole point of being a member of the club is anonymity. Names are on a need to know basis. There are a ton of high-profile members."

"Look…" I bent over until our faces were inches apart. It wasn't pretty. "I'm only interested in one member. This man is wanted by the police for attempted murder. Two counts. And possibly first-degree murder and maybe more. I need his name." I straightened up. "You're obviously a serious, but honorable gun user who has great respect for the proper use of weaponry. Am I right?"

"Of course."

"Then you'll agree we need to get trigger-happy lunatic killers off the street."

Gordon pulled out his cell phone and motioned for me to sit.

"Hello, Gordon Joshua, here. Yes, yes, I'm fine and all that. Look, there's a man that was at the range last week. A fairly decent shot." A beat or two went by. "About forty-five or so. Tall, rail-thin. I noticed he was missing the tippy top of his left index finger, yet his shooting was barely affected. I have a friend…" he rolled his eyes skyward. "…sitting with me and the poor thing just lost the tip of her index finger."

I held my middle finger out to him. It may have looked like I was giving him the bird, but it was to emphasize a point. That's all, I swear.

"I'd like to get some tips from this gent as to prosthetics. May I have his name please?"

Thirty seconds went by with Gordon listening before he finally spoke up. "Okay, then, thank you."

I stood. "Did you get—"

He held up a hand. "Just as I thought. He doesn't wear the fake fingertip when he's on the range. His name is Paul."

"Paul what?"

"Just Paul. The twit on the phone explained the policy of not providing full names, blah, blah. He needed to obtain Paul's permission prior."

That stinks. I was so close. "Thanks." I turned on my heel and made my exit. I pulled out my phone and called Abby. I gave her an update.

"We're going to need more to obtain a search warrant at MTT," she said. "I'll make some calls."

She disconnected and I headed for Gordon's hostess. I had a little something to run by her.

Chapter Forty-Five: Back to Life

The hostess at Gordon Joshua's restaurant was having a tete-a-tete with a server when I waved her over.

"I just left Gordon," I said. "I heard that he visited Big Sam this morning. That was nice of him." I was going full speed ahead with the bait and trap lines today.

"Is that where he went?" She planted a hand on her hip. "I was wondering. I called his cell, but he didn't pick up."

"But he wasn't gone very long, was he? About…"

"Three minutes, tops."

Not enough time to visit Sam's parking lot, shoot a bullet and come back.

"Hope they kiss and make-up," I said. "There's a lot of tension between those two when they could be friends." I meant that last part. I headed back to the diner.

***

Veera waited outside. "Big Sam's hiding out in his office. Which is fine with me."

"What did you say to him?"

"He's not hiding out for my sake. He claims someone tried to run him down when he crossed the street. I didn't see anything. I was examining the hole in the tire."

"The more I think about it," I said. "That wasn't a bullet hole in the tire rim. More like a bolt or a screw got in there. Let's go have a chat with him."

I knocked on Big Sam's office door. "It's me, Corrie."

"How do I know this isn't a trick so Gordy can have another go at me?"

"He's not here," I said. "I was with him at his eatery the whole time."

The door swung open. Big Sam stood there, face drawn, eyes all over Veera before he turned to me. "What're you talking about? Of course he could've done it. By sending one of his flunkies to do the job. And why are you two wearing those jogging outfits?"

"We work twenty-four-seven. These are our hunting down criminal joggers," Veera said. "We don't have the time to change for you." Veera's head cocked and her eyes squinted.

"Where did you go while I was gone?" I asked Big Sam.

"Figured fresh air would do me good." He huffed. "Tried to cross the street and I was nearly run over in front of my own establishment."

"Any witnesses?" Veera asked.

"Plenty." He opened the door wider and stepped aside. We walked into a compact office with floating shelves displaying trophies and framed photos of Big Sam wearing a chef's uniform. "There's a street full of witnesses out there."

"Did you call the police?" I asked.

"I don't need any more bad publicity. That's why I hired you two."

"Were you jaywalking?" I asked. Ocean Avenue teemed with traffic almost all the time.

"He sure was. I saw that much," Veera said. "Only fifteen yards farther and he could've crossed safely using the crosswalk."

"Did you get a look at the driver?" I asked.

"Looked like the guy Gordy uses as security for his place," Big Sam said. "Did you see him at the restaurant?"

"Yes, I did."

"Did you actually see him behind the wheel?" Veera asked.

"Didn't need to," Big Sam said.

"Oh yes, you—" Veera started.

"I know what kind of vehicle he drives," Big Sam said. "It's a retired, unmarked police car, complete with tinted windows, and front and rear stabilizer bars. How often do you see one of them try to run you over?"

Veera and I swapped glances.

"A Crown Vic Police Interceptor?" I asked.

"That's what I said."

"Doesn't look like you were hurt," Veera said.

"I was shaken and stirred up. The only reason he missed was because I dove onto the sidewalk in the nick of time. Lucky I'm fit as a fiddle."

"Can you give me names of the witnesses?" I said.

"I was knocked off my feet," Big Sam said. "You think I took a poll while I was laying there fighting for my life? That's your job."

"Your staff see anything?" Veera asked.

Big Sam rubbed the back of his neck. "Probably got whiplash from diving onto the pavement." He locked stares with Veera. "No, they didn't. That's because they were concentrating on doing their jobs."

We looked out the door at the staff. They were either chatting on their smartphones or staring out the front window.

"I'll go ask." Veera left us alone.

Big Sam slumped into his chair.

"You need to make up with Gordon," I said.

"After what he's done to me?"

"You mean what you did to each other," I said. "He's got a lead on the shooter, but he'll need help." I told him about the MTT club and Paul.

Big Sam rose to his feet. "In the name of all that's good and right and tasty, I'll do it. We'll work together and find out Paul's last name."

"Great, here's the plan."

Ten minutes later I joined Veera outside.

"Either everybody's blind or Big Sam made a big deal over nothing," Veera said. "One witness saw him run across the street and trip and fall when he jumped over the curb. She didn't see any car come close to hitting him. Maybe he got knocked on the head and imagined it." She clicked her tongue. "Did you look at him? Not a scratch, rip or cut on him."

"His palms were scraped like he'd try to break his fall," I said. "Something happened, but was it connected to the shooting or Gordon? Or even a car?

I doubt it."

"I'll see if I can round-up more witnesses."

"Never mind about that," I said. "Have you ever been a referee?"

"No, but doesn't mean I can't do it." She rummaged around in her shoulder bag and pulled out a whistle. "Can I use this?"

"You might have to," I said.

"Who am I reffing?"

"Big Sam and Gordon," I said. "You're going to go with them to a private shooting range and get a name. It needs to be on the down-low."

"I can do that. This could be the turning point in what hasn't been a beautiful friendship for those two." Veera rubbed her hands together and pulled on a pair of aviators. Big Sam joined us outside.

"Here comes our ride." He pointed to a four door Jaguar pulling in front of the diner, Gordon at the wheel. Big Sam put out his elbow for Veera. "You ready?"

She shooed the elbow away. "I got dibs on the front seat." She turned to me.

"Where are you going, C?"

"To visit a higher source."

"Never hurts to ask for some help from above," Big Sam said.

"Amen," I said.

Chapter Forty-Six: Handle with Care

My cell phone vibrated as I motored to the D.A.'s office. It was Michael.

"We called a few more ranges," he said. "And still got nada. No one fitting the shooter's description. What'll we do? We're driving in the dark without head or tail lights."

"Veera's checking out a private gun club," I said. "We're following a tip from Gordon Joshua. He may be able to get us a name."

"The pistol packing celebrity chef?" Michael asked. "Never thought he'd come through."

"He hasn't yet," I said. "It started with a false accusation and an active imagination on Big Sam's part. Please ask James if we can take a look at Beckman's file on Tulep."

"Okay." He repeated my request to James. "He's on his way to see Beckman," Michael said. "Would his file be any different?"

"We'll see."

***

I parked on a side street and used trees, shrubs and shadows to sneak to the D.A.'s office. I even crouched the whole way to keep out of eye level scanning. Just in case the triggerman lurked close by. It took me a little longer to get to my destination, but at least I'd make it alive. Not that I was his target, but it was good practice. I finally slipped into the lobby of the building and texted Michael of my arrival, just as my phone rang. It was

Veera.

"Find anything?" I asked.

"You mean before or after I knocked a few heads together?" she asked. "Once I got everyone to simmer down and play nice, we got ourselves a name. I'd never believe it if I didn't hear it with my own ears, but Big Sam sweet-talked one of the old ladies running the place. Her late husband co-founded the club and she's got a soft spot for veterans. Sam's a navy man, which got him on her good side. Did you know he went straight to culinary school after his last tour?"

The tides had shifted in Veera's assessment of Big Sam. "Sounds like he's a decent guy."

"I would've argued with you yesterday, but I can't disagree now. Gordon Joshua's decent, too. With excellent British manners. They're talkin' like old chums."

Michael held open the door, and I breezed past the lobby and behind the scenes.

"Sam's also a Coast Guard volunteer," Veera said. "Can't argue with that either. And he agreed to put up a thousand dollar reward."

"Sweet, but…did you forget something?" I asked as Michael and I headed for the elevator.

"I think I covered it all," Veera said.

"Uh, what's the last name?"

"Oh, that's right. I got two Paul possibilities. I passed them along to James to check out. Big Sam's dropping me off at the D.A.'s office." Veera giggled. "Talk soon." She disconnected.

"Whose name?" Michael said. "Do we know who the gunman is?"

"Not yet," I said. "But we're getting closer."

***

Thirty minutes later, I'd hunkered down behind James' desk, reviewing Beckman's file on Tulep. Michael pulled a chair next to mine. James had dropped off the file and returned to Beckman's office. This file was thicker and disorganized. Michael and I divided the contents and pored through the paperwork.

"The teen that's on life support," I said. "See if you can find a name."

"Looks like Beckman collected every little detail about the case," Michael said. "Except that."

James joined us minutes later. "Slight bump in the road. Anyone hear from Ramsey? After we left him at the bar last night, he vanished."

"Wasn't that the reason why he staged his own kidnapping?" Michael asked. "To disappear into the night?"

James shoved his hands on his hips. "Beckman says he's fallen off his radar."

"He tracks him?" I asked, surprised Ramsey would agree to being watched, even by his boss.

"We're both on Beckman's tracker," James said. "The tracker showed Ramsey still at the bar."

"So? He left his phone there," Michael said.

"Detective Rosewater was notified early this morning," James said. "She sent an officer to the bar. The phone was located in the trash receptacle. A witness saw Ramsey take off with a guy."

I stiffened. "Description?"

"Male, Caucasian, and a baseball cap," James said. "Dressed in black coveralls."

Was it the gunman? "Anything else?"

"The witness admitted to being a little tipsy," James said. "Ramsey's SUV is still parked downstairs."

"The staged kidnapping turned real," Michael said.

"If anyone can handle it, Ramsey can," I said. He had plenty of tricks up his sleeve. No way to know if he was playing games or not. I sifted through the file, while James looked up the two names Veera had provided.

The minutes ticked quietly until Veera texted that she was downstairs. James buzzed her inside and she joined us.

"Find out anything?" Veera said when she laid eyes on James.

"First Paul name belongs to a Hollywood stuntman. He's been overseas working on a movie for the past few months," James said. "And he's got the whole finger missing, not just the tip."

"What about the guy with the long last name?" Veera asked.

"Paul Salamagucci," James said. "Just checking him out."

"It means, say hello to Gucci," Michael said. "In Farsi."

We all turned to Michael.

"What?" he said. "It does. One day you're going to see me on *Jeopardy* beating the pants off all the big winners who came before me. It's not bragging, if it's the truth."

"Is that why you're soaking up all the trivia you can?" Veera asked.

"No, but I wouldn't rule it out," Michael said.

"Concentrate, people," James said.

"Wait," I said. "There was an Italian surname in the file." My fingers flicked through the pages.

"Beckman's file?" James asked. "I don't recall any witnesses, victims, or anyone with that name."

My mind raced faster than Secretariat approaching the finish line. "Where did I see it? Not in any court documents..."

"I'll do an internet search," James said.

"Veera can you verify you've got the right name?" I asked.

"I'll call." She pressed a button on her phone.

The answer was in my head. I just needed to wade through the muck to yank it out.

"He's checkin'," Veera said a minute later.

James's phone chimed. He sat up in his chair and stared at his phone. He lifted his eyes to mine. I saw a hardness that wasn't there a minute ago. He stood. "I'll be back."

"Who texted you?" I asked.

He tilted the phone sideways so I couldn't see the screen. "It was...Beckman."

Why the hesitation? James never hesitated. "What does he want?"

"Another meeting." James stood.

"I'll come with," Michael said.

Michael must've noticed the change, too.

"Me, too." I stood and stretched out my arms. "Could use a break."

"No," he said. "It's an internal affair."

Michael walked with James to the door. "I'll hang outside."

I followed them.

"I don't need a nursemaid." James blocked the threshold. "Look, I said I'll be…back."

Michael and I stopped in our tracks.

"You're staying in the building, right?" Michael asked.

"Yep." James said, eyes fixed on me.

What was he trying to say? I failed telepathy class every time. I stepped closer.

"Why the secrecy?" I whispered.

Michael's glances shot between us. "Is something wrong?"

"Nothing's wrong." James spoke quietly through gritted teeth like he was trying to mash his words to a pulp. He turned his face and glanced over his shoulder at me. "Charge up my phone later, okay?"

"Didn't you take it with you?" I asked.

"Personal phone's in the drawer. I'm taking my work phone." He held it up in one hand. "Don't forget." He turned and stomped away.

"He must be under a lot of pressure," Michael said. "That was strange."

Veera's phone buzzed. "It's Sam."

Michael and I swapped stares.

"You're on a single name basis with him?" I asked.

"It's hard to call a man 'Big' when I'm bigger than he will ever hope to be," she said and answered the call. "You're on speaker so Corrie can hear."

"I've got to hand it to you," Big Sam said. "How'd you know Thelma gave me the wrong name?"

Veera's eyes widened and I slid closer.

"What's the right name?" I asked.

"She got mixed up with another member. The guy with the missing tip of the index finger is Paul Cuccione. Long-time Club member in good standing. Gulf War vet, an accountant with his own firm…"

"At least she got the Paul part right," Michael whispered.

"Any family?" I asked.

"Didn't say. Should I find out?"

"Yes, please and fast," I said. "He could be the man that—"

"Shot up my place?" he said.

"Do you mean the bullet hole in the back wall?" I said.

"I want him arrested," Big Sam said.

"Working on it." Veera disconnected and turned to me. "Let's look up Cuccione."

I slid behind James' computer, flanked by Michael and Veera.

"That name'll be a cinch to find," Veera said.

"Wait for it..." I said, pounding the keys. "Bingo. Paul Cuccione, sixteen years old?"

"That can't be him," Michael said. "Too young to be a war vet."

"There must be more..." I pounded the keyboard again. "Bingo, part two. That was Paul Junior. Here's his father."

Veera peered closer at the screen. "Doesn't say much about Senior."

"Guys." Michael had moved to the window. "I know the answer. It's right in front of me."

Veera clicked her tongue. "Did you read what I just read?"

"The car that's a pick-up," Michael said.

"Junior's the teen on life support." I caught my breath. "From a drug overdose. That could explain—"

"Why the church witness got mixed up," Michael turned to me. "It's like a truck, but it isn't."

"Motive?" I told Veera and flipped around to face Michael. "What truck?" In two steps, Michael and I stood staring out the window.

"A Chevy El Camino," Michael said. "I should've known. That's the car Alma saw Bianca get into after leaving the sedan in front of the D.A.'s building."

Veera sank into my seat and took over the Cuccione search.

"How did you figure it out?" I asked.

"One just drove by. Here." He held his phone screen. We peered at an internet photo of a powder blue Chevy El Camino, circa 1986.

"The one that drove by," I said. "What color?"

"Silver with a black panel at the bot... oh my—"

"We'll be right back," I told Veera. "Meanwhile, find everything out about Paul senior."

Michael and I rocketed down the hall to Beckman's office. The door was open and the office empty. I ran up to a D.A. type walking by.

"Beckman? Seen him?" I asked.

"About twenty minutes ago. Left in a hurry." The guy pointed to the stairwell. "Beckman never takes the stairs."

"What about D.A. Zachary?" I asked.

The guy shrugged. "He ran down the hall five minutes ago."

It was our turn to run. Michael and I landed on the pavement outside and raced to the back of the building.

We sprinted to the top of a driveway leading to the underground parking. A metal gate prevented entry by anyone without a key card. A security camera pointed toward us.

"It's no use. We're too late." Michael faced me. "The El Camino was driving away from here when I spotted it. Why would James agree to meet Cuccione without telling us?"

"He must've threatened him." That was dumb of James. "Or threatened the whole team."

"Why wouldn't he let you see the text?"

"Trying to keep us out of harm's way." I turned and sprinted back the way we came. "Idiot."

"He must've hacked into James' cell." Michael kept up with me.

"Or sourced his number." Ramsey would've given it away to save his own hide.

"What are we going to do?" Michael ran by my side.

"I need to see James' other phone."

Chapter Forty-Seven: On the Run

A minute later, I flung open James' desk drawers. And there it was. His cell phone.

"Not much about Paul Senior on the Internet, but Sam called back." Veera speed-talked an update. "Paul has a sister. Guess what her name is?"

I grabbed the phone. "Bianca."

"How did you know?"

"I didn't until now," I said.

I handed James' smart phone to Michael to unlock. Fingers crossed that there'd be a location finder leading to James. I gave Veera the run-down.

"We gotta get moving. How are we going to find James?" Veera asked.

"By locating Paul Senior." I stepped back and yanked out my cell phone. I called Eva at Arnold's Dental. It was nearly closing time. "Pick-up, pick-up…"

"Here we go." Veera read another Internet news source. "Cuccione Junior's been hospitalized for four weeks. He overdosed on opioids laced with Fentonyl. That's the motive right there. Revenge, just like you said."

"Pick up, pick up…" I said.

"Unlocking tool is in place." Michael sat on a stool, hunched over the phone in his hand.

"Doctor Arnold's office," Eva answered.

"This is Corrie Locke with the undercover traffic police. Is Bianca there?"

"She bailed again," she said. "Guess it's okay since she's—"

"At the hospital?" I asked.

"No," Eva said.

My heart sank. Was I on the right path? "I read about—"

"Poor Paulie? It's so sad. He's been in a coma. And Paul is such a good dad. He and Bianca went rock hunting together, to find pieces Paulie might like."

I perked up. "They're into geology?"

"No, but Paulie is. Or was. They take rocks to the hospital, hoping Paulie'll wake up if he senses he's in rock heaven. Paul's not a bad driver, is he?"

"No," I said. "He'll get a… commendation." Oh, brother. "Where'd they go rock hunting?"

"Golden Cove Park."

My heart nearly leapt out of my chest. "Golden Cove in Palos Verdes?" I knew P.V. like I knew Paul Cuccione was the gunman. I grew up not far from the park. It was rocky, desolate and the perfect spot to execute a bad deed without an audience.

"That's the place. Good luck arresting her. She can be a handful."

I disconnected and sent a text to Roger, the informant.

How about a ride in the chopper? Be there in thirty minutes.

He answered seconds later.

Runway 21. Does this mean I'm getting paid?

Yes!

I crossed my heart and hoped to die if I didn't pay Roger something. I inwardly shook my head and pictured Big Sam's reward money.

"I'm in the phone." Michael handed me James' phone.

I scrolled through his texts.

"What are we looking for?" he asked.

"Location Tracker." I scrolled some more.

"Shouldn't I call the police?" Michael asked.

"I'll text Abby. Let's go." I dropped the phone in my purse and shot up. I'd take the phone up again once we got to the car. I dove for the door, Michael and Veera close behind.

We scampered out and down the hallway, heading for the stairs. I sent the text while we dashed down the stairwell, telling Abby to meet me at Golden Cove Park in Palos Verdes.

"How are we going to find where he's at?" Veera asked.

"I know where he's headed." At least I think I did. I said a little prayer and pulled out my car keys.

Chapter Forty-Eight: In the Air Tonight

I sank behind the wheel and Michael rode shotgun. Veera took over the backseat and I powered up the engine. My phone chimed. It was a text from Abby. I read it out loud. *Why Palos Verdes? I can't reach Beckman. Where is he?*

"Someone's behind the times," I said

"All of the Beckman team were taken?" Veera said. "It'll be hard to kill three guys at once."

I texted Abby back:

Shooter transporting three hostages to P.V. Paul Cuccione, Senior is our prime suspect.

"Abby'll meet us at the park." She wouldn't miss this for the world. I slammed the gas pedal and peeled out of my parking spot.

"That's a relief," Michael said. "Taking traffic into consideration…assuming they stop at lights…" He tossed me a glance. "…they should be ten minutes away from the 405 freeway right about now."

"In my purse," I said, rolling through a stop sign. "Get James' phone. See if there's location tracking."

Another text rolled in from Abby. Michael grabbed my phone and read the text out loud:

Cuccione has no record. I need hard evidence before I go anywhere. What have you got?

"Is an industrial strength hunch not good enough for you?" I said out loud. "You can quote me. And text her back a description of the El Camino. The more details, the better. Throw in an expletive, too, just because."

Michael shot off the text and turned back to James' phone.

I zipped past a lumbering Acura.

"Whoa, whoa." Michael gripped the dash. "We need our limbs in working order when we get there…"

I didn't need to look at him to know his hair would be graying right before my eyes.

"No worries. I won't be driving the whole way."

Michael laid his head back. "Best news ever." He snapped his chin up. "Only because of the pressure you're under." He stared at James' phone. "No tracking for Beckman."

Why did James ask me to charge his phone? I hit the brake at a stop sign leading to Venice Boulevard. Two seconds later I pounded the gas pedal and made a sharp right, cutting off a cement truck behind me. The driver leaned on the horn.

"Just say the word and I'll take the wheel," Michael said.

He'd get us there, alright, but way behind schedule. Slamming the gas pedal wasn't in his nature.

"The freeway will be jammed," he said. "That'll slow him down."

"So will the surface streets," Veera said.

"We don't need to worry about slowdowns." I sped past a dozing Lexus. "We're going to get there first."

"Don't forget the story of the tortoise and the hare," Michael said.

"That turtle was on steroids," Veera said. "Had to be."

"That's not true," I said. "The race was fixed."

"You mean the bunny was paid off?" Veera asked.

"Guys," Michael said. "I just want to get there in one piece." He scrolled through the cell phone. "Rescues go more smoothly that way."

"We will." I squeezed his leg. "And we'll still get there first." I zipped beneath the 405. "We're going to travel by air. We should arrive at the park in twenty minutes or less."

"You got a lead on a plane?" Veera said. "At LAX?"

"Santa Monica airport." I weaved in and out of slowing traffic. Michael's white knuckles gripped the dashboard again. "In a helicopter." I reminded them about Roger's chopper service.

"I'm stoked," Michael said. "But since we'll be facing a trigger-happy killer soon, shouldn't we come up with a strategy?"

"We'll hide out and ambush him," Veera said.

"That's what we'll do. We finally have our plan," I said. Golden Cove Park was all rocks and sand and sea. I caught my breath. And it had the perfect spot to hide the bodies.

***

We parked in the airport lot and scuttled to Runway 21. But not before I popped open my trunk and reached into a duffel bag. I extracted a few necessities for managing criminals. The thrum of plane engines eclipsed all lesser sounds. The ground rumbled beneath my sneakers. I spotted Roger leaning against a red helicopter on a helipad. He waved us over.

Minutes later, we sat buckled up inside a copter built for four. I rode upfront and gave Roger the nutshell version of where we were headed. And what we'd discovered.

"Man, I can see shooting up the drug dealer." Roger roared up the engine, starting up a low whine and the slow whirl of the propellers. "But going after district attorneys? Wrong play, man."

"The location finder," Michael shouted. "In James' cell. I found it. I know where they are. Nearing LAX."

"Door-to-door, this should take ten, twelve minutes," Roger said. The propellers whirred faster. "No sig alerts, no traffic jams. No worries about slow pokes in the fast lane. We'll soar above it all."

"This is going to be fun." Veera grinned big-time.

We thundered skyward and banked sideways toward the ocean.

"Glad this copter's not vertically challenged." Michael slapped his knee and grinned.

I grinned back.

"Steady now." Roger banked the chopper over the shoreline. Waves sparkled beneath a full moon.

At 120 miles an hour and 400 feet high, the sandy beaches and deep blue waves rushed beneath us. We coasted past Marina Del Rey, dipping low over LAX to avoid the flight path of jets taking off.

"Point Vicente Lighthouse has a helipad," I said.

"I'm landing at Torrance airport," Roger said. "You can catch a ride from there."

"No time," I said. "Veera, get Big Sam on the line. Tell him to call his Coast Guard buddies and say we'll be making an emergency landing at Point Vicente."

She pulled out her phone.

"I don't do daredevilish stunts anymore," Roger said.

"Since when did you become upstanding?" I asked.

"You just never saw the real me."

"The landing pad is near the cliffs," I said. "Far from the parking lot and people. You'll be up again before anyone notices."

"Nothing doing. Coast Guard members live at Point Vicente from what I recall. They'll come running out."

"It's not a choice." I pulled out a pistol from my purse and pointed it at him. "You can say you were held at gunpoint. That'll keep you in the clear."

"Whoa. Doesn't mean you really have to pull a gun on him," Michael said. "I'm sure he'd be willing to play along."

"I'm not playing," Roger said.

"Neither am I," I said. But I really was. I wasn't shooting anyone. And if we were intercepted by the cops, I was ready to take the blame. I didn't want Roger involved.

"Sam's making the call." Veera disconnected.

"Isn't there any place else for us to land?" Michael asked.

"That's the nearest helipad. It's where the Coast Guard practices helicopter rescue training," I said.

"But Corrie," Michael said. "What if we're wrong and Cuccione doesn't—"

"We're not wrong." I gulped.

"Why are you doing this?" Roger asked me. "You're going to be in big trouble."

"It's what friends do."

"You're paying me for the ride?" He coasted downward.

"You take installments, right?"

"We're going to need bail money, too," Roger added.

"Oh, man," Michael sat back in his seat.

"Our GoFundMe is on the rise," Veera said. "So far, we've raised $3,042.61. Wait 'til I add that we're on a rescue mission. I'm inserting live footage on Facebook. That'll bring in more contributions."

"What if the shooter's on Facebook?" Michael asked.

Michael was losing it.

"He shouldn't be on social media while he's driving his hostages," Veera said.

I turned to Roger. "You'll be a hero to the D.A.'s office when this is all over."

"Just what I've always wanted. That's assuming you're able to save the day," Roger said.

"Piece of cake," I mumbled. If that cake were made of sticks of dynamite...that were lit. Oh dear.

Chapter Forty-Nine: Rocky Landing

"They're off the freeway." Michael looked down at the phone. "On Hawthorne. That means…"

"They'll be at Golden Cove in twenty minutes," I said.

"Sam wants to talk." Veera handed me her phone.

I pressed it to my ear. "Can we land at Point Vicente?"

"Not unless you want company," he said. "The place is swarming with Coast Guard personnel. You'll be immobilized before you hit the ground."

My heart sank. We didn't have time to land anywhere else.

"But one of the guys gave me a tip," Sam lowered his voice.

I could barely hear his next words. "What?" I shouted. "Speak louder." My pistol still pointed at Roger.

The next words tumbled out in a broken stream. "Park…go…co." And the phone went dead. I texted him,

What's the tip?

"Nearing Point Vicente," Roger said. "Put that thing away and tell me where I'm landing."

"The lighthouse is a five-minute walk from Golden Cove Park." Michael was staring at the map on his phone. "And that's not counting walking the trail down in the dark, which'll be another five to ten. Will we get there in time?"

Michael grew up in Palos Verdes, too. He knew the terrain even better than I did.

"Can we park in the lot at Golden Cove Park?" I asked.

"Too many trees and too narrow a landing space," Michael said.

Big Sam's text rolled in,

Golf course landing

Yes! "Change in plans," I said. "We'll be landing at Royal Palms Golf Course." The course was next to a hotel where Dad and I had investigated a series of burglaries. "On the hole nearest to Golden Cove parking lot." Back in business again. I put away my pistol.

Ten minutes later, the chopper hovered over a putting green. The whirling blades kicked up a mini sandstorm, thanks to a nearby bunker.

"Hey." Roger leaned over to me. "Pay no attention to what you see when you leave here. Don't come back no matter what." He straightened. "Good luck. Give Ramsey a kick in the pants from me."

I grabbed my handbag. I was armed and bound to be dangerous. The moment the chopper hit the ground, Michael, Veera and I stumbled outside. We landed in a crouch and jogged our way toward the parking lot. The thunder of the copter's propeller rattled my eardrums. The chopper had to have been noticed by now, not just by the hotel next door, but the houses on the hill across the road. I expected the copter to fly straight up, but the propeller slowed, the hum steadied and fizzled. I gazed over my shoulder. Bright flashing lights cast an eerie glow around the copter. Roger hopped out, stumbled and dropped to the ground. I slowed.

"What's he doing?" Michael asked.

"Keep going. He'll be fine," I muttered and picked up speed again, remembering Roger's words. No time to go back. We were on a mission.

When we reached the top of the trail, I took a last look at Roger. A small crowd had gathered near the chopper. Turned out, he wasn't as upstanding as I'd thought. He'd joined right in, acting as our distraction in case we were spotted leaving. I owed him big-time now.

We scrambled down a wide dirt trail to the roar of crashing waves.

Minutes later, we landed at the rocky bottom of a cliff-lined cove.

"Won't that helicopter crowd scare off Cuccione?" Veera asked.

"He walked into a crowded diner and pulled a gun," I said. "He shot at two D.A.'s outside their office with the police standing by. He doesn't spook easily. Besides, all eyes are on the copter. Harder to notice him leading the hostages down the trail."

"Looks like Cuccione's passing the Peninsula Center." Michael stared at James' phone. "Arrival in about ten."

"Cell phones muted?" I shut off my sound.

"Check." They both muted their phones.

"Have your weapon of choice ready," I said.

Michael pulled out his knife and tranq gun. Veera held a can of pepper spray.

"Not ready for shooting bullets just yet," she said.

"I almost forgot." Michael reached inside his jacket and yanked out a baseball cap. He pulled it over his hair. "Now I'm ready. The hostages must've been lying down in the bed of the El Camino. I noticed it had a cover. I bet they're tied up."

"He'll untie their feet to walk them down this trail to the sea caves." I sounded more confident than I felt. He could take them to another deserted beach spot, but this would be my first choice.

"There's more than one cave?" Veera's chin snapped up. "Do these sea caves have bats?"

"No bats," I said.

Veera blew out a breath. "Good news 'cause I don't want any sticky wings getting caught in my ponytail."

"That would never happen," Michael said. "They've got sharp eyesight and superhero flying skills. If they come near you it's because they're chasing insects attracted by your body heat."

"My body heat is none of any bat's business."

"Keep flashlights off unless absolutely necessary." I turned to Veera. "You're going to be our scout, while Michael and I hide in the caves. We know our way around."

"Suits me," Veera said.

"Only one trail leads down…" I stared up at the path.

Michael checked his phone. "They're at Golden Cove, which means they'll be here really soon."

"Veera, find some bushes along the trail to hide in where you can see them, but they can't see you. Report back by text, when you can."

She gazed up the dirt trail. "I don't see many bushes or hiding places around the trail. Not even any rocks up there. How am I going to find one big enough to cover all of me?"

I eyed the bottom of the trail. "There's the spot." I pointed to a group of shrubs at the end. "On the right, past the bench…that'll have to do."

"Guess I can squeeze behind those," she said. "Rattlesnakes sleep at night, right?"

"Not exactly," Michael said. "But the temperature's pretty cool tonight. They won't be slithering around."

"You sure about that?" she asked.

"They've burrowed for the evening." I had no idea if that was true, but we needed to stay on track. "Cuccione should go straight for the caves, which is where we'll be waiting."

Veera picked her way along the rocky shore up toward the trail, mumbling, "Bats and snakes and—"

"Watch out for prickly pears," Michael said.

"Prickly what?" She pulled out her pepper spray.

"Cactus," he said.

Michael and I skipped along the rocks toward our destination.

"Bats and snakes and prickly pears, oh my!" Veera said. "You leave out anything?"

"Don't forget the shooter," Michael said.

Chapter Fifty: Cave Patrol

Michael and I hurried along the rocky shore amid the clickity clack of rocks shifting beneath our soles. My ankles twisted in ways I didn't know were possible.

"Corrie? Do we have to worry about the tide?" Michael asked.

I knew he wasn't worried for himself. He had solid swimming skills. He was asking for my sake. My skills were less than solid. In fact, you could throw a sail on me the size of a small billboard and I'd still tip over and sink.

"It's low enough," I said. Everything would be fine…as long as I didn't fall in.

"Oh man. Here we go." He stared at his phone. "The car's parked in the lot."

My heart thumped wildly in my chest, as we stumbled along toward the cave. Waves slurped along our right, sending up a thin mist that sprayed our clothes. Veera texted a minute later to say she heard footsteps on the trail. After that she texted to say she'd counted five heads coming our way.

"The first cavern, right?" Michael asked. "The big one."

"Yes." The one with the twenty feet deep crevices. Michael and I had explored the rocky cove as teenagers. We'd climbed up and down these cliffs plenty of times. Only back then, it was for fun. "That's the one I'd pick," I said. If I were a killer. The rest were small and shallow caves. The only action they saw were waves dashing in and out.

We climbed up a tilted rocky surface in crouching positions so our moving silhouettes would be harder to spot by enemy eyes. There were just enough footholds to make the trek. The moon lit the way.

Michael waited at the top of a ridge and knelt to lower his hand. I gripped it and clambered upward. We gingerly walked along a steep ledge, wide enough for one person at a time. It led to the craggy mouth of the cave. Fresh seaweed scented the night. Foamy waves shone beneath us. And there it was. The entrance to the biggest of the Golden Cove sea caves.

The ledge sloped downward and ended a few feet from the rocky surface below. We jumped down and scampered through sea puddles. The ground was all pebbles, rocks and boulders. Pieces of driftwood scattered around. Thoughtful Samaritans had placed wooden planks along the uneven surface to make dry, smooth pathways. Graffiti provided the only dabs of color in the gray and white cave.

Beams of light suddenly pierced the darkness and I froze. I turned. Michael's head was all lit up.

"Nice hat," I said.

He grinned. The brim of his baseball cap housed thin beams.

"Isn't it great? I use it when I'm working on my car at night."

Michael was very mechanical, among other things.

"I'm all about hands-free," he said. "Nothing's going to slow my roll."

"Looks like you brought moonbeams inside with you."

"I'd find a way to bring them in if you wanted me to."

"Would've been too much light for our purposes. What you have is perfect."

"I'll turn it off after we pick our posts," he said.

I scanned the surroundings. Moss clung to a few of the larger rocks. Twenty feet ceilings and crashing waves filled the dim cave. Something dark and fluid leapt over a rock and melted into the darkness nearby.

"I'll hide by the entry," I said. "Once they're inside, I'll jump him from behind."

"By 'jump', do you mean you're going to…"

"Hop on his back, put him in a chokehold and-or clonk him on the head with the butt of my gun."

"I can trip him before he gets to you if that'll speed things up."

"Keep an eye on Bianca. She's all yours."

"The driver who can't drive? Easy."

Meanwhile, this was where words of wisdom from Dad usually floated through my mind. A practical gem he'd toss out in the middle of investigations. I never paid attention to them until after he was gone...that's when his voice arrived in my head. I swallowed the lump in my throat. What if something happened to James because of me? I'd had two chances to nab the shooter and both were epic failures.

No such thing as failure, only a delay in results.

"Thanks, Dad," I mumbled.

"Corrie?" Michael slid closer and wrapped an arm around me. "You okay?"

I brushed his arm away. "I'm fine." No time for softness now.

"You know..." He put his arm back around my shoulders. "...I get worried every time we're on a mission, but then I remind myself I'm with you. And worries vanish."

"Maybe you should worry," I whispered back.

"Are you kidding? You're like a homing torpedo, heading straight for the target. You can't miss."

I spun around to face him and was blinded by the LED lights on his cap. He reached up a finger and pushed a button beneath the brim of his hat. It was dark again.

"Homing torpedoes have sonar," he said. "They never miss. Just like you." He lifted my chin. "They adjust and make corrections to follow the target no matter where it goes. Cuccione can never escape the torpedo."

"Thank you." I kissed his hand.

"I'll take care of Bianca."

A text vibrated from in my pocket. It was Veera.

They should be there soon.

"There's a boulder on the right by the entrance of the cave," I said, "with just enough space behind it for me to hide."

"I'll lie under a plank. I saw a spot up ahead."

"Not a good idea. Everyone will look down at their feet to see where they're stepping."

He gazed upward. "Can't exactly hang from the ceiling."

"You're going to be about ten feet ahead of them."

"You have a spot for me?"

It may have been dark, but I knew Michael's eyes had lit up.

"Cuccione will be in the back, hostages up front," I said. "He's going to urge them forward."

"But they'll have nowhere to go."

"Except down."

"So I'll be blocking downward movement? What about Bianca?"

She seemed like the unruly type. "She'll come in first," I said.

"How would Cuccione know about this cave?" Michael asked.

"Sounds like something of an amateur geologist, collecting rocks for his son. I bet he's been here before."

"Which means he knows his way around better than we do."

"But he won't be expecting anyone," I said. "That gives us the advantage." I looked at my phone. Reception had disappeared. "Let's get in place." I scooted to the boulder, climbed on top and dropped behind it. I peeked out. I couldn't see Michael, but his sneakers padded slowly along, then grew quiet. "Showtime," I whispered.

Chapter Fifty-One: Love on the Rocks

Minutes dragged and all I had for company was the bluster of waves licking the rocks, and a foghorn in the distance warning little boats to be careful. If I hadn't known Michael was nearby, I'd think I was alone. The cave seemed sinister, filled with dark corners, rats and a rotten seaweedy stench. My stomach rumbled and I clenched my teeth. What if they were headed somewhere else? I was second-guessing an unpredictable killer. He might do away with them outside.

'What ifs' cause shipwrecks, sweetheart. Concentrate on being ready for whatever comes your way.

"Focus." My shoulders relaxed. It was a comfort to hear Dad's voice in the darkness.

I was about to climb over the rock when a flash of light made me duck. A beam shone from just outside of the cave. A voice drifted through the darkness.

"Can't hide our bodies in a shallow cave," Beckman boomed.

I heard a splash, like the sound of a rubber boot plopping in and out of a large puddle. I peeked out from behind the boulder. A stout, middle-aged woman stood a few feet away, aiming the flashlight into a small bag. The bob, thick bangs, and pasty face could only belong to Bianca. She wore baggy sweats, galoshes and gloves. She spun around, shining a flashlight around the cave. I dodged her beam just as footsteps plodded inside, sloshing and rattling the rock floor. The plodding went quiet and the cave grew brighter.

"Company halt," a man's low rough voice said.

Someone had watched one too many old military movies.

"Do you know how long it takes to find a body in a cave?" he asked without a trace of emotion.

"Cuccione," I muttered.

"Could take decades. One body wasn't discovered for forty years." Bianca's soft voice sounded like it belonged to a young schoolgirl.

But she was right. Bodies in caves could go undetected for a long time. Especially in sea caves with crevices. Ocean smells would overpower the stench of death. I shook off the nasty thoughts.

"I have friends looking for me," Ramsey said. "As in law enforcement friends. You'll never get away with this."

"Yes, we will, sugar," Bianca said. "Your bodies will be dumped so deep, you'll be missing forever and forever."

"Listen," James said. "You're a decorated military veteran. You're an ace with a gun. You could've killed us the first night, but you didn't."

Meaning Cuccione had a conscience? Or was James stalling?

"He was giving you a preview," Bianca said, "of upcoming attractions. Now move."

James continued talking while I crawled to the next boulder. Light slipped through a sliver along the bottom of a smaller boulder lodged between the two big ones. Enough space for me to view the area in front of me about a foot high off the ground. I caught my breath. Cuccione stood in the wrong spot. If I staged an attack, he'd see me coming before I even stood.

"Paulie's birthday is tomorrow. He won't even know it," Cuccione said. "Tulep pumped drugs into children. Your blunder set him free."

"We put him away," Beckman said. "We did our job. We didn't take the law into our own hands like you're doing. You killed Tulep which makes you a murderer."

"Paul didn't shoot him," Bianca said. Waves crashed before she spoke again. "You shouldn't call him names. Just for that, you'll go first. Paul's back's been bothering him so the others can help roll your lifeless body down the hole. I wonder if we'll hear the splash?"

"How can you live with yourself?" Beckman said.

"Having your blood on my hands," she said. "It makes me glow just thinking about it."

Boy, did she get that wrong if that pasty face meant anything. I peeked through the crack between the boulders again. Cuccione had moved forward a few steps. One more step and he'd be in position for me. I tensed my legs.

"You are so going to get it, lady," Ramsey spoke up.

My fingers curled around two large sized rocks.

There were shuffling sounds, a thump and a gasp.

"Why'd you punch me?" Ramsey whined.

"Out of my way." Bianca's voice had lowered an octave.

"I demand to go first," Ramsey said. "I'm the real force on this team."

What was he doing? Nobody's ego could be that big.

"Wrong," Beckman said. "You're just a poor excuse for a gumshoe."

"That's cruel," Ramsey said. "Me first."

"Agreed," Bianca said. "Go ahead."

Cuccione took another step forward. I shot up, rocks in each hand, climbed up and over the boulder and propelled myself forward, toward Cuccione and…I fell with a thud onto the rocky surface.

"Ugh!" Sharp pains knocked the breath out of me. Cuccione had sidestepped in the nick of time. And I'd flubbed it up again.

"No!" I rolled on my back and hurled the rocks at him. The first whizzed by his head, but the second hit him squarely in the chin knocking him backward and down.

Michael rushed forward. He wrapped his arms around Bianca, pinning her hands to her sides. He threw her on the ground and stomped his sneaker onto her back. She gasped. Cuccione tried to sit up, but James raced over and kicked him in the side. Meanwhile, Michael twisted the gun out of Bianca's hand and tossed it. Ramsey quick-stepped over and turned his back. The hostages' hands were tied behind them. Michael pulled out his knife and freed him just as Cuccione scrambled back to his feet. Blood dripped from his chin and onto his windbreaker.

In seconds I was up, pistol in hand. I banged the grip hard over the side of his head. Cuccione shuddered and faced me.

"You," he mumbled breathlessly. "I've seen you before."

"Not during my best moments." I took a step back and pointed my gun at him. "It's aimed at your heart. Since you've evidently got a really hard head."

Bianca squirmed under Michael's foot.

"You've killed before," Cuccione said. "I can see it in your eyes."

So you really can fool some of the people, some of the time. I finally gave off the right vibe. "On your knees. Hands behind your head."

He dropped to his knees. "Who are you?" He linked his hands behind his head and stared up at me.

"I'm the one that hit the rocks and came up with my .38."

"You're ruining everything," Bianca babbled. "We had this all planned out."

Ramsey was cutting Beckman loose just as Bianca made a wild play. She rolled up her knees to her chest, placed her hands above her head and jumped to her feet, ninja style, knocking Michael down in the process.

"What just happened?" Michael said, giving his head a fast shake.

Bianca grabbed a large rock with both hands and threw it at him, narrowly missing his head. She pulled out a smaller gun from inside her sweatshirt and pointed it at Michael. "Drop your weapon or he gets the next bullet." She cut a glance my way.

I slowly knelt toward the ground, locking gazes with James. In one quick move he dove for the rocky floor and Bianca's sneakers, giving me time to fire my shot. I'd aimed for Bianca's gun hand and hit her in the arm, just above the elbow. Like the superhero he was, Michael dashed away and rushed forward a second later, in time to yank Bianca's arms behind her, blood and all.

Chapter Fifty-Two: Almost the End

Paul and Bianca were tied together, back-to-back. There were brief mumblings about dropping the two of them down a crevice (Ramsey's idea), but Michael quickly pointed out there were too many witnesses and one was sure to crack (that would be Michael).

Bianca spent a good amount of time screaming. Like a small child, she seemed to enjoy hearing her echo, pausing after each scream to listen. When she paused to catch her breath, Cuccione's eyes welled up and he sobbed quietly.

"I never collected the barite crystals for Paulie." His body shook. "I came for the crystals."

"Not to get rid of the D.A. team?" I asked. His stumpy index finger was in plain sight.

"That was all Bianca," he said. "I never meant to hurt anyone. I'm no killer. I saw enough of that in Iraq. I just wanted them to know how I felt."

"He has trouble expressing himself," Bianca yelled. "Unlike me."

"Did you mean to shoot me in my rear?" Beckman asked.

"I was aiming for your head," Cuccione said. "But I changed my mind, last minute. I was going to cut you and your team loose…eventually. I wouldn't have let Bianca harm you."

"Likely story," Beckman said.

"Why'd you drop the receipt and leave a calculator behind?" Michael asked Cuccione.

"To confuse and distract you. It worked, didn't it?"

Michael shrugged and shook his head. "Not really."

Bianca resumed her screaming again, which likely helped our next visitors locate us more quickly. Abby and crew splashed their way into the cave, guns drawn. Veera brought in the rear.

"Nice work," Abby said to me, shoving the gun back into her holster.

"Didn't expect to see you," I said.

"We got an anonymous tip about ten minutes after you texted me," she said. "It was pretty detailed. That's what convinced my boss."

"Would've been nice if you'd let us know," Veera told her. "I'd nearly finished my climb up that slippery slope outside this cavern when you yelled out. I slid all the way down. Now I've got scraped fingers and knees, no thanks to you. You owe us."

"I'll make it up to you," she said.

"Who was your informant?" I asked Abby. All kinds of names ran through my head. Roger, Big Sam…

"Me," Cuccione said.

"You tattled," Bianca said. The little girl's voice was back.

"I couldn't kill civilians, no matter how wrongly they handled the case."

"You called the police when I went to tinkle." Bianca's shoulders jutted back against Paul and she banged her head against his. She turned and tried to spit at him. It took two officers to restrain her.

"Does she have a record?" Michael asked.

"She's had more than ten traffic related encounters with the police," Abby said. "But no record."

An hour later, we left Abby and her team and hiked away from the sea cave. James joined us. We started our upward climb on the dirt path, but this time with flashlights and Michael's cap to guide the way.

"Our ride'll be here in fifteen minutes," Michael said. "I called for a Lyft."

He and Veera chatted their way to the top. I dropped back and joined James.

"Why did you go to Cuccione?" I asked. "You should've let us help."

"He had Beckman and Ramsey," he replied.

"I can't see Beckman going to Cuccione willingly," I said.

"Cuccione said that if Beckman didn't come out, he'd go in and shoot everyone in the building. Said the same to me."

"Still, you could've been more helpful without becoming just another hostage." I punched him in the arm.

"What do you want me to say?" he asked.

"The truth." I was betting he did it just to keep the rest of us safe.

"Someone once told me the truth was overrated."

"That was Corrie 1.0. Before the update. You should've trusted me. No one would've gotten hurt." My schoolgirl crush had long evaporated, but I needed to tell him something. "I've never thanked you properly for all the times you stepped up to the plate to help me."

James' expression didn't change.

"And for being such a good friend to Michael." I turned to walk uphill.

Footsteps pounded the path beneath us. Michael's LED lights beamed on the uniform bounding up the trail.

Fisher paused in front of me, panting. "Mind stepping aside for a few moments?"

"She's finished for tonight," James said.

"It'll be quick," he said.

I nodded and walked down the hill with him. My three musketeers stood rooted in place, watching.

"After you left, Abby discovered an important piece of evidence." His voice went low and he dropped his chin. "About another case. You need to hear it for yourself."

"Why didn't she call or text me?" I asked.

"It's sensitive and we haven't checked it out, but you might be able to tell us if it's true or not."

"We'll talk tomorrow." I turned my back to him.

"It's about your father," he said.

I put on the brakes and pivoted on my heel. "What about him?"

"We were about to leave the cavern when Bianca Arnold blurted out something. She got everyone's attention."

"So?"

"She said she knew who poisoned your dad. She even mentioned the type of poison. Ricin. She said a large amount was mixed into his coffee. The heat made it more potent."

I caught my breath. How could she know? "That's not possible." Evidence gathered by police as part of an ongoing investigation is confidential. Dad died a year ago, but the case was still open.

He planted a hand on his hip. "If you want to go back, you can find out everything she knows. Personally, I think she's not as crazy as she seems."

"What's going on here?" Veera joined us.

"You'd better not be giving her a hard time for what went down in the dental office," Michael said.

"What dental office?" Fisher glanced around.

"I meant—" Michael started.

"I know the law," Veera said. "I just finished my first semester of night law school. You scoot and we'll overlook this violation of her civil liberties."

"I'm going back to the crime scene with Officer Fisher," I said. "Apparently, Bianca has information about my father."

"What?" James said. "Why would she know anything?"

"That's what I'm going to find out," I said.

"We'll all come," Michael said.

"Look, I'm just following orders," Fisher said. "The detective instructed me to only bring Miss Locke. You're welcome to wait here for her. Shouldn't be long." He turned and trekked back toward the sea cave.

"Bianca could be playing you," Veera said to me.

"She mentioned something the average person wouldn't know." I threw back a wave. "See you soon."

Minutes later, I followed Fisher's flashlight up the rocky shoreline to the boulders bordering the cave.

"Ladies first," Fisher told me when we got to the rock-climbing part.

I retraced my steps up to the plateau. I wasn't looking forward to walking the ledge again. Fisher stood close behind me. As I stepped forward, he grabbed my arm and yanked me back, twisting my other arm in the process.

"Hey!" I wiggled my arm free and swung it toward Fisher. He dodged the blow by stepping sideways. His grip on my right arm got tighter as he steered me toward the sea cave. He cut off the light.

"You're not the detective I thought you were, Miss Locke."

"You're the second person who's said that to me today." Gordon and now Fisher. "Maybe that's because I'm not a detective." Missing puzzle pieces dropped into all the open slots.

In one quick move, he grabbed my wrist in a vise-like grip with both hands and dragged me up the boulders. His thumbs locked across each other at the back of my hand.

"One hand should be enough for a wristlock," I said. "I'm not nearly as big and strong as you are."

"Shut up."

Instead of heading for the cave entrance, he trekked in the opposite direction, toward a cliff where hissing waves crashed below. I dug in my heels to slow him down.

"You're making a big mistake," I said.

"You made the mistake," he said.

I had one chance to do this right. No replays or it was all over. The blurry picture came into focus. How the shooter stayed ahead of us. Fisher was the inside man.

"You killed Tulep," I said.

He grinned. "I should get a commendation for that. He deserved to die."

"You smoked the cigar in the barbershop. Where'd you dump your cigar butt?"

"Outside," he said. "In the dumpster your boyfriend was pawing. No one bothered to look."

"Why would you be involved with Bianca and Cuccione?" I asked, heart pounding. I could taste saltwater on my lips.

"I'm the baby brother," he said. "Their parents fostered me as a teen. Paul and I are close."

I dropped to the ground and wrapped my free arm around the piece of a boulder jutting out like a cone. "Owww! You're hurting me." I wasn't keen on playing the role of the helpless female unless it served a noble purpose. Like saving my skin. "Why me? I'm not responsible for setting Tulep free."

He bent close to me. The stubbles on his chin scraped against my cheek.

"No, but you got in Paul's way each and every time he could have finished a D.A. off. You're a nuisance."

"He wasn't shooting to kill." What was my next move? Think of something. "This'll ruin your career. Your chance of becoming a detective."

"Who's going to know I'm responsible? You're the one that can't swim. And you won't be able to tell anyone."

"Paul wouldn't want you to do this."

"If you didn't interfere, he'd never have been caught."

Fisher gripped my wrist with one hand and reached his other hand around to loosen my hold on the cone. He jerked me back on my feet and I kicked out hard. He lurched back and forward again, re-fastening his two-handed grip on my wrist. He squeezed my palm with his fingers. My eyes teared from the pain. I yelled out and lunged my left leg behind him, following with my right. In one quick move, I snapped my arm toward his back, freeing my wrist. I jammed my sneaker against his butt, sending him reeling forward. I left him sprawled across the rocks, but not before I conked him on the head with the grip of my pistol.

"Finally," I muttered.

Michael padded up the boulder as I made my way down. "I heard you yell. Is everything—"

James and Veera barreled toward us with Abby coming from the other side.

"How could you possibly hear over the waves?" I asked Michael.

"He's got the same hearing as dogs and cats," James said. "Where's Fisher?"

"Studying the rock formations," I said. "And now if you don't mind, I'd like to hobble my way home. I've got a few wounds to mend."

***

I wasn't permitted to head home for another hour, but Michael patched me up using the police team's first aid kit. I declined paramedics since I was itching to go.

More statements were taken, and Fisher was cuffed and hauled off, up the pathway, but not before I made a final statement.

"Excuse me," I interrupted as Abby was thanking me. I rushed after Fisher, holding back until the cops were about to toss him inside the rear seat of a patrol car. As he bent over to get in, I landed a hard kick in his tailbone. He cried out and dove headfirst into the car. I marched off, leaving the officers speechless. Another gift from Dad; knowing the most sensitive spots to land a blow.

None of us had figured Fisher as the insider. He was fostered as a teen, taken in when Bianca and Paul's parents needed some extra funding. A drifter that went from job-to-job and finally settled in as a cop. He never lost touch with his foster siblings. Cuccione offered his services as a witness against the other two. Fisher used my father's homicide as bait to reel me in.

"You know our GoFundMe campaign?" Veera whispered.

She sat with Michael and me in the back of a police SUV on our way home.

"We're at $17,459.23. We got a lot of action once I let it be known we were taking down a criminal. I shared live footage when I was waiting for Cuccione."

"Guys, it's still going up." Michael stared at his smartphone. "I added the part about uncovering a rogue cop. We're at nearly $20,000."

"It's like we've cured a disease that could've gotten way out of hand," Veera said. "We have enough to pay a whole lotta informant money and rent for our PI agency."

"I have a better idea," I said. "We can fund housing for people with nowhere to go." I'd made promises I wanted to keep. "And pay back Roger for the helicopter ride."

"I have an even better idea," Veera said. "We can give them jobs in our new P.I. agency. They can make enough money to pay for their own housing. We'll be flooded with clients once people see how good we are."

"I like that," Michael said and turned to me. "Don't you?"

"Let me see," I said. "No more regular paycheck, no studio perks, no more gourmet lunches at the commissary…"

"But plenty of cases to solve," Veera said. "We've got us some police connections, informants and restaurateurs as fans. Don't forget Sam's reward money. I bet we can get Gordon to pitch in. We'll be in the big leagues in no time. Now all we need is a name."

"How about Head Locke Private Investigators," I said. "As in Bankhead and Locke."

"That's the best name yet," Michael said.

"We're going to rock it," Veera said. "I'm feeling some major joy."

"Me, too," I said. I could say that again. "Me, too."

Acknowledgements

My never-ending gratitude for the support and guidance of so many incredible individuals who helped light the sometimes dim and meandering path of writing a book – thanks and more thanks to:

Librarian Extraordinaire Kim Pendleton – For sharing your time, your eagle eyes and for being my trusty first reader. Your good-natured commentary always puts a smile on my face.

Assistant Deputy District Steven Pomeroy for patiently and thoroughly answering my D.A. related questions, and providing authentic touches in my fictional story, so I could keep it "real".

The lovely and brave Sofi Reyes – for making my day by performing an unexpected and large act of generosity that made my heart swell.

To the gracious, big-hearted and ever-wise Marilyn Metzner – for always providing smiles, inspiration and hugs.

To the good, kind and thoughtful Judge Tom Anderle – for promoting my series when least expected. Your never-ending humility and caring for others are unsurpassed.

To the vivacious, fun and energetic Alyce Scerbo – for reminding me of the importance of an excellent attitude and friendship.

To my indefatigable, hardworking publishers and editors: Verena Rose & Shawn Reilly Simmons – always capably adding the finishing touches to my manuscripts.

And where would I be without the three marvelous men in my life, my lovely daughters-in-law and my wonderful sister, always there when I finally cross the finish line.

About the Author

Lida Sideris' first stint after law school was a newbie lawyer's dream: working as an entertainment attorney for a movie studio…kind of like her heroine, Corrie Locke, except without the homicides. Lida was one of two national winners of the Helen McCloy Mystery Writers of America Scholarship Award for her first book. She lives in the northern tip of Southern California with her family, rescue dogs and a flock of uppity chickens. To learn more about Lida, please visit her website: www.LidaSideris.com

9 781947 915923